The Day Hunters

Mark A. Keith

The Day Hunters

The Day Hunters

To my Grandmother, Mary Ann,
Who loved the cowboy way

The Day Hunters

The Day Hunters

chapter 1

West Texas, 1869

"Come on, boys. We've gotta keep goin'," Bass Reed demanded. "I ain't gonna sit here, and wait for 'em to kill us."

"To hell with you, Bass. You led us out here, and we're gonna die out here. What difference does it make if it's today or tomorrow?" Carter said. "Damned if I know why the Captain put you in charge."

Carter wasn't alone in his thinking. Bass himself wondered why the Captain had put him in command. In all his years as a Texas Ranger, he had never been in charge of so much as a cleanup detail. Now, here he was on the frontier with four greenhorns, all looking to him for leadership. But when the Captain looked at you with those hard, grey eyes, and a face that could've been carved from granite, you just naturally did what he said.

The Rangers had followed Merejildo Zendejaz and his band of gunrunners, deep into the Llano Estacado, in an effort to locate his Comanchero stronghold. When Zendejaz split his forces, Captain Ellsworth did the same. The Captain and the more seasoned fighters continued west in pursuit of the larger group, while Bass and the greenhorns were ordered to "follow, but not engage" the smaller. The second day, after leaving the troop, the outlaws killed the Rangers' horses. Afoot, they became hopelessly lost. Bass was surprised his own men hadn't killed him for his failure. He was sure the outlaws had been watching them the past few days, just waiting. But why? They could've just as easily killed the Rangers as their horses. What were they waiting for?

"Hell, we'd be dead already if we hadn't eaten the horses," Carter continued.

"How damned long have we been out here?"

Bass couldn't remember. The sun was playing tricks with his brain. "I don't know, but I ain't just gonna quit. We'll rest

3

The Day Hunters

awhile, wait for sundown."

"There ain't a inch of shade in a hundred miles of here," Ramey said.

"Well," Carter said, "you're wearin' a hat, ain't you?"

"Yeah. And if you don't shut your mouth, I'll be wearin' yours, you son of a bitch!"

"Shut up, both of you!" Bass said. "Sit down. Try to get some rest."

The Rangers had been drinking their own piss for two days. Bass knew they wouldn't last much longer. He'd become so lightheaded and confused, he wasn't sure what was real anymore. He wondered if the Captain and the rest of the troop fared any better. What he wouldn't give to see Stone Horse, their scout, coming to save them as he had so many times before. But he knew Stone Horse wasn't coming. No one was coming.

The dry earth of the Llano Estacado didn't yield much in the way of survival. The game knew where the water was, and so did the hostiles, but somehow they all seemed to vanish out here. The land was so bleak and desolate, a man could ride for days and not see a single thing to give him direction.

Bass looked around, taking stock of his men. They all appeared to be sleeping, but might well be dead for all he knew. He wondered if they had anyone to miss them or even care if they were dead.

Carter, the oldest of the four, was only twenty, a full eight years younger than Bass. A native Texan with a suspicious background, Carter had been with the Rangers about a year. It was rumored that he'd killed a man while robbing a stagecoach in Colorado, then returned to Texas and joined the Rangers, feeling the organization would be a good place to hide.

Ramey hailed from New Hampshire, having come to Texas in search of adventure. Too young to fight in the Civil War, Ramey felt he had missed the grandest adventure of them all. At seventeen he left his comfortable home, and worked his way to Texas. Bass wondered if dying of thirst on the llano would be considered an adventure in New Hampshire.

The Day Hunters

Josh and Jody Cameron, two tall, raw-boned brothers from Nacadoches. The boys had good voices, and loved to lead the singing around the fire at night. The consensus was that there was not a song or a joke they didn't know. They would often recite a poem, or sometimes re-enact funny arguments they'd seen their parents have, to entertain the troop. Bass hated to think their young lives would soon be wasted. And that it would happen under his command. He lay back, pulled his hat over his face, and tried to sleep.

Jody had just begun to stir. He'd no more stood to his feet when the rifle slug tore through his belly, splattering Ramey's faded shirt with blood. He fell across his sleeping brother, who awoke in such a panic both Carter and Ramey had to subdue him.

"Stay down, dammit. Stay down!" Carter said.

"Oh God, get him off!" Josh cried. "Get him off me!"

Bass pulled Jody off the boy, taking note of the severity of the wound. Jody would die, though he might suffer for hours.

"Is he dead?" Ramey asked.

"No. He's alive for now."

"Oh God!" Josh said, when he saw the wound. "They killed you, Jody. They killed you."

"They didn't kill him. He's still alive, can't you see?"

"Oh God, Jody, they killed you."

"Shut up, godammit!" Carter shouted. "We've gotta think about stayin' alive ourselves!"

Ramey inspected the blood on his shirt, and stared off into the distance. "I can't see a damn thing out there," he said. "I wonder where they are."

Bass knew they could be anywhere. The llano looked as flat as a frozen lake, but that was deceiving. The country dipped and rolled, and everything seemed to disappear. Many a man had become lost out here, and starved or died of thirst as a result. Bass wondered if that was the outlaws' plan, to hold them here until they died. Couldn't the bastards have done that without cutting this boy in half?

5

The Day Hunters

Bass removed Jody's gunbelt, and rolled it up to make a pillow for his head. The boy stared vacantly at the searing white sky, his fingers buried in his own entrails as if holding himself together. He had not yet said a word, though his mouth had hardly stopped moving.

Keeping low, Josh crawled to his brother's side. Having retrieved Jody's hat, he placed it over the boy's empty eyes, then removed his bandana and covered the wound.

"I don't know, Jody. I don't know," he repeated.

"It'll be dark in a few hours," Bass said. "Maybe we can sneak out then."

"And go where?" Carter said. "I've gone as far as I'm goin'. If they're gonna kill me, they can do it right here. We couldn't get Jody out anyway. Let the boy die in peace."

"He's right, Bass," Ramey said. "No need to wear ourselves out even more crawlin' around this desert. We're dead men. They know it, and we know it."

Bass had all but lost the will to go on. He just felt he should try to lead, though it was much too late for that now.

"Let's at least spread out, and try to give 'em a fight," he said. "We likely won't hear from 'em 'til mornin', but they might come in after dark."

"I'm gonna stay with Jody," Josh said.

"Yeah," Bass agreed. "I think that's a good idea."

The Rangers checked their guns and moved out to form a perimeter, each man preparing himself for the coming attack.

After a quiet hour alone with his brother, Josh Cameron said goodbye. He removed Jody's hat, neatly folded his bandana, and placed it over the boy's face. He held it there until Jody stopped breathing.

#

"Hell, why don't we just leave 'em?" said Emmett the Idiot, so named for his maniacal laugh. "Let the damn desert kill 'em. I want a drink o' whiskey."

6

The Day Hunters

"Because Lean Wolf wants to kill them," Fast Elk said. "You know we will do what he wants, not what you want."

"I think he's crazy."

"If he hears you say that, he will kill you too."

"Maybe I'll just kill him when he gets back, and that'll be the end of it."

Fast Elk knew there was little chance of Emmett killing Lean Wolf. The man was such a savage that few could look him in the eye, much less choke up the nerve to kill him. Zendejaz gave Lean Wolf plenty of room, though with one order from him, his men would cut Lean Wolf to pieces. Hearing a single horse approaching, Fast Elk snickered, "Maybe now is your chance."

The horse Lean Wolf rode in on was laden with canteens of fresh, cool water. The Brazos River was no more than two miles from the Rangers' location. They could have easily walked there in an hour, if they had known. Dismounting, he pitched the canteens to the ground.

"There's one less Ranger now," he said. "I shot his guts out."

"I wish we'd just go kill 'em all, and get outta this damn desert," Emmett said.

"Tomorrow. Make some coffee."

Fast Elk felt the mere presence of Lean Wolf was enough to make anyone nervous. He was squat and thick, like his father's people, the Comanche. His powerful arms could easily drive his big knife up to the hilt. Fast Elk had seen him do it many times. He carried numerous scars on his body, the ugliest being a long knife scar on his face, angled downward across both lips.

Lean Wolf's mother had been a Mexican captive whom he murdered when he was fourteen years old. She was treated with such disdain by the Comanches that Lean Wolf learned to hate his Mexican blood. He cut her throat one day while she was making water, then blamed the murder on another captive woman. The captive was then raped and murdered by his father. Fast Elk knew Lean Wolf would kill on a whim. Though he too would rather go kill the Rangers now, he kept his mouth shut.

The Day Hunters

"They still outnumber us," Lean Wolf said. "Tomorrow we'll surround 'em. Let the sun cook 'em awhile, then we'll move in and kill 'em all."

"I wonder if the rest o' them Rangers are headin' this way," Emmett said.

"Hell, Zendejaz led 'em so far out onto the llano, they'll never get out," Lean Wolf said. "When he finds a good place to kill 'em, he will, just like we'll kill this bunch tomorrow."

#

The heat of the morning sun finally woke the exhausted Rangers. Every man had fallen asleep. Had the renegades attacked in the dark, none of the Rangers would have survived. Carter and Ramey had accepted their fate, but the fear in Josh's eyes was almost too much for Bass to bear. He wished there was something he could say.

"Do you think they're still out there, Bass?" the boy asked.

"Yeah, I'd say they are. Only way to know is to stand up and start walkin' outta here. I don't think we'd get very far."

Carter blew sand from his pistol, and gave the cylinder a spin. "Y'know, Bass, I've a mind to blow your damn head off."

"Shut up," Ramey said. "We need every man."

"For what? So we can stay alive another ten minutes?"

"Goddamn you, shut up!"

Josh Cameron rolled over, hid his face, and cried.

"Aw, to hell with this," Carter snapped. He jumped to his feet and ran out into the open, only to be cut down before he fired a shot. Not a single word was spoken. Josh cried that much harder.

The stench of the dead bodies was unbearable by midday. The Rangers crawled a short distance, but it didn't help much. Any further and they would risk exposing themselves. Josh patted his brother's hand as he crawled past the body.

8

The Day Hunters

With tears in his eyes, Ramey whispered to Bass, "Why don't we just shoot each other? It'd be better than this damn waiting around."

"I don't think Josh could do it."

"I can shoot him, then we'll shoot each other. Dammit, I can't take it anymore. We've gotta do something, or we're gonna cook out here."

"Maybe the Captain'll show up and run 'em off," Bass said, though he knew there was not a chance of that happening. Ramey knew it, too.

"Hell, how would he ever find us? That's just foolish thinking. We've gotta look out for ourselves."

Bass had no idea what to do, he just couldn't bring himself to give up. Ramey was ready to end it, though Bass was sure he would stick it out if they could come up with a plan. There was nowhere to go, and no one had the energy to travel if there was. They hadn't eaten in days, but he still couldn't quit.

"I'm not wastin' another night sittin' here," he said. "When it comes full dark, I'm leavin'. Hell, what if they take us prisoner? That'd be worse than dyin'. I'd rather die out there, than stay here and have my hide cut off. I'm leavin' after dark," he repeated. "If you're goin' with me, get some rest."

Bass awoke with the burning sun and heat waves distorting his vision. His tongue was so thick and dry, he could barely swallow. He didn't think he could piss anymore, and had vowed to kill himself before he would harvest from the corpses. He knew his life was slipping away.

"That you, Horse?" he mumbled.

"No, not Stone Horse," Lean Wolf said. He plunged the heavy blade deep into the Ranger's chest, pushing him onto his back.

Bass groaned. The knife punctured his lung. He could hear the screams of his dying men. No shots were fired. Only screaming.

9

The Day Hunters

Ripping out the big knife, Lean Wolf tore the man's pants open, and slashed at his crotch. Cursing and laughing, he spit in his face.

Bass Reed lived long enough to be glad he was dying.

#

"By God, Cole, wouldn't you think that one damned settler in Texas would provide a Ranger with a decent mount?" Harley ranted. "This bar o' soap I'm ridin' couldn't run fast enough to scatter his own shit."

Captain Cole Ellsworth might have chuckled at that remark, if he hadn't already heard a hundred just like it in the last twenty-four hours. But, as was more often than he cared to admit, Harley was right. They'd been friends all their lives, nearly thirty-three years. Harley was right most of the time.

If they were caught out in the open, poorly mounted as they were, they'd be slaughtered for sure. The few settlers living along the upper Brazos were keeping their good horses close to hand in the event they would have to flee the area. The Quahada Comanche seemed unlikely to surrender any time soon, but that was the army's problem now. The Comanche wars were about over for the Texas Rangers.

They were a rough looking bunch, heavily armed, with little distinction between themselves and the outlaws they pursued. Sturdy breeches to withstand the brush, vests for the added pocket space. Wide brimmed hats and high heeled boots, made for a life in the stirrup.

The black man, Moody, was the exception. The brogans he wore were a size too big. He'd taken them off his father's feet, after he was hanged for defending himself against the attack of a white trader. He preferred the large Mexican sombrero. Long hours in the fields had given Moody an appreciation for lots of shade.

They'd made three stops to acquire four horses, as they'd

The Day Hunters

lost three in the skirmish with Zendejaz, and finally had to eat the other one. The pack mule was the last to go. Captain Ellsworth rode the mule at the end, his hip badly bruised by a rifle bullet that struck his holstered pistol. If they made it back to Austin, he would have to buy a new weapon.

The fight with Zendejaz was brief, each side losing horses, the outlaws losing one man. Moody made the kill, a clean shot through the head. The Rangers, outgunned as usual, could do little but watch their quarry ride away, as the renegades kept them pinned down with heavy rifle fire.

Since the end of the war, Texas could scarcely afford to mount a troop of Rangers. Their numbers throughout the state had dwindled to almost nothing, especially on the Northern Plains. The results were predictable. Mexican bandits had all but taken over the border country. Texas ranchers mounted small armies, but could do little to protect themselves. The bandits had them greatly outnumbered.

On the plains, the Comanches gained an even stronger foothold when the army pulled out to fight in the east. Now, the Henry repeating rifle, which had once given the Rangers tremendous advantage, was finding its way into the hands of the hostiles. Cole could think of little more frightening than a horseback Comanche with a Henry repeater.

"When we get a little farther down river we can breathe easier," he said, more for the sake of Eli Plummer than Harley Macon. Eli's nerves were stretched to the limit, and Harley's complaining was wearing on everyone.

"Breathe easy?" Harley said. "Hell, Cole, you're crazy. There's too damn many guns floatin' around out here to get comfortable."

Cole agreed. If the Comanches continued trading for rifles, it would certainly take the army to defeat them. They had terrorized Texas for many years, with no more than primitive weapons. What would it be like if they all had Henrys?

There had been no reports of the army losing weapons, and few of the settlers had Henrys. Most kept Spencers or

The Day Hunters

Springfields. Some still carried their old Kentucky flintlocks. A poor choice of weapon to engage hostile Indians. A Comanche warrior could easily shoot more than a dozen arrows a minute, while an old flintlock was maybe good for three or four rounds, if you were a fast reloader. The Texas Rangers had buried many a man who wasn't. The hostiles were plainly getting the guns from Zendejaz, but where was he getting them?

Merejildo Zendejaz was a cold-blooded Mexican, who had spent most of his life living with and learning from, the Apache outlaw, Golonka. On a raid into Mexico, the Indian had stolen the boy from his parents. Merejildo was nine years old at the time. He lived the next fifteen years as an Apache, learning every trail throughout New Mexico, and how to live off land that could kill anything. He found water where none could be found, food where little could live. The boy quickly became an accomplished raider, often riding south across the border alone, to steal horses and cattle, sometimes even women and children. He had no loyalty to the Mexican people, nor to anyone else for that matter.

Golonka had been proud of his Mexican son, but one day Zendejaz decided to kill the old outlaw, and leave the wickiup for good. He shot the man dead, helped himself to anything of value, and rode away leaving Golonka for the dogs to eat. Cole knew he would be a hard man to take.

"Up yonduh, Cap'n!" Moody shouted from the flank.

More than a mile ahead, Cole saw the buzzards circling. There was a black dot on the endless prairie, but he couldn't identify it. Reaching into his well worn saddlebags, he withdrew the spyglass given to him by Harley Macon. Harley claimed to have taken it off a dead Yankee colonel, and Harley was not one to lie about such things. Cole knew his friend had seen plenty of action with the 8th Texas Cavalry. He saw no reason to doubt him. He took his time focusing the glass, scanning the horizon carefully.

"What the hell is it, Cole?" Harley snapped.

"It's Stone Horse. And he's found somethin'."

#

The Day Hunters

Stone Horse had been waiting for the Rangers a long time. He'd waited so long he became bored and went exploring, which was as normal for Stone Horse as flying to a bird. In his wandering, he found something so awful he wished he did not have to tell Captain Ellsworth. He knew he would see the Captain's war face—an unpleasant experience. The Captain could readily deal out justice as simply the duty of a day's work. But sometimes he would wear his war face. It was easy to believe that most men who had seen it paid an awful price.

The five men the Captain sent to follow the renegades had not covered much ground. The renegades got them lost, then killed their horses. Stone Horse found the dead horses earlier that same day. The Rangers walked circle after circle while Lean Wolf waited for just the right time to attack. There were many tracks in the area. The men must have been here a day or two, never knowing they were so close to water. But why would Lean Wolf wait? Why not just kill them and be done with it?

Stone Horse could see the bodies had been mutilated, even though there was not much left. Coyote and buzzard had been there. The frontier produced many outlaws, but few were butchers. Maybe Lean Wolf just did it for fun. As he watched the approaching riders, Stone Horse could tell by the Captain's actions that he could now see the massacre. The Rangers would reach him soon enough. Stone Horse thought while he waited, he might take a few moments to pray.

"Dammit, Cole, this is my fault," Harley said.

"I shouldn't've pushed so hard to send 'em after those villains."

"We both sent 'em, Harley."

Cole was shocked at what he saw. In all his years chasing the Comanche and the Kiowa, he'd seen murderous brutality time and time again. But this time the victims were under his command.

The Day Hunters

Men not killed in battle, but murdered in cold blood, butchered, and left to rot in the sun.

He could see no sign of a fight. No shell casings, no dead horses to hide behind, nothing to suggest the Rangers had fired a single shot. Every weapon gone, every stitch of clothing. Nothing left but dead men, and blood stains on the ground. From the looks of it, the killers simply rode in and slaughtered them all without warning.

"One of 'em tried to run," Harley said. "That's Carter, ain't it?"

"Yessuh," Moody said. "Castrated him. Castrated all of 'em."

While Harley and Cole gathered the remains, Moody and Eli hobbled their horses and started digging the grave. They found a spot under a cut bank where they could dig the hole and cave the small bank in on top of it. There were plenty of rocks to make it look nice.

Moody fought hard to control his emotions. He'd been especially fond of the Cameron boys. "I'm sure gettin' tired o' buryin' folks. Ain't you, Mistuh Eli?"

"Yeah. I hate to think we could end up like this. Just a hole in the middle o' nowhere. It makes me sick to look at 'em. I expect the Cameron boys'll be leadin' the singin' in Heaven tonight."

"I just hope they in Heaven. Men butchered like this might have restless spirits. I prefer to avoid restless spirits."

Eli's staunch upbringing didn't allow for restless spirits. When you died, you either went to Heaven or you went to Hell. You didn't wander around the world scaring folks. But he knew Moody worried about such things. "God hath not given us the spirit of fear," his mother would say. Eli never saw any need for it. Texas had the Comanches for that.

"It was Lean Wolf who killed them," Stone Horse said. "He led the bunch the Rangers followed. I found where he waited to kill them. He has two men with him."

"Lean Wolf? That breed is runnin' with Zendejaz? By

14

The Day Hunters

God, Cole, look what we've done." Harley walked to his horse, pulled his rifle from the boot, and began shooting at the buzzards circling overhead.

Cole stared at the distant horizon. Lean Wolf and Zendejaz. Things couldn't get much worse.

Stone Horse wanted to give the Captain time, but there was little. He spoke cautiously as he made his report. "I think Lean Wolf is going to his camp in the river country, Captain, or maybe to the Nations. He is celebrating in blood because he killed your Rangers. He is traveling fast."

How Stone Horse knew all this, Cole couldn't say, but over the years he had stopped asking. Somehow the man just knew.

"Well, if he's travelin' fast, we won't catch him on this crow bait we're ridin'," Harley said. "We're gonna need some decent horses."

Stone Horse was anxious to be on their way. "I think we should be moving," he said. "I know a good camp site out of the wind not far from here. A fire will not be seen there. We can reach it before dark, if we start soon."

Eli and Moody were just finishing the grave. They would be ready to ride in minutes. They bordered the grave with fist-sized rocks, and with smaller stones made a crude Ranger star in the middle. If they said any goodbyes, they said them to themselves.

Harley Macon spoke a few words over the grave, then the bedraggled troop started southeast at a walk, the only gait their sorry mounts could muster. Only a few stars twinkled in the Texas sky, as the sunset turned the ugly prairie a magnificent golden hue. Stone Horse pointed to one of the stars and told the Captain to follow it. He would trot ahead to make the camp.

"Why you reckon he'd cut them boys up like that?" Eli asked. "I couldn't do that to somebody no matter what he done."

"That's because you ain't a blood drunk Comanchero," Harley said, "but that son of a bitch is. Why, you're a fine fella, Eli. And a member of the finest, most underpaid law enforcement outfit in the world. The damn Texas Rangers, by God."

15

The Day Hunters

"Very funny. You reckon they're waitin' for us up ahead?"

"I doubt it," Cole said. "They wouldn't know we were comin'. Besides, Stone Horse said they were movin' fast. I expect they're long gone by now."

Moody rode quietly behind the others, his horse being the poorest of the lot. The conversation worried him He felt it best not to speak of the dead, especially those murdered so brutally. Moody didn't understand Comanches or white folks, either one, very well.

The Rangers rode into the darkness, the only sound the creaking of saddle leather, jingling spurs, and horse hooves in the dust. They knew there would be no talk of women at the fire tonight. No joking or teasing. No poker game for pebbles. Captain Ellsworth was wearing his war face.

Merejildo Zendejaz had six men with him, one of them seriously wounded. The Comanche, White Hand, had been hit bad down low in his belly. The bullet was still inside him. The other Comanches tended him the best they could, though none of the men wanted to try to take the bullet out. Ruiz and Ugly John were in favor of shooting him, but Zendejaz wouldn't have it. He and White Hand had been together too long. They'd saved each other's lives, loved each other's women—killed each other's enemies.

They were hard men, living a hard, dangerous life. Every one of them knew the chances they took, riding with an outlaw like Zendejaz. The man was known far and wide throughout the Southwest as a killer with neither mercy nor compassion for his enemies. It only stood to reason that he would expect the same from his men.

Ugly John had killed, robbed, and raped all over Wyoming before making his way down south. He was a man with a taste for cruelty, and a fierce aversion to bath water. His own brother shot

The Day Hunters

him in the face when they were boys. The brother, tired of the constant beatings, took up their pa's pistol and shot Ugly John, blowing away part of his jawbone. The shot left gunpowder imbedded in his skin.

Ruiz was a dangerous man of intemperate disposition and many skills, one of them being the ability to keep captives alive for long periods of time under torturous conditions. Zendejaz was often amazed at the tortures Ruiz could dream up. He felt Ruiz was the only man he knew to rival Lean Wolf when it came to such things.

Delgado was different. Hard, but not cruel. Quick to fight, but not antagonistic. He could sit transfixed and watch torture by the hour, but would never inflict the torture himself. He was Zendejaz's most trusted man.

Lately, Zendejaz was feeling more pressured than ever. With the Civil War over, the army was back in the West again. Soon it would not be just the Rangers looking for him, but the army as well. His stronghold was remote and well hidden. But he'd heard tales of great balloons the army had. Balloons so big that men could ride in them, and shoot from the air. Balloons that gave man the eye of an eagle. Zendejaz knew the eagle could find him. Maybe the balloons could find him, too.

White Hand coughed and spit up blood. All the men had seen this before. They knew it wouldn't be long. In another place, at another time, Zendejaz would have been as anxious to leave as his men. But he was sure Ellsworth was dead. He'd shot the man with the buffalo gun. He didn't believe Ellsworth could survive such a wound and besides, they'd killed most of the Rangers' horses.

"Let's shoot him and get on with it," Ugly John said.

The scowl on the faces of White Hand's Comanche friends made it plain they didn't like the idea.

"He will die soon," Zendejaz said. "Make a fire. I want some whiskey. We will camp here tonight. Ride for the stronghold in the morning."

"In the morning, *Jefe*? We have plenty of daylight left,"

The Day Hunters

Ruiz said. "The Rangers could still be close. We haven't traveled very far."

"The Rangers won't come. Ellsworth is dead. We killed too many of their horses. They'll die in the desert."

"I wouldn't count on that," Ugly John said. "Ellsworth ain't an easy kill."

"He is dead, I tell you!" Zendejaz was tired of the talking. He wanted the men to shut up, so his friend could die in peace. "This is a .50 caliber Sharps, you fools. He bled to death. They could never save him out on the prairie. They buried him where he fell."

Ruiz and Ugly John looked doubtful. They didn't believe Ellsworth was dead, and weren't sure Zendejaz did either.

"Well, whether he is or he ain't, Macon ain't, and he'll hound us to Hell if you killed Ellsworth. Some day he'll just ride in and slaughter us all," Ugly John said. "I'm for gettin' outta Texas for a while."

"We'll ride to the stronghold. If Macon lives and comes after us, I'll kill him, too," Zendejaz said. "Besides, the stupid *gringos* are still coming west. They are easy to rob and kill. I like their yellow-haired women."

The men had seen that look on their leader's face many times. Whether raping or killing, the look was the same.

Zendejaz could appreciate the men's uneasiness. Though he tried to hide it, he too was worried about Macon. The man had left a trail of dead outlaws all over Texas. The stories Zendejaz heard about his combat skills were extraordinary. Harley Macon was a famous man, and he didn't get that way because of some eastern writer's imagination. Macon's story was written in the blood of his enemies. Zendejaz concluded that more information might be a good idea, after all.

"Delgado, my friend, I want you to take a long ride. Find the Rangers. See how many are left, and what they are doing. The rifles will be coming soon. I'll want to know if the Rangers are in the area."

"*Sí, Jefe*. But they may have a big lead, by now. If I cannot

18

The Day Hunters

find them?"

"Ride all the way to Austin if you have to. Maybe there you will hear news of them. The rest of you men split your provisions with Delgado. He has a long trip ahead."

Each man gave Delgado a few bullets and some jerky. They filled an extra canteen with water. After sacking a little coffee and tobacco, Delgado rode south with neither goodbye nor handshake. Before he was out of sight, White Hand breathed his last. The Comanches carried him away from camp, and rolled him in his blanket. There was no way to build a scaffold, so they left him to be consumed by the earth.

"*Adios, compadre,*" Zendejaz said. "I will meet you in Hell."

Zendejaz tried to reassure the Comanches. They looked worried. White Hand had been their leader.

"You will ride with me," he said. "We will get more guns and drive the whites out of this country. Every Comanche will have a rifle that shoots many times. We will drive the whites back across the muddy river. I doubt Macon will even come after us without his friend."

The Comanches shouted and whooped it up, but Ruiz and Ugly John were not so sure.

The Day Hunters

Chapter 2

In only eight years of living, Boone Randall was already acquainted with death. He walked to the graveyard on a dismal gray morning in Austin, Texas, to visit his mother, Louise, and tell her the news around town. It had been almost a month since his mother died, and Boone liked to talk to her often. He wanted to tell her about the old pocketknife he found down by the creek. The boy had just reached his mother's grave when he saw his friend, Toad Phinney, running up the hill for all he was worth.

"Boone, did you hear about Opal?"

"Nope, what about her?" Boone tried hard to sound matter of fact, like Captain Ellsworth, one of his many Ranger heroes.

"She got shot last night." Toad was so excited, he tripped and rolled back down the hill, cussing all the way, trying to sound like a grownup.

"Why would anybody shoot Opal? Are you lyin'?"

"No, I ain't lyin'. Two men had a gunfight in the alley, and shot her in the neck. She was out for a walk and got shot down dead."

"Who told you that? They're lyin'!"

"Uh-uh. I seen her. She's dead."

Boone felt his eyes welling up. He didn't want to cry in front of Toad, so he did the only thing he could think of. He punched his friend in the nose. The boys went to the ground in a tangle, wrestling, and punching, and kicking up dust.

"Dang you, Boone. Quit!"

"You take that back, or I'll poke you in the eye."

"Quit! My ma's gonna whip me if I tear my shirt."

When the boys finally ran out of air, they let go their grasp and rolled onto their backs. Both began to cry at the loss of their friend.

"Who done it, Toady?"

"Charles Milner. The storekeep over in Mex town," he said, wiping the tears from his dirty face. "He gun fought Malcolm

The Day Hunters

Thorndyke, that old farmer, but he missed and shot Opal. The swamper at the saloon said they were fightin' over her."

"How come?"

"He said they both wanted to marry her."

"What happened to old Thorndyke?"

"Nothin'. He didn't get a scratch. I gotta go home." Toad stood up and walked away without saying another word. He left Boone lying beside his mother's grave.

Opal Calvin had many friends in Austin. Every kid in town came to her door for cookies and treats. Her death would be a hard blow for all, but especially for Boone. Opal had been the only woman in his life since his mother died. She promised Louise she would see to it that Boone was cared for, and had been as good as her word, though most others in town were not. People often made promises to the dying, and Boone was likeable enough, but Louise had been in a downward spiral since the day she and the boy arrived.

She came to Austin five years before, a mail-order bride filled with hopes and dreams of a better life. Her husband was killed in the first year of the war. Boone hadn't even been born. She struggled to make it on her own in New Orleans, but in time her options ran out, so she advertised herself in the Gentleman's Catalogue. Mr. Josiah Hennessey replied, and sent her the money for the trip within four months.

Mr. Hennessey wasn't handsome, but he owned a prosperous farm and seemed to say all the right things. He didn't say anything about his drinking. On the day she and Boone reached Austin, Mr. Hennessey, after too much celebration, stepped into the street and was run over and killed by the very stagecoach that brought them to town.

Once again left with no money and few options, Louise began working the jobs available to women. Laundry, bakery, cafe, and eventually saloon. There was no place left to go but whoring, which she refused to do. All the while, her own drinking increased until finally it took her life.

Boone loved Opal, and would often stay with her when his

The Day Hunters

mother worked at night. But if she worked during the day, he would usually go to the Rangers' bunkhouse, where every boy in town ended up sooner or later. He had been living there since his mother's death.

Eddie Roberts, an old Ranger who no longer took to the field, would fill the boys' heads with wild tales of Comanches and Mexican bandits. Boone had even heard Eddie tell one of the older boys how Opal Calvin had once been raped by a Comanche buck. Boone didn't know what rape was, but he knew what dead was—and Opal Calvin was dead.

Eddie told so many stories, Boone thought he must be at least a hundred. He didn't know how anyone, especially a Texas Ranger, could live to be that old. At the rate people died in Texas, Boone considered this a miracle.

The boy dried his tears and got to his feet when he heard Eddie making his way up the hill. Eddie had become so rheumatic in his old age, that Boone didn't have to see him to know he was there.   He grunted and groaned with every movement, adding plenty of cussing for emphasis.

"They're gonna bury her this afternoon," he said. "I'm sure gonna miss her, ain't you?"

"Yes, sir."

"She had a pretty smile, and a gentle good nature. Them two things don't always go together in a woman. Remember when she'd cook supper for you? Why, she'd always ask me to come along. She must've been a fine wife. I know Wesley really loved her."

Opal's husband, Wesley Calvin, had been a good friend to Eddie and a good Ranger to Texas, but one day he just shot himself. Boone didn't know why. He heard stories around town, but he didn't understand them. To him, Wesley was just one more dead man in Texas.

"Did you know him, Eddie? The man that shot her?"

"Yeah, I knew him. He came to Texas from Alabama after the war. I don't know why. Life ain't any easier here than it is in Alabama. Though they ain't got any Comanches there."

The Day Hunters

"I hope they hang him."

"It was an accident, son. Besides there's no need. He cut his own throat in jail last night. I expect he felt hopeless."

Boone, at the moment, felt hopeless himself. He wished the Rangers would come home so he could talk to Harley, because Harley always knew what to do when things went bad.

Harley Macon had been a Confederate captain in the war. Afterward, he returned to Texas to rejoin the Rangers and his friend Cole Ellsworth, who stayed behind to help keep the lid on the Comanche problem. Though he held no official rank with the Rangers, it was clear that Harley was second-in-command to Captain Ellsworth, as his combat exploits were the stuff of legend. It was said that his lofty stature and absolute courage inspired his men to fight. It was also said that his handsome face and charming way encouraged women not to.

Though he'd once been a captain, he didn't like to be called captain, unless of course, he used the title himself. All the Rangers just called him Harley, except Moody, who called him Mister Harley. But then, Asa Moody called all white men Mister.

Moody met Captain Ellsworth when he was still a slave on a farm south of Austin. The Captain had been tracking a known horse thief, who mistakenly took refuge in the master's barn. When questioned, Moody informed the Captain of the thief's hiding place and soon, without ceremony, the man was hanged from the rafters. Moody buried the body himself.

"If I can ever help you, call on me," the Captain said, so on the day Moody got the news that slavery had been abolished, he dropped his hoe and walked to Austin. He'd been with the Texas Rangers ever since. A brawny man of rare good humor, Moody was easy to talk to and knew many things. But Boone wanted to talk to Harley, who seemed to know everything.

His mother had been well liked by all the Rangers. He was sure they would be sad when they heard she was dead. And now, Opal Calvin was dead, too. Harley and the Captain both liked Opal, and the Captain had visited his mother a lot. Many men came to visit his mother, but she turned them all away. The only man she showed any interest in was Captain Ellsworth.

The grave diggers strolled up the hill, laughing and joking, dragging their shovels on the ground. It seemed like rude behavior to Boone. His mother had taught him that a funeral was a place to be quiet, so he thought a graveyard should be, too. Boone hoped Eddie would say something to the men, but he didn't. Either way, the quiet moment with his mother was over.

As the gravediggers began their task, still laughing and joking, Boone and Eddie, hand in hand, started down the hill back to town. The storm clouds were blowing up, and it was turning chilly. Boone hoped the noisy gravediggers would catch cold in the rain.

#

Sergeant Marcus Teague had spent enough time in the army. He was thirty years old when he joined up to fight for the Confederacy, serving as a lieutenant under General Thomas "Stonewall" Jackson. He was present the night the general was wounded by friendly fire, and stood beside the operating table while the surgeon amputated the arm. But the general's life could not be saved, and neither could the Confederacy.

The war had been a long, desperate conflict, one bloody engagement after another. As much as he wanted it to end, by the time the war was over, soldiering was about the only thing he could remember how to do. He'd signed on with the blue bellies as a means to travel west, and here he was. Fort Riley, Kansas. What a hell of a place.

Upon arrival, Teague's rank was immediately reduced to sergeant—another point of contention. Wearing the blue began to rub him the wrong way. He felt the army owed him something, so he started scheming to steal the mules. Shortly after arriving he met Corporal Bullock and Private Daniels, two young, bored misfits. The army was full of them. Convincing them of his plan took little effort. They were just waiting for the right conditions.

"Sergeant of the guard! Post number one!" Corporal

The Day Hunters

Bullock shouted, his voice nearly lost in the wind. The cavvy of forty mules he guarded became more and more restless as the thunderstorm drew closer. The storm could work well to the thieves' advantage. The weather was perfect for what they had in mind. Once the mules started moving, they would cover ground quickly. The storm would drown out the noise. Maybe tonight, after all the planning, they would steal the mules and drive them south. Bullock had never done such a thing, but compared to army life, it sounded far more lucrative.

He heard the sucking sound of horse feet in the mud as Sergeant Teague approached, his rain slicker blowing in the breeze.

"We gonna do it tonight, Sarge? The weather couldn't be much better, could it?"

"You're right there. When's the last time you saw Daniels?"

"When we started our watch. He's ready when you give the word. It's gonna storm like hell."

"That's just what we want. Wash out all our tracks. The mules are in good shape. We can drive 'em hard. They'll bring a good price in the territory. I heard Lean Wolf pays with gold."

"And then trades 'em for rifles," Bullock confirmed.

"Right."

"Kinda sticks in my craw to put guns in the hands of them Indians."

"We ain't sellin' 'em guns. We're sellin' 'em mules. What they do with 'em is their business."

"What time is it, Sarge?"

Teague checked his father's gold watch. "Ten thirty."

"Perfect. No shift change 'til two. If we leave soon, we can be hours from here before we're found out."

The thunder grew louder. It was just starting to rain again, the lightning flashes as bright as day.

"I'll go find Daniels," Teague said. "Give me five minutes, then start driftin' 'em southwest, slow and quiet."

Bullock checked the load in his pistol, buttoned up his

slicker against the chilly rain, and started easing around to the east side of the cavvy.

Private Orry Daniels was a jumpy man. The storm only made him more so. He hoped this would be the night, but Teague had backed out before, citing any number of reasons. Daniels was beginning to doubt the man's conviction.

All the talk of gold to spend and freedom from the army, had convinced Daniels that Teague's plan was sound. But there were other things he needed to be free of.

He'd joined the army to flee a rape charge in Michigan, and only recently had raped and killed a young Lakota girl right here at Fort Riley. The girl seemed willing at first, but then Daniels got rough. She fought him hard, threatened to tell her father, so when he'd finished, he strangled her, and dumped her body in the woods. Though no one in particular was suspected of the crime, Daniels thought it best to get away. The Indians at the fort were in an ugly mood, vowing quick vengeance if the killer was identified.

Mexico sounded good to him, the warm climate, and black eyed *señoritas*. Daniels had never been with a Mexican girl, but he'd heard they were fiery, passionate lovers. He looked forward to the new experience.

The rain was falling steadily when Sergeant Teague rode up. Daniels could tell by the look on his face that they were about to leave.

"I guess this is it, huh, Sarge?"

"Yeah. This is it. I'm headin' for the point. Give me a minute, then start 'em slow. We'll walk 'em quiet for a mile or so, then let 'em run. You ready?"

"More than ready."

The theft took place just as Teague ordered, but they didn't make a mile before a huge clap of thunder set the mules off. In a flash, the whole bunch were at a dead run, charging through the storm, headed southwest.

The Day Hunters

Chapter 3

Delgado rode throughout the night, reaching the battleground just before daylight. He found the outlaw's remains and the Rangers' dead horses, but there were no graves. That meant Ellsworth was alive. At least, he didn't die here.

The outlaw's name was Carlisle, a man Delgado held in contempt for his rudeness. The fool seemed to have no manners at all. Picking his nose and scratching his ass were two of his favorite pastimes.

Delgado knelt to search Carlisle's pockets, holding a bandana over his nose against the smell. He found twenty-five dollars in gold coin, and a fine ruby ring. The ring would make a nice gift for a willing woman. He stripped the man's gunbelt, gathered his weapons, mounted, and rode away. What the buzzards hadn't eaten wasn't worth burying.

The Rangers would likely ride south to the Brazos. There were a few settlers brave enough to live there, though it was a precarious existence. Everyone needed water in this country, good men and bad. There was no telling who might show up at your door, the prophet, or the predator.

Delgado filled his hat with water from his canteen and offered it to his horse. The horse drank it down without hesitation, then looked to Delgado for more.

"It is twenty miles to the river, *caballo*. There you can drink your fill."

The Rangers' camp on the Brazos was easy to find. Delgado was pretty sure where they would go. The campsite was used by every traveler on the river. He'd used it himself a few times. He was certain the Rangers would just follow the river to Fort Belknap, then down to Waco. From there, the last leg of the trip to Austin would be easy.

But how bad was Ellsworth wounded? He saw no sign of any blood in the camp. No fresh holes dug to bury the bandages. Maybe Zendejaz was wrong. Maybe he hadn't wounded Ellsworth

27

The Day Hunters

at all. Zendejaz seemed certain that he'd hit him, but anyone could make a mistake in a gun battle. Besides, Ellsworth had made it this far. He couldn't be hurt very bad. If he made it to the settlements, he could get whatever medical attention he needed.

Delgado rested a while at the camp, then pushed on until about sundown. The following morning, he found another dead horse along the Rangers' trail. The horse had been shot between the eyes, the hindquarters butchered for food. Soon, the Rangers would reach the settlements, where they would probably get more horses, then ride on to Fort Belknap. Delgado could not show his face there. If he did, he would surely be hung—a matter of twelve stolen horses.

Would the Rangers remount, and head back to the field? He thought it unlikely. Delgado felt sure they were bound for Austin. Disobeying Zendejaz, he crossed the river and headed southeast. There was no need to follow the river. After all, Zendejaz didn't own him.

The Rangers' layover at Fort Belknap was brief. A bath, a shave, two meals, and a night's sleep were all Cole would allow time for. He intended to wire a report to the governor, but the lines were down, as they often were. Between people shooting the insulators for target practice, and the Indians cutting the wires, it was not uncommon for communication to be hampered.

Cole took a chance at being laughed off the post when he attempted to trade their broken down horses. "There's not enough feed on this post to fill out these glue bags," was how the remount officer put it.

"We ain't gonna get any help from the army," Harley said. "The Texas Rangers are a joke to them."

"Well, I had to try," Cole said. "As slow as we're travelin', we'll head straight to Austin. No need to go to Waco. Plenty o' water between here and there."

"I'm ready to get back, too. I swear, I've never seen uglier

The Day Hunters

women than them that whore at an army post."

"We need to be thinkin' about horses and supplies. Anything you're plannin' on doin' in Austin, you better do it fast. We ain't gonna be there long. Just long enough to get gathered up."

"You know it don't take me long to do my business, Cole. I'd like a drink o' good whiskey, though. I'd need a while to build up a tolerance for the swill they serve around here."

"They probably didn't expect a man of your high standards. I'm sure if they'd known somebody special was comin' by, they'd've had somethin' sent in from St. Louis."

"The point is, if they expect these blue bellies to come down here and fight injuns, they oughta, at least, get 'em some decent refreshment."

"Let's get goin'. I've enjoyed all this place I want."

The Rangers walked to the stable to saddle their horses and put Fort Belknap behind them. One night's rest and feed hadn't done much to improve the animals' condition. They looked like they'd just been *unsaddled.*

"Stone Horse," Cole said, "I want you to ride up north. See if you can find any sign of Lean Wolf. I expect we'll meet you on the trail somewhere in eight or ten days. We'll hold our course due north of Austin."

Stone Horse nodded his agreement, mounted, and rode away. The Rangers set their sights on Austin, leaving a group of soldiers leaning on the fence, laughing at the Rangers' poor horses.

#

Stone Horse found Lean Wolf's camp three days after he split off from the Ranger troop. Captain Ellsworth would be glad to know that Lean Wolf was now using the camp of Crooked Foot, the Comanche chief the Captain had killed in this very place only a year ago. The Rangers could make good time, already knowing the camp's location. But Lean Wolf was not there.

The Day Hunters

Lean Wolf and his renegades had turned the place into a shambles. It did not look like the camp of a prosperous outlaw. The whole area reeked of human excrement, poorly disposed carcasses, and rotten guts. The few people in the camp wore tattered rags for clothing. All were in poor flesh. Broken women, dirty, drunken men, and a few nearly naked, half starved children were its only inhabitants.

Stone Horse wanted information on Lean Wolf's whereabouts, and he knew only one way to get it. He waited until he saw an old man wandering off into the woods alone, then quietly began to stalk him. He found the Old One on his knees, pleasuring himself, holding a tintype of a very shapely, bare breasted woman. No doubt the picture was stolen from some murdered settler. Stone Horse hated to interrupt, but managed a smile as he lay the blade to the old man's throat.

"Where is Lean Wolf?" he demanded.

The Old One shriveled instantly. "Lean Wolf is not here."

"I know that, you fool. *Where is he?*"

"I do not know where he is. He comes and goes as he pleases."

"*I am Tonkawa!*" Stone Horse threatened. "Cutting the throat of a stinking old Comanche will not trouble me."

"Nor will it trouble me to die by the hand of a stinking Tonkawa," the Old One said, "if you would only grant me a few more minutes."

Stone Horse held back his laughter. "All right, old man. I will leave you to your pleasure. I am going to find the Rangers. If you are still here when we return, you will be killed," he said, disappearing into the brush.

#

The faint smoke rising from the chimneys of Austin was a welcome sight to Captain Ellsworth and his men. They'd been five days on the trail from Fort Belknap. Tired and numb from the long hours in the saddle, each man longed for comfort in his own

30

The Day Hunters

way. But all thought a trip to visit the girls was in order. The weary men had spoken of little else through the day, and Cole was glad of it. The troop needed a distraction from the memory of their butchered friends. He knew they would not be in town long. As soon as they could remount and provision, he intended to head north to find Lean Wolf and kill him.

Cole saw the boy kneeling beside a cheap wooden cross, tending the flowers, as the graveyard came into view. "Look there, Harley. Ain't that Boone, Louise's boy?" A shock wave ran through him as he said it. The day he'd dreaded had finally come.

"Yeah, looks like. Damn, I expect she finally gave it up."

A deep sadness came over Cole. "I swear. I remember the day she and the boy came to town. I think she was the prettiest girl I ever saw."

"Well, she lived a hard life, Cole. Too much liquor catches up to all of 'em, one way or another. Damn, she was pretty, though."

The Rangers rode close enough to read the marker. Harley spit and hung his head. Neither Eli nor Moody knew how to read, but they could see the grave was right beside Wesley's.

"Dern, is it Opal, Cap'n?" Eli asked.

"Yeah, it's Opal."

"What happened here, Boone?" Harley asked the boy.

"A man shot her when he shot at another man. And my mama's dead, too," Boone added. The tears streamed down his face, at the sight of his returning friends. Harley promptly dismounted and went to the boy, holding him, letting him cry.

Cole had no idea what to say. Both he and Harley had remarked as to how poorly Louise had been looking. They knew she had only a slim chance of recovery. But they also knew that Opal had promised Louise to care for the boy in the event of her death. Now Opal was gone, too. She couldn't keep her promise.

"Have you been stayin' with Eddie?" Harley asked.

Boone nodded, but didn't stop crying.

Harley struggled for words to comfort the boy. "Remember when we talked about your mama, son? How she wouldn't be sick anymore, after she was gone? Well, she ain't sick anymore, Boone, and we're all proud of you—the way you stood up to it. You're a good, brave boy."

Two rows over Cole found Louise's grave. He stared at the marker as if in a trance, his mind flooded with memories of the many hours he'd spent with the pretty girl from New Orleans. Her soft brown eyes and coal black hair, captivated him from the moment she stepped off the stage. He immediately took a shine to her, as did every other man in Austin.

"Eli, you n' Moody stable these nags. Take Boone down with you," Harley said. "Me n' *Captain* Ellsworth'll be along shortly."

"Yes sir," Eli answered, happy to be away. When Harley used that tone Eli knew there would be an argument. He gave Boone a warm hug, lifted him up on the Captain's horse, and the three of them rode down the hill.

"Well, Cole, what're you gonna do now?"

"About what?"

"By God, you know what. Somebody oughta look out for that boy. You want him cleanin' spittoons for a penny a day? He's a good boy and his mama cared about you. Don't tell me you didn't care about her. Hell, he's at the bunkhouse half the time anyway. We oughta take care of him. Opal can't do it now."

"Dammit, Harley, how are we gonna take care of him? You wanna answer me that? We're hardly ever in town more than a week or two. And this time only a few days."

"What's the harm in lettin' him stay with Eddie? He can help the old cod with the chores, and Eddie can teach him plenty o' things he'll need to know, like how to make a decent cup o' coffee. That's more than anybody else in this outfit can do."

Cole was too tired and sad to argue with Harley. The trip had been long and slow. They needed to report to the governor, though he certainly wouldn't like the report. Cole started to speak, but Harley was already halfway down the hill.

"Where you goin'?" he shouted.

Harley turned quickly, glaring at his partner. "I'm goin' to see the damn governor, *Captain.* You comin'?"

#

Governor Elisha M. Pease had been staring out his office window for an uncomfortably long time. The news of the murdered Rangers struck him a hard blow. Cole waited, trying to be patient. He had even thought of excusing himself and coming back later, but finally the governor turned and spoke.

"Do we know any more about who's supplying Zendejaz?"

"No, sir. No idea where he's gettin' the Henrys."

"And that bastard Lean Wolf is still free. The thought of that murderer running loose is almost more than I can tolerate. I can only imagine how you and your troop feel, Captain, having lost so many in your command. But you did exactly as I would have done. 'Seasoned troops to the front, green troops to the rear.' You made the right decision, though I'm sure that makes it no easier to live with." The governor returned to the window and slipped back into his silence.

The clock ticked. Cole grew anxious, waiting for Governor Pease to say something. He didn't want to be rude and interrupt the man's thinking, but things needed to be done. The Rangers needed fresh mounts and provisions. They should leave as soon as possible if they were to pick up Lean Wolf's trail again. He and Harley had discussed this on the trip back to Austin.

The future of the Texas Rangers was uncertain at best. Congress didn't want to fund them, and Texas couldn't. They'd been ready to quit the Rangers and try their hand at something else, but the loss of their men changed that. Now they wanted Lean Wolf's scalp more than ever. Harley had remarked that he would take great pleasure in hanging the man "a little at a time". Just as Cole was about to speak, the governor shocked them both with his statement.

"Captain, I hate to let that scoundrel escape, but I need to send you and your men to the border. The few Rangers we have

The Day Hunters

down there can't hope to control it. The army won't help. They claim they're too busy with the Indians up north. The ranchers are raising hell, what with all the rustling and killing going on."

Harley exploded. *"Rustlin'* and *killin'*? With all due respect, Governor, we need to be after Lean Wolf. That son of a bitch murdered five Rangers. By God, he needs to pay for it!"

Cole could hardly believe his ears. Surely the governor couldn't mean what he said. Five dead Rangers, and they were being sent to the border? Cole knew there was plenty to do there. He just thought their business more urgent. The border wasn't going anywhere, but Lean Wolf was hard to keep track of.

The southern border of Texas had long been disputed. The United States claimed the Rio Grande, Mexico claimed the Nueces River. In between lay a long stretch of bloody prairie, known as the Nueces Strip. In the aftermath of the Mexican War, the strip became, essentially, a lawless battleground. Rustlers and horse thieves from both sides of the Rio Grande spent their lives chasing livestock back and forth, killing anyone who tried to stop them.

For the past ten years, thousands of cattle had been driven to Mexico by a highly organized band of thieves, their leader a ruthless bandit known as Juan Cortina. A cunning, fearless, self-proclaimed patriot, Cortina showed his enemies no quarter, leaving any number of dead Texans in his wake.

Though he was speechless, Cole knew it wouldn't matter now if Harley was talking to President Grant. He would have his say. Cole thought to intervene for a moment, but reconsidered. To hell with it. Harley would have his say, and he would back him. That's the way it had always been. There was nothing to do now but let Harley get his wind up.

"With your permission, Governor, we'll give chase to Lean Wolf and his killers, then we'll take the border. Without your permission, by God, we'll give chase to Lean Wolf, and you and the border can go to Hell...*sir!*"

Harley turned on his heel, and stormed out of the office, throwing the door wide open as he left.

With nothing else to do, Cole stood up and put on his hat,

The Day Hunters

waiting to see what the governor would do or say. As the man seemed to be in shock and slow to speak, Cole excused himself and strode to the door.

"Captain," the governor said. "Round up some men. You have thirty days."

#

Cole nailed up a request for volunteers outside the broad, swinging doors of the Top Drawer Saloon. A wiry Mexican lounged on the boardwalk. Cole gave the man a suspicious nod before he stepped inside.

Harley sat at a corner table playing solitaire. The place was a cool retreat from the hot summer sun, furnished with padded leather chairs and a forty foot bar, with mirrors from Kansas City the full length behind it. Faro, roulette, and even a pool table kept the customers occupied. The Top Drawer was one of the finest saloons in all of Texas. Cole knew whenever the Rangers were in Austin, he could find Harley there. He walked to the bar, picked up a glass, and crossed the room to join his tipsy friend. Harley had consumed nearly half a bottle of whiskey. He was feeling a little better.

"Sit down, Cole. You ain't gonna get any taller," he chuckled. "Let's have a drink."

Cole filled the glasses, and Harley made the toast.

"To die is but to live again."

The look on Cole's face barely passed for amusement.

"I never thought I'd hear somebody tell the governor to go to Hell."

"Why not? He's the governor. He ain't God. I expect you'll be runnin' for the Lord's office when we quit Rangerin'."

"I didn't say he was God, Harley. But hellfire, he sure looked shocked when you told him off. Besides, we ain't quittin' now. At least, not for a while. When we catch up to Lean Wolf, I hope God ain't lookin'. The governor gave us thirty days to get him, so we need to get busy."

The Day Hunters

"I'll get busy after I've had a bath. A meal and another bottle don't sound bad neither. While I'm here, I expect I'll get me a poke," Harley chuckled, eyeing the pretty brunette at the bar. Normally the girls came straight to his table when he came in, but not today. For whatever reason, he had to blame it on his partner.

"Hell, a bath wouldn't hurt you none neither, Cole. I swear, you're repellin' the whores."

#

Cole Ellsworth was not the kind of man who would shirk his responsibilities just because he needed a little sleep. But the real reason he was standing guard, was that he couldn't take the crying in the bunkhouse. Austin was no longer under Ranger security. The bandits didn't come this far north anymore, nor the Indians this far south. Whatever law needed enforcing in Austin, Sheriff Pence could handle it.

But the boy cried all evening. The death of his mother weighed heavy on him. And Opal's too. Bass Reed had been kind to him, and he was fast becoming friends with some of the murdered Rangers. Cole knew a boy like Boone would need a good friend, as he'd suffered many of the same hardships himself.

His pa died in Arkansas, when a tree he was cutting down fell the wrong way. His mother, left alone with a young son, went to making and selling moonshine whiskey. It kept the wolf away from the door for a while, but when she started sampling too much of the product, her many male customers took to spending the night. Soon a constant parade of men stopped by, not only to purchase the shine. What killed his mother, he didn't know. Maybe the whiskey, maybe something she caught from the men, or maybe she just quit living. He found her naked in her bed one morning—buried her that afternoon. He left for Texas the following day, one week before his twelfth birthday. His friend, Harley Macon, ran away from home to go with him. They'd been together ever since.

36

The Day Hunters

He deeply regretted not being in Austin when Louise gave up the ghost. He had never been there when she really needed someone. He was always off chasing Indians with Harley. He'd been familiar with her for several years, and over those years they had become good friends. It was more of a kinship than a love affair, as he'd watched his own mother live the same life. Often, he found Louise drunk, crying in the dark, pretending she wasn't home. He never knew what to say to her at those moments, but he would hold her, and that seemed to be enough.

Nearly every man in Austin made a play for her, whether married or single. It was her good looks that made the men want her. Afterward, when she'd turned them down, they only wanted her more. He'd wanted her himself, maybe more than the others. He just didn't know why. After witnessing his own mother's lingering demise, why would he entangle himself with a drunk? And a drunk with a child, at that?

His partner would have ridiculed such reasoning, since according to Harley, the boy's worship was obvious to the blind.

"Hell, Cole, you're his hero," Harley would scoff. "He walks like you, talks like you, he even sits around sharpenin' his damn knife blade away like you do. What else do you want?"

Cole didn't claim to know what love felt like, but he had always liked and respected Louise. He knew he would dearly miss her. She held her head up when Austin looked down on her. He recognized the courage in that. In a few days, he knew his own courage would be tested again, when the Rangers rode out after Lean Wolf. The boy would have to stay with Eddie, at least until they returned—if they returned. He didn't know what else to do. None of it made any sense. How could the Rangers care for a boy when they could be killed at any time? When all they could think about was Lean Wolf, or Zendejaz, or some other damned bandit?

He'd never thought of himself as a caretaker to a child. Nor as anything other than a Texas Ranger. Mostly because, as the name implied, he purely loved to range. He had always felt his first duty was to the citizens of Texas. And now, to Bass Reed and the boys. It was time for Lean Wolf to die.

The Day Hunters

Chapter 4

Harley awoke, well before daylight, in the arms of Isabella, the brunette whore at the bar. He preferred to spend the entire night with Isabella, rather than go back to the bunkhouse and listen to the Rangers farting and snoring. Her charms proved this to be the right decision, as she had put him to sleep, completely satisfied, in a bed far more comfortable than he had in the bunkhouse. Harley hadn't taken any comfort in a good, long while. He knew it might be even longer before the opportunity presented itself again.

The smell of Isabella's hair, her soft gentle breathing, the rise and fall of her shapely breasts were all things Harley yearned for. He partook of women's favors as often as they were available, but none satisfied the longing in his heart. Harley lay still, quietly thinking of all the women he had woken up next to. And of Abigail Mendenhall, the one woman he dearly *wanted* to wake up next to.

After the Perryville, Kentucky fight, the 8th received orders to cover General Bragg's tedious withdrawal from the state into Tennessee. The march was made particularly difficult due to an October cold snap, accompanied by an early snow. The locals graciously opened their homes to the battle weary Texans in December of '62, providing the men with good meals, warm fires, and plenty of pretty smiles. It was in such a home that he met her.

Harley felt there was not a woman in Texas that could rival Abigail's beauty. She moved with a grace beyond compare, looking to the needs of the soldiers in an almost angelic fashion. She nursed their wounds, cooked for them, mended their clothes, even entertained them on the spinet in the evening. Every man sat in awe of her, but it was Harley she chose to walk with.

They had long talks about everything, and danced when her mother supplied the music. Harley even helped her with the Christmas decorations. He was sure he'd found the only one, but then the war interrupted and the 8th moved out. They never saw each other again. Though he'd no more than kissed Abigail's cheek, Harley knew he would always remember the tall, willowy blonde with the flashing blue eyes.

Neither Bass Reed nor the boys, would ever wake up with a woman again. Some were so young, maybe they never had. It was a thought that grieved Harley's soul. He felt he had seen enough dead boys for one lifetime.

Harley reached for the whiskey bottle on the nightstand, surveyed the contents left from the night before, and polished it off in one long drink. Returning the bottle, he slid from Isabella's arms, covered her bare foot, and stepped behind the privacy screen to use the chamber pot. With just a streak of gray in the sky, Harley could see the graveyard from the window of the little room above the saloon. Louise was there, along with Opal and Wesley. Bass and the boys, and a lot of other friends, all dead and gone now. Well, life was for the living and he was alive. It was time to get moving.

Harley stepped out from behind the screen just as Isabella sat up in the bed, yawning, stretching her chubby arms to the ceiling. Her sleepy smile and naked breasts, enticed him to stay a while longer. But he reasoned that he would need nourishment before he could do himself justice, as Isabella had surely weakened him. She snuggled back down in the covers as he began to dress.

"Mornin' honey. You sleep good?" he asked her.

"I surely did, darlin'."

Her answer brought a smile to his face. "Hell, if you slept that good, maybe you oughta pay me."

"Goodness, if I did that, I'd have to raise my own prices to pay my bill. I can't do that, sugar."

Isabella's playful expression changed to melancholy. "We sung at Lou's funeral. Me and some of the other girls. But the town didn't want us at Opal's."

"Sounds about right. Did she suffer much?"

"Yeah, but not alone. One of the girls was with her most of the time. Annie was there when she died. So was Boone."

"Well, I expect I'd better get goin'. Cole's likely chewed

The Day Hunters

through his leash by now." Harley dug into his pocket and laid ten dollars on the nightstand, just before strapping on his pistol.

"It's only five dollars for the night, darlin'." Isabella was surprised by the man's generosity. "Most men would've argued about the five."

"Ain't you heard? I ain't most men." Harley bent and kissed her on the cheek. "A workman's worthy of his hire, honey. That's in the Bible."

He walked out the door and down the back steps, into the street just coming to life. It was not much different than any other main thoroughfare in any other western town, with the exception of the capitol building at the far end of the street—a shabby looking structure denounced as the worst firetrap in Texas. A wide area for turning wagons around, hardware, a dry goods store that doubled as a post office, barber shop, a saloon or two inferior to the Top Drawer, bakery, cafe, feed and grain, and sundry shops filled with ladies knick-knacks and do-dads.

Old Man Pearson creaked along, snuffing out the street lamps. Sheriff Pence stepped around the corner, offering a wave as he returned from his morning trip to the privy. The merchants, out early, swept the dust from the boardwalk.

Harley ambled down the street in the direction of the Rangers' bunkhouse, but stopped short when he saw the large doors of the blacksmith's shop swing open. The scrappy looking little man with the big moustache waved him over.

His name was Beau Hackler. After the war, both he and Harley had returned to Austin, arriving in town the same day. Beau served as one of Captain L.H. McNelly's Confederate guerillas in Louisiana, often operating behind enemy lines. The two shared the feelings all soldiers shared. He grinned a grin Harley could barely see behind the moustache.

"Howdy, Beau."

"Harley," he said, sticking out his hand. "I heard you boys got in. Sorry about your men."

"Yeah. Not as sorry as we are. We just plain did that wrong."

40

The Day Hunters

"You know how it is. You give your orders and you hope they're good ones. Sometimes they are...sometimes..." he shrugged his shoulders.

"We'll be leavin' soon. Tomorrow, I reckon. Cole's got blood in his eye. Me too, I guess."

"Don't let it cloud your thinkin'. No luck findin' Zendejaz?"

"We found him. We had some lively shootin', but he got by us. The son of a bitch just disappears out there."

A hungry looking Mexican approached the shop, leading an outstanding chestnut gelding, in dire need of being re-shod.

"Well Beau, looks like you're about to go to work," Harley said. "I'll meet you at the Top Drawer tonight for a drink."

"All right. Bring your money. We'll play some cards."

Beau Hackler was intolerant of folks who put off their horseshoeing. He looked the horse over as Harley walked away. He was disappointed in what he saw.

"Now son, there's three kinds o' horses in this world," he said to the Mexican. "Them that's been lame, them that are lame, and them that's gonna be lame...like your horse was about to be. If you'd waited much longer to get him shod, you'd be walkin'."

"*Sí, Señor*. How much?"

"Two dollars. I oughta charge you more for the shape he's in."

"I will pay three dollars. I am in a hurry, *Señor*."

"Don't crowd me, son. You might be in a hurry, but I ain't. You wait 'til he's purt near barefoot, then you're in a hurry. Get comfortable. I ain't even built my fire yet."

Delgado rolled a cigarette while he waited for the farrier to build his fire. He was in a *big* hurry. Zendejaz would want to know that Captain Ellsworth was not only alive, but mounting a troop to go after Lean Wolf. The news of the Rangers' massacre was the talk of the town. It didn't take him very long to find out that Ellsworth was heading back into the field. Citizens walked the streets preaching revenge, though Delgado doubted many of them had the courage to go looking for it.

The Day Hunters

He'd been in town only two days when the Rangers arrived. After taking his pleasures with the girls, and spending most of Carlisle's money, he sat leaned back in a chair in front of the Top Drawer Saloon when Ellsworth nailed up the sign. He could've reached out and stabbed the man, but knew he'd never get out of town alive.

He would leave the horse, and go get some breakfast. As soon as the shoeing task was finished, he would ride for the stronghold to warn Zendejaz.

#

Harley drifted to the lots behind the bunkhouse to find Eddie Roberts leaning on the top rail of the corral, nursing a cup of coffee that looked hot enough to cook over.

"Mornin', Eddie."

"Mornin', Harley. Glad you made it back. Boone's been missin' you somethin' awful."

"Is he up yet?"

"Naw. He cried a lot last night, so I let him sleep. The Cap'n left. Couldn't stand the cryin', I expect."

"Yeah, I expect," Harley scoffed. "Looks like you've been doin' some horse tradin' while we've been gone. There's some good mounts in there. Glad to see the damn legislature finally found some money somewhere."

"Yep, I favor that dun geldin', and that little grulla mare. They'd be my picks if I was pickin'. But I ain't." Eddie knew he'd never ride out with the Rangers again. The thought always made him sad.

Harley nodded. "Who's in the bunkhouse?"

"Eli and Moody, and two new young'uns. They been hangin' around town awhile. Saw the sign, and come in last night. I think one of 'em's got the makin's, but the other one looks kinda squeamish."

"Moody make the coffee?"

The Day Hunters

"Nope, made it myself."

"Good, I'll have some." Harley threw the bunkhouse door open and stepped inside. "By God," he shouted, "you boys better get your ass in the saddle. Cole's already got the mules packed!"

All four men leaped off their bunks. They ran, grabbed, stumbled, and fell out the door amid a chorus of "damns, oh lawds, and aww hells."

Harley laughed aloud as he closed the door, wedging a chair up under the knob. He poured himself a steaming cup, then took a seat in the one decent chair in the filthy room. Boone, awakened at such a noisy entrance, walked over and climbed into the Ranger's lap.

"Careful with that coffee, son. It's hotter'n Hell on Sunday mornin'." He saw no reason to question the boy, as he'd heard all about both Opal and Louise in the saloon the night before. "You all right, Boone?"

"Yessir, I reckon I am," the boy said, his brown eyes filling with tears.

"Well, you'll dry up pretty soon. Has Eddie been takin' good care of you?"

"Yessir, but he can't cook like Opal."

"I'll bet on that," Harley laughed. "Opal was our good friend, wasn't she, son?"

"Yessir, and she was mama's friend, too."

Harley felt bad for the boy. He was sure off to a rough start. "Well, I reckon you'll just stay with us, now. We'll teach you what we can, and we'll start with makin' coffee. Now the first thing you need to know is, *don't let Moody teach you!*"

#

The Rangers lined up at the fence like magpies, talking, looking over the horses, when Harley and Boone stepped out into the morning sun. The two young Rangers snapped to attention in preparation to meet the mythical Confederate captain, Harley

The Day Hunters

Macon, who, to their regret, completely ignored them.

"Better get breakfast workin', Moody. Boone looks hungry," Harley said.

"Yessuh." In passing, Moody gave Boone a rub on top of the head. "That's good luck," he chuckled.

Eli swung Boone up onto his shoulders, and trotted around the corral. The boy shrieked with laughter. Boone was so happy, he was beside himself. He just didn't know what to do first. Show the boys how he'd been practicing with his rope, or show them where he'd dug the trench around the stable, so the stalls wouldn't get wet after a big rain, or tell them he'd made almost a dollar doing odd jobs around town. After the sadness of the last few months, Boone was overjoyed that the boys were back.

Maybe this was how the people at the church felt when they danced with their hands in the air. His mother had taken him to church on Sunday mornings, but he never saw her dance with her hands in the air. They always sat way in the back because they came late, and left early. Sometimes the men in the church would look at his mother in a way Boone didn't understand. The look seemed to make all the other women mad. Harley said the women were mad because his mother was prettier than all of them put together, and Boone believed it. To him, his mother was the prettiest woman in the world.

"Look," Boone shouted. "The Captain's comin'."

Stepping out of the bunkhouse with a fresh cup of coffee, Harley looked to the east to see Cole approaching, his big Henry rifle cradled at his elbow. He chuckled as he spoke to the young Rangers. "I'm gonna give you boys some real good advice. Find somethin' to do, quick."

"Yessir, Captain," they harmonized, trotting off to the stable.

"And, by God, don't call me captain!" he snapped, giving Boone a playful wink. "Better put that boy down, Eli. Looks like

The Day Hunters

the fun's over.

"Why, good mornin', Captain Ellsworth. I trust Austin is secure?"

"Yes, Austin's secure, no thanks to you."

"Y'know, Cole, spendin' the night curled up with a woman don't make me the crazy one. Did you n' Henry have a good time?"

"No, we didn't. I'll bet I killed that damn Lean Wolf a hundred times last night."

"You should've gone and got your ashes hauled. It might put you in a better mood. We can't kill him from here."

"All the more reason we need to get busy." Cole gave Boone a firm squeeze on the shoulder, as he stepped into the bunkhouse. "Let's eat it, Moody. We need to get movin'."

"All right, we heard you the first time," Harley said. "We need to get movin'. You get that, Moody?"

"Yessuh, we movin'," Moody replied, his customary grin intact.

Harley turned to the boy. "Go tell them in the stable they better come and get it, Boone. This bunch is liable to eat the table."

"Yes, sir." Boone left the room, his hands in his pockets. His face looked pouty and sad.

"Damn, Cole, we could've prepared him before you said we were leavin'. He's havin' a hell of a time."

"Well, you're right," Cole agreed, promptly returning to Ranger business. "Eddie, you list what we need to provision for a month in the field. Four of us, and Stone Horse. These boys are too young to go. You can keep 'em on if the state's got money to pay 'em, or let 'em go. It's up to you."

Harley nodded in agreement. They would lead no more green troops into the field.

Boone came quietly back into the room, and climbed up into his chair. "They said they'd be here when they finished the stalls," he reported. Moody served him a plate of bacon with cornbread and jam, and a small cup of coffee and milk. The boy devoured it all in an instant.

The Day Hunters

"We about outta coffee," Moody said. "I'll make some more."

"Oh lord," Harley said. "Can you handle that, Eddie? Give Moody a chance to eat?"

Moody laughed out loud as he sat down to his breakfast. Mr. Harley surely hated his coffee.

"Take one o' them new boys with you when you go to collect that stuff, Eddie."

"Yessir, Cap'n." Eddie lit a cigarette, and coughed up phlegm all the way to the stove.

"Make sure you don't get that in the coffee," Harley said.

"Eli, you take the other one. Get to work shoein' them horses."

Eli had been wolfing down his breakfast, hoping not to keep the Captain waiting.

"Yessir," he said, and headed for the door, a dab of jam still on his chin.

"Moody, pick two good mules for this trip. No jugheads. We can't afford any mistakes."

"Yessuh. I'll get started right now." Moody rushed out the door, taking his breakfast with him.

"Well, Harley, let's take a look at the horses," Cole said, gulping the last of his coffee. "Looks like Eddie found us some good ones."

"Don't you have somethin' for me to do, Captain?" Boone asked.

The question caught Cole off guard. He wasn't sure what to say. "Well, why don't you wash the dishes, and sweep the floor," he said, smiling at the boy's reaction.

"Yes sir, Captain!" Boone exclaimed, proudly mimicking the Rangers. He promptly gathered the dishes, and gave Harley a big smile. "At least the boys ain't gone yet," he whispered.

Cole and Harley made their way to the door, just as the young Rangers stepped inside, hungry and anxious for their breakfast.

"Too late, boys," Harley said. "Breakfast is over. We've

The Day Hunters

gotta get movin'."

#

Trailing the stolen mules through the Kansas hills seemed easy enough. One man, usually Private Daniels, would ride out to survey the countryside. He would then return and report. If all was clear, the men would drive the mules up onto the flats—there they would make good time. If anything suspicious was sighted, the cavvy was driven into the nearest depression and held there, or, if possible, driven more slowly through the lowlands.

So far, a few Cheyenne hunting parties had been seen, but at a safe enough distance the cavvy could easily be concealed. The deserters had seen no sign of the army, nor much of anything else, as they did their best to avoid contact with anyone. At the moment, Sergeant Teague and Corporal Bullock pushed the mules across the plains at the trot, while Private Daniels scouted the country.

"Let's walk 'em awhile. Let 'em blow," Teague shouted. When the mules had slowed their pace, the two men drifted together and, as was normal for most men, the conversation turned to women.

"You ever been married, Sarge?" Bullock asked.

"Yeah, I was married once. To a gal I'd known all my life. We were neighbors growin' up, so it seemed real handy. She died of typhoid seven months after we were married."

"Sorry. Was she pretty?"

"No. She wasn't pretty at all. She was plain as homemade soap. But she was kind, and gentle, and that's more important. She'd have made a fine mother. Just didn't get her chance. Her name was Caroline."

"I ain't ever been married. But I was with a woman once. I'd sure like to do that again."

"That's a good part of bein' married, all right. But it ain't the best part."

"If that ain't, what is?"

47

The Day Hunters

"Holdin' her close to you under the blankets, when it's freezin' outside. Havin' her say she loves you, and knowin' she means it. Or sayin' it to *her* and knowin' *you* mean it. Knowin' she ain't never gonna leave you. That's the best part."

"Well, I still wouldn't mind doin' that other part again."

"Me neither," Teague chuckled. "I guess we can have all we want when we get to Mexico."

"Look, there's Daniels!"

Private Daniels approached at an easy lope. He was in no particular hurry, but he carried important information.

"Indian village. Five miles ahead, Sarge. Big one. I'd say about a hundred, give or take."

"That means twenty warriors. . . or more," Teague said.

"We'd better cut south before they see us."

"You know where we are?" Daniels asked him.

"No, not for sure. But they say the Cimarron runs red. I guess we'll know when we get there. It's a good ways yet, I imagine."

They pointed the mules due south and left at the lope, putting as much ground as they could between them and the Indians. They had been lucky so far. Teague hoped their luck would hold out.

The Day Hunters

"Well, that's four, Eli. I expect you better lend a hand," Harley chuckled. He referred to how many times the mean-eyed bay had kicked the young Ranger, Milo Simms, across the pen. Milo had never shod a horse in his life. Harley was starting to think this one would probably last him. The youngster sweated through every dry thread. After four trips to the ground, he had sand stuck all over himself—a sight not wasted on Harley Macon.

"Damn, son, if you was to lay down out there in the pen, I doubt we could find you," he said.

According to Eddie, Milo had been in Austin only a short while, but everyone seemed to like him, especially Boone. He was eighteen years old, handsome and tough. Boone looked up to him like a big brother.

The talk was that Milo sometimes fought for money behind the cantina on the west side of town. But when Boone asked if he could go watch, Eddie had told him no.

"Your ma wouldn't want you there, son," Eddie said. "But I'll tell you all about it."

Harley and the boy sat perched on the fence, where Boone watched with fascination as Eli took over the shoeing. Eli had handled the farrier work ever since becoming a Ranger. Although he was far too tall for the job, he just had a knack for it. In a few minutes, the bay settled down and the work began to progress.

"Well, Milo, looks like you're gonna live through the day," Harley said.

"Yeah. Damned if I wouldn't rather fist fight than shoe horses. A horse is a little outta my weight class."

"Don't feel bad, son. Maybe the farrier's art just ain't your callin'. What'd you do before you threw your life away to be a Texas Ranger?"

"I've mostly just been prize fightin' since I left home," Milo said, a touch of bravado in his voice. "I do all right."

"Where's home?"

The Day Hunters

"Cleveland, Ohio. I got into the fight game there."

"Well, we don't fight for prize money in this outfit. We mostly fight for our damned lives. You ever had to do that?"

"No sir," Milo answered, somewhat offended by Harley's tone.

"Why'd you sign on with this outfit?"

"Me and Carl just been sleepin' out. I ain't had a fight in a while. We figured if we were gonna sleep outside, we might as well get paid for it."

"There's more to bein' a Ranger than campin' out, y'know. There's ridin' all day, 'til you're nearly broke in half. Guardin' all night, so some injun don't slip in and steal your horse. Eatin' dust and wishin' it was mud."

With Harley's remarks, the young man fell silent.

"Lean Wolf ain't no fist fighter, son. He's a murderin', rapin' Comanchero, and he'll cut you into fish bait, if he gets a chance. I could show you twenty graves we've dug on his back trail over the years."

Harley recalled the lonely prairie where he and Cole had seen their first Comanche war party, many years before. They'd been on their very first patrol. The Comanches had kept them pinned down for hours in an arroyo west of the Pecos River. Two Rangers lost their lives that day, along with three horses, one of them Harley's. He and Cole rode double all the way back to Austin. They'd been only a little older than Milo then, and although they still lived, the Comanches, for the most part, had taken their lives, too.

"You ain't goin' with us. That's final," Harley said.

Milo started to argue, but thought better of it. After listening to Harley, hearing about the five dead men, he wondered if he had what it took to be a Ranger. Maybe Harley was doing him a favor by not letting him go. "Whatever you say, sir," the young man replied, inwardly breathing a sigh of relief.

Harley turned his attention back to the pen. "Eli, how's it goin'?"

"Well, there's one," he said, dropping the last foot on the

mean-eyed bay.

"Shoe that dun next. I need to take a ride."

"Now where the hell are you off to, Harley? We've got work to do," Cole said to his partner. He'd just returned from the hardware store sporting a spanking new Walker Colt .44 pistol.

"Yeah, and part of it is tryin' this horse. I ain't trailin' Lean Wolf on a horse I don't know. In case you don't recall, I ain't no bronc rider."

"Oh, I recall all right," Cole chuckled.

"To hell with you, *Captain* Ellsworth!"

"He's broke, sir. I rode him from the ranch where we got him," Milo announced, hoping to win some small favor with Harley.

"Well, Milo, you don't mind if I try him myself, do you? Let me know when he's done, Boone. I'll be catchin' a nap."

Eddie rounded the corner in a squeaky buckboard filled with provisions, but no young Ranger.

"Where's your helper, Eddie?" Cole asked him.

"AWOL, I reckon, Cap'n. I come outta the store, and he'd lit out. I reckon the stories were too much for him."

Harley laughed aloud from inside the bunkhouse, "He's the only one of us with any damned sense. If I knew where he went, I'd go with him."

"Hellfire," Cole snorted. "I didn't even get his name."

"It was Carl," Eddie said, "Carl Flood."

The renegades attacked the small farm at sunset as the family played a game, kicking a ball around the yard. They rode up quietly to get as close as possible when suddenly the dog began to bark. Fast Elk shot the dog. Emmett shot the father as he sprinted for his rifle. His shot was low. The bullet struck the man in the hip, spinning him to the ground. Lean Wolf jumped from his horse. He stomped and kicked the wounded man, as he gamely crawled to his rifle. With a bloody war cry, Lean Wolf drew his big knife and stabbed the man repeatedly, until he could crawl no more.

Lean Wolf tore open the father's pants, and slashed off his privates. He threw them at the fat mother, so paralyzed with fear she could do nothing but scream. Her sons ran to her side, but couldn't help her. Emmett and Fast Elk grabbed the two young boys and tied them together back to back, viciously throwing them down to tie their legs. They mocked the boys, kicking, and threatening them.

Lean Wolf laughed at the fat mother who could neither run, nor fight, nor protect her children. She screamed so loud and hard, her fat body shook all over, amusing the outlaw.

But as he walked toward her, his mood changed. His look became vicious and mean. He no longer found the woman amusing. Now he saw her as just another white coward in his country. The closer he came, the louder she screamed, her face twisted with fear.

The men encircled her, and tore her dress off. They teased and touched her, poked her with their guns. The poor woman tried to hide herself, but there was too much to cover with her hands. She sobbed and begged, but it did no good.

Grabbing her by the hair of her head, Lean Wolf shoved his pistol in the woman's mouth and shot her, much to the delight of Fast Elk and Emmett. She hit the ground with a heavy thud. The boys screamed uncontrollably. The renegades laughed all the more.

They ransacked the cabin, finding only the bare necessities. Flour, beans, some dried venison, clothing, and a few pictures. Ammunition for the rifle, two bottles of whiskey and the white man's Bible, which Lean Wolf immediately threw in the fire.

The Comanches would often stuff Bible paper between the layers of their war shields, to use the whites own medicine against them. But Lean Wolf didn't believe the paper had power. He thought the whites were stupid to believe a book written by other lying whites. Lean Wolf didn't believe in any god other than his

The Day Hunters

belly. He gave one bottle of whiskey to his killers, and kept one for himself.

Lean Wolf knew what his companions had in mind for the boys, by the ugly looks on their faces. He ordered them out of the cabin, and sat down to rest in the big rocking chair by the fireplace. After a few pulls on the bottle, he felt the effect he was seeking. He heard the cries and screams of the boys, as the men began their demented outrage. Under the influence of the whiskey, he was soon shouting encouragement to his men, laughing at the pitiful screams, as if the boys were squealing pigs.

How long it all went on, Lean Wolf didn't know nor care, but finally the screaming stopped. An eerie silence replaced the din. Emmett and Fast Elk stepped through the door, laughing, slapping each other on the back. After taking their pleasure, they had cut the boys' throats, and left them in the dirt where they lay.

"Let the damn coyotes eat 'em," Lean Wolf said. "I'm gonna get some sleep."

Emmett and Fast Elk drank whiskey for another hour. They soon wished they'd let the boys live a while longer.

After a sound night's sleep in the beds of the murdered family, eating all their food, and drinking their whiskey, the men felt it was a fine morning to be an outlaw. They stepped out of the cabin to see that the varmints had been in the yard overnight—a ghastly scene which barely caught their attention. The farmer's horses were very poor. They would only slow the outlaws down, so they turned them loose. The man's rifle was the only thing they kept from the raid. Lean Wolf decided not to burn the cabin.

Fast Elk blew up at the decision. "Why not burn it? I thought you wanted to drive the whites out of this country. I say we burn it to the ground!"

"No. If we leave the cabin, soon more stupid whites will live here. Then we'll come back and kill them, too."

Mounting leisurely, the killers rode away to the sound of Emmett's muttering, "I wish we'd got more than just this dern rifle."

The Day Hunters

Moody sang softly, methodically packing the mules, wondering how this patrol might end. The Rangers waited on the dawn as they saddled the horses and checked their weapons, each man alone with his thoughts. Moody tried to be steady and loyal to the Captain, since he'd hired him on years ago, but this patrol worried him. He'd never seen Captain Ellsworth in such a dark mood. The Captain himself said a man needed a clear head for this kind of work, but Moody didn't think the Captain had a clear head. The sight of the butchered Rangers had frightened and sickened them all, but the Captain was like a different man, now. He'd become obsessed with killing Lean Wolf and his outlaws. Captain Ellsworth was a man known for his fiery temper. Moody hoped Mr. Harley would keep things under control.

Eddie stood at the dilapidated old stove cooking breakfast, a cigarette that was mostly ash dangling from his mouth. Boone sat outside the door, a very worried look on his face.

"The troop sure is gettin' smaller," he said.

Eli could see the boy had a lot on his mind. "We'll be all right," he assured him.

Boone felt like everyone in his world was dying. He didn't want to lose anyone else. "The last time you rode out, there were five more men with you. Now they're dead. Why would you go after outlaws with just four men? What if this time none of you come back?"

"Don't you worry, Boone. I expect we'll be back in no time."

"He's right, son," Harley said, trotting up to the pen on the stout dun gelding. His test ride the day before, had ended with the dun standing three legged all night in front of the Top Drawer Saloon. "Climb up here. We'll eat at the cafe." Harley pulled Boone up behind him and kicked the dun into a lope, both of them laughing as they rode down the street.

Cole was saddling his horse on the far side of the pen when

The Day Hunters

Harley and Boone rode off. He wondered where they were going, but more so what Harley was telling the boy. Cole let himself be distracted for only a moment, and the bay horse tried to bite him. He cuffed the horse on the nose for his effort. He thought the mean-eyed bay might be too much for Eli, so he chose to ride the horse himself. Eli would ride the grulla mare, Moody an ugly, tough looking appaloosa.

"Double check your gear, boys. We'll leave after breakfast," Cole ordered.

Eli and Moody walked to the bunkhouse. Neither man looked very settled.

"I don't like this, Mistuh Eli. No suh, I don't like this. The Cap'n's tracked down and killed many a man, but I never seen him wantin' revenge before."

"Me neither, but. . .well.. . .I expect we better eat."

Boone was absolutely thrilled. He had never eaten at the cafe before, nor even been inside for that matter. He looked around with wide-eyed amazement, at the people so quickly coming and going, spending more money than he had ever seen.

Harley was touched by the boy's innocence.

A waitress relayed an order through a window to the cook, then made her way to their table. Her hair was like corn silk, tied up in a bun, her eyes a deep sea blue. Her fine features captured the eye of every man in the room.

"Why, Harley, who's your handsome friend?" the waitress asked. She gave Boone a pretty smile, and smoothed out his dark, curly hair.

"This here is Boone Randall, future governor of Texas," Harley answered, playfully poking the boy in the ribs. "Boone, this is Miss Rebecca Tate."

"Good morning, Boone. You need to come and see me more often, honey."

The Day Hunters

"Thank you, ma'am." Boone's face turned a crimson red.

"We'll have flapjacks 'n bacon, coffee 'n milk. That sound all right to you, son?"

"Yes, sir."

Rebecca walked back to the kitchen, and Harley began the speech he'd been rehearsing much of the night.

"Y'know, Boone, you've been through a lot these past few months, and we're all mighty proud of you. I don't know how any more could be asked of such a young fella. Sometimes things happen to make a boy grow up fast. That's what you'll have to do. Your mama would want you to be strong, and act like a man to make her proud, too. Do you understand?"

"Yes sir, I reckon." Boone's tears began to flow again, leaving tiny spots on the front of his shirt.

"Besides, if you're goin' to the border with us, when we come back, you'll have to be brave and work hard, all right?"

"Go to the border? With the Rangers? Yes sir! I'll work hard, and won't cry no more, I promise," he said, wiping the tears from his face. Boone had never been anywhere to speak of. He had no idea where the border was, except south, but he would do whatever his heroes asked of him. He was riding to the border with the Texas Rangers.

Harley admired Rebecca's graceful form as she returned carrying the breakfast tray. "I swear, Rebecca, I wish I had one more night in Austin."

"Well, such is life, honey," she said with a smile. "You come and see me when you get back."

"I might just do that. Let's eat, Ranger Boone. Captain Ellsworth's a' waitin'."

#

Eddie leaned on the top rail of the corral, as the Rangers rode out of Austin. He had a sad, faraway look in his eye. Milo Simms stood beside him, possibly contemplating a change of occupation. And Boone Randall sat the rail, waving and smiling as

56

The Day Hunters

if he might burst.

"Boone sure looks happy," Cole said. "What'd you say to him?"

"I told him we'd take him to the border with us when this is over."

"What? Have you gone crazy, Harley? You had no right to tell him that."

"Why not? I expect I've got as much right as you, Cole. You ain't his pa, are you?"

The two men glared at one another, then Cole put the spurs to the bay. The bay bogged his head, and threw a bucking, bawling fit, much to Harley's amusement.

"Defend yourself, Lean Wolf," Harley laughed. "The Texas Rangers ride again."

#

Eddie sat alone in the cantina, with only a bottle of tequila for company. It was all the company he wanted for the moment. He'd been a Texas Ranger, off and on, for most of his life, having served with McCullogh, Ford, and even Jack Hays. Vera Cruz, Contreras, Monterrey, Mexico City, all held a place in his memory. He'd even wrapped the first bandage on General Sam Houston's foot, when the General was wounded at San Jacinto. Now, it was all over. He'd known it was over for quite a while, but today, watching the boys ride out, it finally hit him.

Eddie threw his cigarette on the floor, and rubbed it out with his boot heel. He poured a drink, tossed it down, and took out the makings to roll another.

The old Mexican woman, watching Eddie from the kitchen, seemed to recognize his sadness. Eddie was a regular in the cantina, preferring tequila to whiskey, enchiladas to beef steak, and, oh, how he loved to watch the girls dance. Usually, he was in a festive mood, but today it wasn't so. Eddie smoked and drank until the bottle was empty, left some coins on the table, then wobbled out into the sun.

The Day Hunters

He made it back to the bunkhouse and fell on his bed, his mind swirling with scenes from his life. He had fits for a while, shouting curses in Spanish, but the tequila soon left him snoring. When he came to, Boone stood beside the bed looking at him.

"Are you all right, Eddie?"

Eddie tried to focus his blurry eyes. "Why sure, young fella. I'm just fine."

"Want me to get you some coffee?"

"You bet. Thank you. You're a good boy, Boone."

Boone poured the coffee and gave it to Eddie. The pot had been sitting on the stove all day. The coffee was cold, but Eddie drank it down in one gulp, then gave Boone a big woozy smile.

"Will you go get Ol' Dan for me, son?"

"Ol' Dan? You goin' for a ride, Eddie?"

"Well, I thought the ol' boy could use a little stretch."

Dan was Eddie's buckskin horse, probably at least twenty years old. Though he didn't ride much anymore, Eddie took excellent care of the horse, brushing him daily, checking his feet, exercising him in the pen on a long line. When he had Ol' Dan groomed and saddled, Eddie turned to Boone. "You ready to ride, Ranger?"

Boone looked a little confused, so Eddie lifted him into the saddle. "Now, I'm gonna work your horse on the line," Eddie said. "You just sit up there and ride."

Ol' Dan trotted around the pen as easy as you please, with Boone holding the saddle horn, smiling ear to ear. After a few minutes at the trot, Eddie called, "You wanna lope?"

"Yes, sir!"

Ol' Dan picked up the rocking chair lope that Eddie loved so much. Boone laughed, and Eddie cried, both their hearts filled with joy. When the ride was over, Boone stuck out his hand.

"Thanks for lettin' me ride your horse, Eddie."

Eddie accepted the handshake. "Didn't you hear me, son? I said this is *your* horse. You take good care of him, now. Go give him a drink o' water."

Boone was speechless, flabbergasted. Eddie pulled the

The Day Hunters

saddle, gave the boy a big hug, then walked up the street whistling a happy tune.

#

Milo Simms had been summoned on urgent business by Sheriff Nolan Pence. The boy who delivered the message to the bunkhouse didn't give any details, just that Milo was to hurry to the rooms above the Top Drawer saloon.

He took the back stairs three at a time. When he reached the top, he found a crowd in the tight little hallway. Four whores, Sheriff Pence, and Rex Bailey, the owner of the Top Drawer, stood staring into the last room on the left. The sight that greeted Milo was the strangest he'd ever seen. Eddie Roberts sitting straight up in the bed, stiff as a board, and dead as a beaver hat.

"What happened to him?" Milo exclaimed.

"Well, what do you think, honey?" Susan placed her hands on her tightly corseted waist, thrusting her full hips side to side. Seductively, she whispered, "I killed him."

The hallway burst into a fit of laughter, leaving Milo feeling odd, not knowing what to do. "Well, I guess we should get him outta there."

"I've sent for the undertaker," Sheriff Pence said. "Someone should be here soon."

"He told me his time was up, and he wanted one last poke," Susan said. "It only took a minute. He had a nap afterward. Must've been dead when he sat up. Just a reaction, I suppose."

Two young men arrived with a canvas stretcher. Both had been drinking. They carelessly loaded Eddie like a sack of feed, and started down the stairs. Milo led the way. The first person he saw at the bottom was a very frightened Boone Randall.

"What happened, Milo? Somebody said a whore killed Eddie."

Boone desperately wanted to cry, but he had promised Harley just this morning that he wouldn't, so he bit down hard on his lip instead.

The Day Hunters

"No, she didn't kill him. It was an accident. He just died. Come on. Let's go home."

The boys walked back to the lots behind the bunkhouse. They sat on the fence for a while, looking at the moon and feeling sad. Boone just couldn't understand what was happening.

"What do whores do, Milo?" he asked.

Taken by surprise, Milo hardly knew what to say. He did his best to answer Boone's question, after a few moments of careful thought.

"Well, say a fella doesn't have a wife, like Eddie, or maybe he's lonesome, or sad, or somethin'. He could go visit a whore, and she'd be nice to him, and talk to him, get drunk with him, or maybe rub his sore back. Just be his friend mostly, I guess."

Boone raised his damp eyes to the man in the moon. "My mama was a drunk. But Eddie told me she didn't wanna be one."

The Day Hunters

The news of the Rangers' murder and Lean Wolf's escape, spread across the plains like wildfire. Many of the Old Ones thought such a brutal act would provoke the whites into all-out war. They had lived past the days when the Texans rode into their camps and attacked them. Now, they wanted to live in peace. But Lean Wolf did not want peace with the Texans. He only wanted to run and fight. The Old Ones believed it was Lean Wolf's Mexican blood that made him so hard to catch. They knew all Mexicans were cowards, and good at running. Blood Hawk believed the man had the luck of a demon.

Blood Hawk was to the Kiowa what Lean Wolf was to the Comanche. A half breed, outcast renegade—half Kiowa, half Comanche, and all bad. A man of cruel and wicked spirit, he suffered banishment from the tribe due to his lustful nature. It was rumored that he had even raped his own sister, though for fear of him, she would never tell. Blood Hawk had ridden with Lean Wolf for a short time, and was well aware what kind of man he was—a murdering, raping bastard, just like himself.

He hated Lean Wolf almost as much as he hated Ellsworth and Macon...almost. The two had dealt death and destruction to the plains tribes for a dozen years or more, discounting Macon's service with the gray riders. Consequently, their scalps were the most coveted on the Southern plains. But Blood Hawk wanted Macon's scalp for another reason. When he was a young man, Blood Hawk saw Macon kill his mother as the Rangers charged into the camp of his people. Though he felt no particular love for his mother, he was obligated to avenge her death.

The war between the Comanches and the Texans was hot and bloody then. One revenge raid would spark another, with terrible atrocities on both sides. The Rangers, accompanied by U.S. troops, struck when most of the warriors were off hunting. Many in the camp died that day. They recaptured a large herd of stolen horses, and Cynthia Ann Parker, a white girl captured years

61

The Day Hunters

before, and now the mother of Quanah, the war chief of the Quahada band.

Captain "Sul" Ross had been their leader then. That day the Rangers fought like cougars, killing many of the people, along with Peta Nocona, the father of Quanah.

But Captain Ellsworth was the most hated of all the Rangers. Almost nothing could make him turn back. If he captured his enemies, they would die by the rope, a ghastly death to be sure. How could the spirit escape if hanged by the neck?

Watching the Rangers cross the prairie, Blood Hawk recalled the many stories he had heard of them over the years. How every warrior he had ever known vowed to be the one to take their scalps. How the women had threatened to boil them if they were ever captured. But the men still had their scalps, and neither had ever been captured.

Blood Hawk hated the Texas Rangers for their relentless pursuit of his people. He hated Lean Wolf because the man had cut off his left ear. Lean Wolf accused him of cheating while they were gambling with the dice. A fight ensued. When it was over, Lean Wolf had a knife wound across his belly, and Blood Hawk had one ear. That night, Blood Hawk escaped from the camp, knowing he would be murdered if he tried to leave. Lean Wolf was not one to just let people come and go.

But now, Blood Hawk had nowhere to go. Though he did not want to ride with Lean Wolf again, he knew there was safety in numbers. With so many blue coats in Texas, it was becoming harder to move around. Now he saw Ellsworth and Macon riding north at a quick pace. They were on the trail of someone, and they were in a hurry to find them. He was sure that someone was Lean Wolf. The Tonkawa was with them, but he did not seem to be doing much tracking. They traveled as if they knew where they were going. Blood Hawk was sure he *too* knew where they were going.

Maybe, if he could find Lean Wolf and warn him that the Rangers were coming, he would be welcomed back into the band. Of course, the man might just kill him outright— it was hard to

The Day Hunters

know. After losing the ear, Blood Hawk had thought many times of killing Lean Wolf himself, but he did not want the Rangers to do it. That would only give them more power with the other whites. He decided to take his chances. He could reach Lean Wolf's camp after dark if he rode hard enough. If the renegades were there, he would warn them. They would ambush the Rangers and kill them all. Then he would kill Lean Wolf.

#

Delgado had been riding hard for all of four days. Maybe a little too hard. His horse was nearly played out, but he couldn't stop to rest as long as there was daylight. It was another three days to the stronghold. He slowed to a walk for the last few miles, and was nearly asleep in the saddle when he smelled the smoke from the little cabin. He quickly dismounted, hid his horse behind a low rise, and crawled to the top for a better look.

The country didn't provide much cover, probably why the settler had chosen such a spot. A rider could be seen for miles from the cabin, but Delgado saw no movement there. No movement except the two horses in the pitiful rawhide-bound corral.

The horses stood three legged in the afternoon heat, swishing their tails, stomping at the flies. They looked to be well fed, in much better shape than the ranch structures. But not in nearly such good shape as the woman who stepped out the door.

She searched the horizon, shading her eyes with her hand. She then walked to the well for a bucket of water, and promptly returned to the cabin. A few moments later, she repeated the act, and again, and still again, until finally she disappeared inside.

"That is a lot of water," Delgado said to his horse. "*Aiee*, I think she is taking her bath."

The woman relished her afternoon baths. Though she

The Day Hunters

didn't get them every day, she enjoyed the cool respite from the hot Texas sun. Her husband had gone to the neighbors early that morning to help with some cattle chore. She missed him, longed for him. Sometimes she could convince him to join her in the tub, and relax in the cool water. She wished he was there now, to kiss her and wash her, to love her.

The woman thought she heard a horse in the yard, but dismissed it. Her husband couldn't be home yet. Maybe it was just one of the horses in the corral. She heard the jingle of the big roweled Mexican spurs just as Delgado kicked the door open. He held a pistol in his hand, so she didn't move.

"My husband's coming back any minute!" she screamed. *"Get out of here!"*

"Ah, *Señora*, this will only take a few minutes."

The small tub couldn't hide much of her, which was just fine with Delgado. He enjoyed looking at naked women, especially when they had that terrified look. He stared into her frightened eyes, holstered his pistol, and dropped his gun belt to the floor.

"It has been a long hard ride. I think I would like a bath myself," he said, throwing his hat across the room.

As he did, she grabbed the pistol lying on the floor beside the bathtub. But she was too slow to save herself.

Delgado threw the dagger he kept hidden beneath his shirt collar. The blade sank to the hilt at the base of her throat. She pulled hard at the knife, trying to scream, gagging on her own blood. Her convulsing body splashed water on the floor. She stared her hatred into his eyes, tried to speak, and then she stopped moving.

Sorely disappointed, Delgado spent a few minutes sidling around the cabin, looking for anything of value. He found eight dollars gold in an old sock in the dresser. He then helped himself to all the woman's clothing. Though she didn't have much, the women at the stronghold would enjoy them. He took what food and whiskey the couple had, and tied it in a pillowcase. It was enough to get him home.

The Day Hunters

The killer walked to the tub, and carefully, even gently, pulled the dagger from her throat. "I did not want to hurt you, *Señora*," he said to the bloody corpse. He kissed her on the forehead, retrieved his hat, strapped on his gunbelt and walked outside, quietly closing the door behind him.

Scanning the horizon, Delgado quickly switched his saddle, and rode off with all the horses. As he rode, he considered the sight that would greet the woman's returning husband.

#

Fast Elk and Emmett watched fearfully as Lean Wolf stormed around the camp in a rage. His ugly face turned menacing as he searched the lodges, cursing and shooting off his pistol. The camp was empty. The lodges looked even more ragged than before. The people had left in a hurry. They abandoned many of their belongings, leaving all the assorted white man's junk. It looked as if they'd been driven out, but by who? Tracks could not be distinguished due to weather and wildlife. But Lean Wolf needed no tracks to tell him that someone had located his camp.

"Spread out. Look around," he shouted.

Each man rode a hundred yards looking for sign, but not a trace could be found.

"Long gone," Emmett said.

Lean Wolf sneered. "I can see that, goddammit!"

Fast Elk dismounted and started building a fire, while Emmett brought out some whiskey and took a long pull. He needed the whiskey to settle his nerves, but he would not get drunk tonight. Not with Lean Wolf in such a mood. One wrong word could set the man off, then the killing would commence. He passed the bottle to Fast Elk, who also had a hard time controlling himself. The two stared at one another, each man reading the other's thoughts. This would be a good night to stay sober.

The outlaws stripped saddles, and tied the horses. Lean Wolf cursed and threatened all the while. In short order they were

The Day Hunters

set for the night, the hind quarter of a stolen calf roasting over the fire. Fast Elk and Emmett took every precaution, what with Lean Wolf getting drunker by the minute.

"Where you reckon they went?" Emmett said. "Looks like there'd be some kinda sign."

"Big rain washed everything out. Maybe they went to one of the Caddo villages, or the Chickasaw. They're not far," Fast Elk said.

"They'd need protection. There wasn't no fighters among 'em."

"Who cares where they went?" Lean Wolf said. "I care who found this camp. And why they didn't kill 'em instead of runnin' 'em off."

"Maybe they took 'em prisoner," Emmett said.

That was a possibility, but Fast Elk didn't think so. White settlers would have killed them. Other tribes could barely feed themselves. It was unlikely they would take any captives. That left the army. Or the Rangers. But there were so few Rangers now, that Fast Elk doubted it. Ellsworth and his men were likely the last Rangers in north Texas, and now, he was sure, they were dead. Maybe the army moved the people to Fort Washita. It was the only thing that made sense.

"We'll round up a few more men and ride south," Lean Wolf said. "We'll kill every Texan we see on the way. If we find any more Rangers, we'll hang 'em."

"I don't know, Wolf," Fast Elk said. "The blue coats are in Austin now. It ain't like the old days."

"You shut your damn mouth, or I'll kill you right now." Lean Wolf cocked his pistol, and let the hammer down slowly. "I have killed the Texas Rangers. Nothing can stand against me now."

Fast Elk didn't see how killing a few Rangers could defeat the blue coats, but chose not to argue the point.

#

The Day Hunters

The Rangers made camp beside a small creek, under a canopy of softly blowing willows. A fine camp indeed, if not for the mood of the men. None of them had slept much since leaving Austin, nor even while they were there. Both Eli and Moody were more nervous than Harley had ever seen them. They were far more worried about the Captain than Lean Wolf, as there seemed to be no settling the man. He couldn't sit down for more than a minute or two, then he'd be up pacing again, checking and rechecking his weapon.

"We oughta keep movin'," Cole said. "We don't need the moon. We know where his damned camp is. Stone Horse already told us that."

"We know where his camp is, but we don't know if he's there. Besides, the horses need rest, and so do these men," Harley said. "If he did go back there, he's likely gone by now. Stone Horse oughta be back soon. Maybe he's found somethin'."

"Yeah, and maybe not."

"Dammit, when have you ever known that injun to miss a sign? He's the best tracker there is, you said it yourself." Harley was tired of arguing with his bullheaded friend. "Why don't you relieve Eli if you need somethin' to do?"

"I've got somethin' to do, but sittin' here ain't gettin' it done!"

"Well, we sure as hell ain't gonna catch him on foot. And that's where we'll be if we don't rest these horses. He's gotta sleep too, y'know."

Exasperated, Cole filled himself a plate of unfinished stew, and walked out to relieve the guard. He had always liked the solitude of guard duty, and much preferred it to arguing with Harley. But, by God, he wouldn't wait much longer.

"Cap'n's determined," Moody said. He put the finishing touches on his jackrabbit stew, adding a little bacon grease he'd brought from the bunkhouse for flavor.

"Yeah," Harley said. "But too much determination can cloud a man's judgment. Even *Captain* Ellsworth can make a mistake."

The Day Hunters

Moody recalled the lonely grave on the llano. "Yessuh," he agreed.

Harley glanced toward the guard post to see the lanky silhouette of Eli Plummer approaching the fire. He moved slowly, dragging his big feet, exhausted.

"I swear, Eli, you look like you're about to fall over," Harley said. "You're so tall, I expect if you fell down, you'd be a full minute hittin' the ground."

"Well, if I did fall, I expect I'd be asleep before I got there."

"We'd all better get some sleep tonight. We're about a day from Lean Wolf's camp. We'll wear these horses out tomorrow," Harley said. He noticed Eli was already dozing. "Better eat before you sleep, Eli. Cole ain't likely to give us time for breakfast."

With one last taste of the jackrabbit stew, Moody filled two plates, handing one to each man, then filled one for himself. The men ate in silence, the only sound the clinking of spoons on tin plates, and Harley occasionally gagging on Moody's coffee.

"By God, Moody, when we catch ol' Lean Wolf, I'm gonna make him drink a gallon o' your coffee, then let the son of a bitch hang *himself*."

"Cap'n say he like it strong," Moody laughed, as if Cole's opinion were the only one that mattered. "I'll take him a cup." He poured the coffee, and walked out to the guard post, whistling softly so as not to startle the Captain.

Eli helped himself to another plate of stew. "You think Lean Wolf's at the camp, Harley?"

"Sure suit me if he was. There's a lotta good hangin' trees there. But you can't raid from your camp. I expect he's out gettin' bloody. Our best chance is to find some tracks, if he went back there at all. But if he did, Stone Horse'll find 'em." Harley was well aware of Eli's loyalty to Captain Ellsworth, so he chose his next words carefully. "Eli, I've seen Cole's temper get him in trouble in the past, so when we catch up to Lean Wolf, you keep your eye on me. I fear Cole may go overboard."

Eli, lost in thought for a moment, simply answered,

68

The Day Hunters

"Yessir, I will."

Stone Horse suddenly appeared at the fire, quickly and quietly, as was his habit. It was a habit that unnerved the Rangers, each man drawing and cocking his pistol.

"Dammit, Horse! You better hello the camp on this patrol, or you might get shot down. This outfit's jumpy," Harley said.

Seeing Stone Horse arrive, Cole ran to the fire, anxious for a report.

"What is it?" he demanded.

"I have seen the tracks of one rider, Captain. The tracks point towards Lean Wolf's camp. We have been seen. The rider is going to warn Lean Wolf."

The troop exchanged bitter expressions.

"Break camp," Cole ordered.

#

The arrow made a soft thud as it sunk into the roasting hindquarter, causing each man around the fire to dive for cover. Lean Wolf kept his head down, peeking out from behind the rock that hid him. He could easily recognize the markings on the arrow.

"Blood Hawk," he said. "Can you hear me with only one ear?"

"I can hear you, Lean Wolf. I can see your men, too. If they move, I will kill them." He fired a pistol shot at each location for emphasis. "I have come to tell you that Ellsworth and Macon are coming after you. I saw them this morning riding north."

The statement shocked Lean Wolf. "Ellsworth?" he shouted. "You are lying!" He felt sure that Zendejaz would have led Ellsworth and his men far into the llano and finished them. No one knew the llano like Zendejaz.

"Would I risk my life, and come to you with such a lie? I saw them this morning, riding straight for this camp. Stone Horse is with them."

"Do they know that you saw them?"

The Day Hunters

"No. I was far off. They did not see me."

"How did you get here so fast?"

Blood Hawk shrugged. "I stole a fast horse."

Lean Wolf could think of no reason for Blood Hawk to come into his camp and lie. But things being what they were between them, he had to wonder why Blood Hawk brought the warning in the first place.

"Why did you come here?"

"I came because the Rangers are my enemy also. I thought together we could kill them all, and be rid of them."

"Are you alone?"

"Yes, I am alone."

After some thought, Lean Wolf called to Blood Hawk, "Come in to the fire, slowly, hands up."

Each man stood and stepped into the firelight, cautious and ready for trouble. Hard glances were traded, as four dangerous men sat down to plan an ambush, and eat their stolen beef.

"How far away are the Rangers?" Lean Wolf asked.

"They would camp at the willow creek, one days ride from here. They will be here tomorrow afternoon."

Emmett laughed his idiot laugh. "They'll bog down in the quicksand when they cross the Red. We'll have 'em dead to rights."

"No! They were here before," Fast Elk said. "They will know about the quicksand. They will cross two miles upriver. We should wait for them there, and kill them."

"Fast Elk is right," Lean Wolf said. "They will cross upriver. How many are there?"

"Four Rangers, and Stone Horse. He is the one we should kill first."

"Yeah," Emmett said. "That damn Tonkawa is the one who keeps findin' us. We need to kill him."

"We will kill him tomorrow," Lean Wolf said, "And all the Rangers, too. Now, let's eat."

The men went at the roasted beef as if each were afraid he might not get his share. They eyed one another like starving coyotes, their sharp blades slicing through the bloody meat. Emmett reluctantly passed the jug, aware of the tension between Blood Hawk and Lean Wolf. Though nothing vindictive was ever said, it was obvious that the meeting could quickly turn into a throat cutting. Blood Hawk took a pull on the jug, and walked off to bring in his horse.

"You trust him?" Emmett whispered.

"No," Lean Wolf said. "Why should I? I don't trust you."

# #

The Rangers traveled at a ground-eating trot, Captain Ellsworth as silent as the dead.

"Dammit, Cole, we're wearin' these horses out. They need rest and so do we!" Harley railed.

"Well, if Lean Wolf ain't at the camp, we'll stop to rest. If he is, we'll rest after we kill him. We should reach the crossin' by daylight."

Harley had been stirrup to stirrup with Cole Ellsworth for a good many years. He'd seen Cole fight harder and longer, than any man he'd ever ridden with. Cole would do his duty, no matter what it cost him. But Harley had seen the man's temper, too. A tougher, more determined man had never lived. But Harley was worried about his angry friend.

"Duty is a cruel master, ain't it, Cole?"

"What?"

"I said, duty is a cruel master."

"Yeah, I reckon."

"We're pretty shorthanded. Maybe we should've waited for more volunteers."

"No need to wait. There ain't many who'd volunteer to go after Lean Wolf. Or Zendejaz."

"You got a plan? These are damned dangerous men, y'know."

"Yeah, I've got a plan. I plan to find 'em, and kill 'em all."

The Day Hunters

"Simple."

"What?"

"Why nothin', *Captain* Ellsworth. Nothin' at all."

The Day Hunters

chapter 7

The mules stood in a bunch, their tails turned to the wind, on the flat, barren Kansas Plains. Sergeant Teague and his men could only try to keep the fire going while waiting for the oncoming storm. Just another of many storms that had plagued them since leaving Fort Riley. The wind, at times, would become so harsh that the mules balked, refusing to drive. Then, for one reason or another, they'd be racing across the prairie at breakneck speed, the deserters doing all they could to control them. At such times, they just tried to keep the mules pointed south. For the moment, all the men were dismounted, half circling the fire, trying to keep the coffee hot. They'd been all day without food, and their patience was wearing thin.

"How much farther you think it is, Sarge?" Bullock asked.

"I ain't sure," Teague said. "We've run so many circles, I don't know if we've gained ground, or lost it. We'll just keep drivin' south, I guess."

"Just keep drivin' south," Daniels sneered. "Would that be southeast, or southwest, or just plain straight south? Half the time it's so cloudy, I don't know which damn direction we're goin'. The Indian territory's a hell of a big place. How you plannin' on findin' Lean Wolf if you can't even find the Cimarron?"

"We'll find it. I'm more worried who might be on our trail. We're leavin' a lotta tracks in the mud, until the next rain washes 'em out. Don't forget, there's a lotta damn Indians in Kansas, too."

Nobody needed to remind Corporal Bullock of that. The thought occupied his mind constantly. Up to this point, he felt it almost miraculous that the Indians hadn't found them. The Cheyenne and the Arapahoe had not yet forgotten Custer's massacre of Black Kettle's village on the Washita River. The Cheyenne dog soldiers felt it was their duty to balance the scales. Small bands roamed throughout Kansas and the territory seeking revenge for the sleeping village.

73

The Day Hunters

"I wonder if Fort Riley sent somebody after us?" Bullock said. "Hell, maybe they wired down here. They might have troops waitin' for us."

"Dammit!" Teague snapped. "You boys didn't think we'd just ride off with these mules without a hitch, did you? If you ain't bitchin' about the weather, it's somethin' else. We're in it now, so let's ride it out."

"I could ride it out a lot better if I had somethin' to eat," Daniels said. "I say we shoot one of the mules."

"And I say we don't. You won't starve. We'll find somethin' tomorrow. Let's try the coffee."

The coffee was mostly just brown water. With the wind whipping the flames like it was, they couldn't keep enough fire on the pot to get it to boil. The poor quality of the brew didn't improve the men's disposition much.

"There's bound to be settlements to the east," Daniels said. "Somebody's gonna have to go find some food."

"How would we explain the uniforms?" Teague asked.

"We could tell 'em we got lost from our outfit. Got lost and need some food to get back to the post."

"Might work. But I don't know what posts are around here. I ain't even sure where we are."

"We've gotta do somethin'. It's that or shoot one of these mules. I've been wet since leavin' Riley. I don't aim to be hungry much longer."

"We'll see in the morning. You'll live that long."

Corporal Bullock thought himself the perfect fool. Here he sat on an empty plain, drinking brown water, waiting to get drenched again. Certainly the army must be looking for them, by now. On top of that, they could well be surrounded by hostile Indians. Yes sir, he thought, the perfect fool.

Stone Horse loved the early morning hours more than any

74

The Day Hunters

other time of day. The sky turning gray put the crickets to bed, while waking the birds to sing. The night hunters went into their dens to sleep, and there wait for the moon to come again. The world came alive with the rising sun, as did man, the day hunter. Stone Horse had long ago concluded that man would never stop killing, if he could only see in the dark.

He crossed the Red River without incident, though it was a little higher than usual. Maybe there was rain coming from the west—a depressing thought, to say the least. Now, Stone Horse hoped more than ever that the renegades were in the camp. He hated traveling in the rain, but he knew it would make no difference to the Captain. Once the Captain struck a track, he was like old Ben Lily's bear dogs. He wouldn't stop until he treed Lean Wolf. There was no need to think otherwise.

Stone Horse liked to spend the rainy days with his woman and little girl. He would tell the girl great stories of the Tonkawa people. They would play games, and eat, and laugh the day away. When the girl was asleep, he would love his woman. She would always tease him that he was too fast. He would tease her for making him wait so long.

Stone Horse dismounted, tying his animal a safe distance from the camp, in case there were other horses. He proceeded on foot until he could smell the camp. He could see no smoke, but he could smell it. Someone was there. Maybe Lean Wolf. Or maybe the old man had not heeded his warning. Maybe it was the same pitiful bunch that was here before.

He approached with caution, downwind from the horses. Though the early morning haze was thick, Stone Horse could make out four men sleeping in Lean Wolf's camp. He recognized Lean Wolf and Fast Elk, but could not see the faces of the other two men. One was probably the idiot man Fast Elk was known to travel with.

The camp was a mess, whiskey bottles strewn about, the fire burned to ashes. A sneaky coyote was even stealing bites of the leftover meat on the spit. These men were drunk.

For a moment, Stone Horse was tempted to sneak in and

The Day Hunters

kill Lean Wolf himself. But he knew the others would get him. He could never take all four of them. He could easily kill Lean Wolf with his bow. But if he yelled out when the arrow struck him, it would wake the others, and that would be the end.

Stone Horse felt it better to let the Rangers do the killing. He would do the tracking. Another quick glance around the camp and he was ready to leave. The Rangers should be waiting for him at the crossing, by now. The Captain would be glad to know that Lean Wolf was in the camp. Maybe the Rangers could ride in quietly and capture the drunken renegades, though he doubted it. Lean Wolf would never surrender to the rope.

Fast Elk woke to the sound of the horses shuffling their feet at the picket line. He needed to relieve himself, but didn't want to get up yet. His head hurt bad, and he thought he might throw up. The four had consumed a lot of whiskey while plotting to kill the Rangers. He thought it best to just lie still a while longer.

The sight of the coyote startled Fast Elk, but at least now he knew the reason for the horses' nervousness. The coyote wasn't doing any harm, and Fast Elk just didn't have the energy to run him off. Besides, he feared waking Lean Wolf. The news of the Rangers, coupled with Blood Hawk's presence, had put Lean Wolf in an even uglier mood. He'd watched Blood Hawk suspiciously all evening. Afterward he went to sleep with a pistol in his hand. Fast Elk did not want to wake him suddenly.

His swollen bladder became more uncomfortable. He'd about decided to get up, when, through a tiny slit in his blurry eyes, Fast Elk saw Stone Horse watching the camp. Panic seized him out of his stupor, but he caught himself before he moved. The tracker looked to be alone. Fast Elk could see no one else.

Sick to his stomach, he wondered if he was having a drunken vision. Maybe Stone Horse was not really there at all. He had heard of people having visions when they were drunk, but he never had. One thing was certain. If Stone Horse was really watching the camp, the Rangers couldn't be far away.

The Day Hunters

He wanted to shout, to wake his cronies, but he was afraid Stone Horse would kill him before he could move. Fast Elk closed his eyes for just a moment, to ease the throbbing in his head. When he opened them again, Stone Horse was gone.

"Get up. Get up," he said, keeping his voice low. "Hurry, the Rangers are close!"

The men rolled out of their blankets quickly, causing them to stumble and curse their pounding heads. The coyote scrambled to get away from the outlaws, taking one last bite before he vanished into the timber. Struggling to rise, Emmett tripped over his own rifle. He fell on his face into the burned out fire, cursing, spitting ashes out of his mouth.

"Where are they?" Lean Wolf asked.

"I don't know where the Rangers are, but the Tonkawa stood right over there." Fast Elk pulled his breech clout aside, to relieve his bladder discomfort. Emmett had to jump to the side, to keep from getting his boots wet.

They all hurried to the spot where Fast Elk had seen the tracker. Sure enough, his footprints were plain.

"Dammit! He's gone to get the Rangers," Emmett said, his ugly face still covered with ashes.

"Get these horses saddled," Lean Wolf demanded.

In the flurry of confusion, Lean Wolf pulled his big knife, grabbing Blood Hawk by the hair in one quick, whirling motion. He pressed the point of the blade just below Blood Hawk's breast bone.

"I'll be watching you," he threatened. "If you betray me, I will never let you die, understand?"

"I understand." Blood Hawk feared his chance to kill Lean Wolf had just slipped away. The Rangers must have ridden all night to get here this early. Blood Hawk knew this made him look like a liar. Lean Wolf smelled a trap. He would be watching closely from now on. Maybe he could take a shot at Lean Wolf when they ambushed the Rangers. Or maybe Lean Wolf, or one of the others, would kill *him*. Either way, Blood Hawk was sure someone would be dead very soon.

The Day Hunters

The men led their horses on foot to the edge of the clearing, keeping well under cover of the trees. One could hardly find a better place for an ambush.

"We'll wait for 'em here instead of the crossing," Lean Wolf said. "We have better cover here, anyway. Wait 'til they're in the middle of the clearing before you shoot, or we'll lose 'em. There are five of them and four of us, so pick a target and kill him. But I want Ellsworth alive. Spread out!"

In his drunkenness the night before, Lean Wolf had begun to think of capturing Ellsworth instead of killing him. He could think of many horrible tortures he would like to try on the famous Ranger. Lean Wolf had been so sure that Zendejaz would kill the Rangers on the llano. Soon, Ellsworth would wish he had.

#

"Well, Cole, it's a fine mornin', ain't it?" Harley said.

"Seems like it was a fine day when we were here before, too."

Cole stared in the direction of the camp without a word, remembering the layout, picturing the confrontation in his mind. As best he could recall, they would have cover most of the way. But he also knew there was a small clearing, where they would have hardly any cover at all. They had been lucky before and crossed unseen. If they could do it again, they could take the camp, providing the killers were there.

Lean Wolf had wisely chosen Old Crooked Foot's camp, as it could not be breached from the south or southeast, due to the quicksand in the Red River. But neither could he retreat in that direction. The renegades could only retreat to the north. If they escaped, the Rangers would be forced to pursue them through standing timber. That would be quite a challenge in itself. If they could surprise the camp, maybe there would be no pursuit. They would simply capture the renegades and hang them. Cole hoped for the best. Their horses were exhausted from the all-night ride.

The Day Hunters

They would have to rest them soon.

"You think he's there?" Cole asked his companion.

"We're about to find out," Harley said. "Here comes Stone Horse."

The scout approached the crossing at the gallop, a fine sheen of sweat on his mount. He began shouting his report before he reached the Rangers.

"Lean Wolf is in the camp with three men, Captain. One of them is Fast Elk. I could not see the others. They have fresh horses, but they are drunk and sleeping off their whiskey."

"By God, that's good luck," Harley said. "We got him this time."

Cole's expression didn't change. In his mind he watched as Moody and Eli dug a grave for five butchered Rangers.

"Check your gear, boys," he ordered. "This is it."

The men dismounted quickly, checking saddle girths, horses' feet, rifles, pistols, and anything else they could think of. Eli cut himself a fresh plug of chewing tobacco, his habit before going into action. Moody hummed "Life's Railway to Heaven."

Cole and Harley each produced an extra pistol from their saddle bags, and stuck them into their belts. Cole remounted. The men followed his lead. There was no order given, nor needed. The Rangers rode quietly through the timber until they reached the clearing, where they paused to survey the terrain.

"Let's get at it before they wake up," Cole said. "Moody, tie them mules back in the trees. We'll cross the clearing at the trot, then charge in and take 'em. No quarter."

#

The rifle shots came in rapid succession, kicking up dirt in front of the Rangers' horses just as they stepped out of the trees. Moody's appaloosa reared so high he nearly fell over backwards. Moody had to slide off the horse's back, and retreat to the treeline on foot. A barrage of gunfire then chased the Rangers back into

The Day Hunters

the timber. The bullets whined through the air, knocking bark off the trees all around them. Scrambling, Cole shouted, "Get these horses under cover!" his voice all but drowned out by the gunfire.

Harley was already on the ground, firing his rifle from a prone position to cover the Rangers' retreat.

"It's a trap, Cole! Hell, they were waitin' for us!"

"Dammit," Cole snapped. "Have you ever seen a man with such luck? Anybody hit?"

"No, sir," came the replies.

"Check them horses, Moody."

"We'd all be dead if they'd waited another minute," Harley said. "Whoever the first shooter was, he was a damn poor shot."

Cole was thinking the same thing. Why hadn't they waited? He knew it only took one shot to set off the whole bunch. He'd seen it any number of times in combat. If they were drunk and hung over, maybe their nerves had gotten the best of them. Or maybe they were just poor shots, like Harley said.

All firing had ceased for the moment as Moody came forward to report. "The horses are fine, Cap'n. But Mistuh Eli got a hole in his saddle."

Leaving Cole to stand watch, Harley walked to the horses to find Eli leaning on his saddle, visibly shaken.

"Lookee there, Harley. Right through the cantle."

"Well, Eli, you're lucky today yourself. We could be diggin' a bullet outta your ass."

Eli didn't think that was funny, but he laughed a nervous laugh anyway. He surely had been lucky.

With the horses secure, the Rangers spread out along the treeline, ready for whatever came next.

"Anybody seen Stone Horse?" Moody asked.

#

The renegades had been waiting in deadly silence when the Rangers stepped out of the trees. The plan was for each man to

The Day Hunters

take down his target, leaving Ellsworth to the tortures of Lean Wolf. But those first shots had spoiled the plan. The renegades opened fire at will, when the Rangers retreated into the timber.

"Goddammit, who fired those shots?" Lean Wolf shouted. "Now, we'll never get 'em outta there."

"Let's get the hell outta *here*," Emmett said. "By God, I don't wanna corner this bunch. Macon and Ellsworth won't be as easy as them boys on the llano."

Lean Wolf looked left and right, but could see neither Fast Elk nor Blood Hawk. He wondered if any of the Rangers had been hit, what Ellsworth was planning, and who the hell had fired those shots? His suspicions naturally went to Blood Hawk. Fast Elk would have no reason to warn the Rangers, and Emmett had been in sight the whole time.

Why would Blood Hawk risk his life riding into the camp to warn them, and then, in turn, warn the Rangers? It made no sense, but who else could it be? Stone Horse, maybe? Lean Wolf hadn't seen him when the Rangers rode out of the timber. Blood Hawk had taken up position to his left, the direction he believed the shots came from.

Lean Wolf called for his men. Within minutes they were gathered around him. None had been hit, neither did they know where the shots came from, nor who had fired them. Lean wolf stared coldly at Blood Hawk, as did the other men.

"You stay here and keep their heads down while we move up the treeline," he said. "When we gain a hundred yards, we'll open fire while you catch up. We can run from that position, understand?"

Blood Hawk took a careful look at the men. It was plain they wanted to kill him.

"Understand?" Lean Wolf repeated.

"I understand. I will open fire when you mount up."

Blood Hawk thought he understood perfectly. He was being left to the enemy. His murderous plan was falling apart. One

81

The Day Hunters

wrong move and Lean Wolf would shoot him. Though the Rangers would likely do worse if they caught him, he thought it better to do as he was told, then attempt an escape. He was sure he would never see Lean Wolf again, after the men rode out.

They sprinted to their horses as Blood Hawk took his position. When they were mounted and headed north, he opened fire as fast as he could lever his rifle, spacing his shots throughout the treeline. The renegades raced off without a backward glance.

For a moment, he thought to shoot Lean Wolf in the back as he watched them ride away. He had shot men in the back before. It did not bother him, as long as they were dead. But Lean Wolf and the others were long gone. He planned to fire just a few more shots, then he would attempt his escape. But to his surprise, the renegades opened up from the north just as Lean Wolf said they would.

Blood Hawk was confused, though thankful the renegades would cover his retreat. What would happen next he did not know. From now on, he could not take his eyes off Lean Wolf. Now, it would be cat and mouse to the finish.

Blood Hawk raced to his horse. The nervous animal pawed the ground, more than ready to run. He jumped into the saddle and galloped away, whipping the horse on the rump with his rifle.

The Day Hunters

"Dammit, Cole, do I have to knock you in the head? We're not gonna catch him on these wore out horses! We need to rest 'em awhile," Harley said. "Pull them saddles, boys. Let's get breakfast workin'. Eli, you make the coffee."

Cole felt he might burst from the anger boiling inside him, but he bit down hard and contained it as best he could. He'd counted five rifles, all Henry repeaters. Where had the fifth shooter come from? It was unlike Stone Horse to give an inaccurate headcount. Maybe one man had been off in the bushes while he watched the camp. Stone Horse hadn't said anything about extra mounts. And where the hell was he?

Cole desperately wanted to be alone to think it all through, but dare not leave his position. Maybe the outlaws hadn't really gone that far. Lean Wolf might be waiting for just such a mistake. He and Harley had made many mistakes since becoming Texas Rangers, but none like they'd made on the llano. The very mistake that brought them here.

Keeping the troop together would have only given Zendejaz more targets to shoot at. The boys might have been killed, anyway. But Cole and his bunch survived, with only the loss of the horses. Maybe, if he'd kept the boys with him, they would have survived, too. He didn't know what else they could have done. He just felt they had bungled the job. Now the men responsible for the murders had escaped again, their own horses were exhausted, and by nightfall the renegades may have a lead impossible to make up.

"We need fresh horses," Cole said to his partner. "You reckon Stone Horse knows anybody up this way?"

"I expect he does. He claims he's been as far north as the Sioux country. I expect he's been through here," Harley said. "If he ever comes back, we'll ask him."

"Where you reckon he is?"

"I hope he's on Lean Wolf's trail, but who knows? Maybe

The Day Hunters

he's decided we spend too much time gettin' shot at.' "

The men had finished eating, their heads beginning to nod, when they heard the pistol shot. The sound came from the west, not too far away.

"Want me to have a look?" Moody asked.

"No, they can smell our fire. If they want us, they can find us. We'll wait for 'em here," Cole said. "Keep an eye peeled."

The Rangers didn't have long to wait, before they saw Stone Horse approaching the camp, leading two horses. Both looked exhausted. The roan horse carried a man slumped over, tied to the saddle. The man looked familiar to Harley. He quickly recognized the young Ranger, Milo Simms.

"Well, good mornin', Milo. I see you've met Stone Horse."

Eli and Moody worked to free Milo from his bonds, and pulled him down from the horse. He had quite a knot on the side of his head.

"I told him I was scouting for the Rangers," Stone Horse said. "But he tried to shoot me, so I hit him with a rock."

"Are you all right, son?" Harley chuckled.

"Yes, sir. Dang, he hit me hard."

"I believe you. Horse is apt to get cranky under fire. What're you doin' out here?"

"I come to tell you, Eddie's dead. He died that same evenin', after you left."

The death of Eddie Roberts came as no particular surprise to anyone. He had been ailing with rheumatism for several years, and had long since stopped riding with them. None of the men even knew how old he was.

"I expect the rheumatism finally stopped his heart," Harley said.

"Well, maybe, but not before he got his last poke."

"What? You mean Eddie was still seein' the ladies?" Eli said.

"He did that night. Died right there in her bed. He was layin' in bed, and sat straight up and died. He was sittin' up stiff

The Day Hunters

as a board when I went up there."

"Well, I swear," Cole said. "Did Boone see him like that?"

"No sir, Captain. I made sure he didn't."

"Thank you, Milo. I appreciate that."

"What about Boone? Where's he?" Harley asked.

"Of an evenin', he's stayin' with Rebecca Tate from the cafe. She took him in after Eddie died. He spends the day at the sheriff's office, cleanin' up, and runnin' errands."

"From the looks of those horses, you've been doin' some hard ridin'," Cole said. "When'd you leave Austin?"

"The mornin' after you did. I ain't hardly quit ridin' since. I kept Eddie's weapons. Is that all right?"

"He'd be proud for you to have 'em, son."

The troop slipped into silence for a few minutes, then Harley quietly began to laugh. "Cole, you recall Eddie havin' them Comanche dreams back when he was ridin'? He'd sit straight up in his sleep, with that surprised look on his face and start cussin'?"

"Yeah. You reckon that's what happened?"

"If it did, I'll bet it scared the hell outta that gal."

The idea of Eddie, sitting up in the whore's bed with the surprised look on his face, became the funniest thing the men could imagine. Soon all the Rangers were laughing, even Cole. Stone Horse poured himself a cup of coffee, gulped it down then poured another, while he waited for the laughing to stop.

The laughter released the Rangers pent up frustrations, but was quickly followed by the sadness of losing another friend. Eddie Roberts had ridden with them for many years. He'd been a good companion and a damned hard fighter. In his own way, Eddie had been especially kind to Moody, teaching him many of the useful skills he was now known for.

"I'll take the watch, Cap'n," Moody volunteered. He walked away from the camp forlorn. How many more of his friends were going to die?

"Milo, did you fire those first shots?" Cole asked.

"Yes, sir. It was just pure luck that I found you. I ain't no

85

The Day Hunters

tracker, but that appaloosa's wearin' a bar shoe. He was pretty easy to follow. That's what got me this far. One of them Indians was wearin' a red shirt, and I just happened to see it. I didn't know what else to do."

"You did good, son," Harley said. "You saved our lives. If we make it back to civilization, the festivities are on me. Well, now what?"

"We need fresh mounts," Cole said. "Lean Wolf'll be miles from here before ours are rested. Do you know where we can find some, Horse?"

"There are settlements to the northeast," Stone Horse replied, pouring his third cup of coffee. "Fort Washita is close. There will be horses there. I don't know if they have good ones."

"How far?" Cole asked, impatiently.

"Thirty miles."

"Harley, you take the boys north to the Canadian," Cole said. "Wait for us there. I'll take Eli and head for the fort. I doubt we'll get there before dark, but we'll catch up as soon as we can. Eli, saddle up."

"Yessir, Cap'n." Eli hoisted his saddle up on to his hip and walked out to catch his horse, wondering if he would ever sleep again.

#

The renegades rode north at a fast clip. Lean Wolf took great pains to keep Blood Hawk out in front where he could see him. Blood Hawk often glanced behind. Soon they rode out into a long open valley where they picked up the pace, pushing their horses even harder.

"Somebody keep an eye on him from now on," Lean Wolf said.

"You think he's workin' for the Rangers?" Emmett asked.

"I don't think he just showed up."

"Hell, he coulda been killed just as easy as us. Why wouldn't he just tell 'em where we were?"

The Day Hunters

"I'll know that after I torture him a while."

"You think we hit any of the Rangers?" Fast Elk asked.

"I doubt it, you drunken bastards. You can't shoot worth a damn."

After an hour of hard riding, the outlaws stopped to relieve themselves in a shady stand of cottonwoods. A sizeable bunch of unshod horses had been there not long before. Their tracks led straight to the north. The tracks were too deep for wild ponies. That meant either a hunting party, or a warrior band. Lean Wolf wanted to see neither.

"Keep your eyes open. We'll follow the horses at a distance," he said. "The Rangers will lose our tracks in the bunch. We'll break off somewhere up the trail. Even Stone Horse couldn't separate all these tracks. Let's ride."

Back in the saddle, they headed due north at the walk, giving their horses a chance to breathe. They checked their back trail frequently. Ellsworth was not one to give up so easily.

"I wonder how those Rangers found us so early," Fast Elk said. "You said they wouldn't show till this afternoon."

"Maybe they didn't camp where I thought," Blood Hawk said, showing his anger at Fast Elk's tone. "Maybe they rode all night."

"Or maybe somebody led 'em to us," Emmett said.

In an instant Blood Hawk drew his pistol and struck Emmett in the mouth. The blow broke the idiot's teeth out and knocked him from his horse. He quickly fired three shots into the dust around the man's head. Emmett wadded up in a tight little ball, his hands cupped over his ears.

"I did not bring the Rangers," Blood Hawk stated. "If you accuse me again, I will leave you for the buzzards." He then calmly turned his horse and rode away as if nothing important had happened.

Lean Wolf roared with laughter at the sight of Emmett, balled up on the ground, cursing, spitting his teeth out. "If you're gonna roll up in a ball and whine, maybe we'll call you Armadillo Emmett."

The Day Hunters

Lean Wolf rode away laughing, leaving Emmett trying to catch his horse.

#

Every whore in Austin had stopped by Rebecca Tate's home in the past few days, dropping off articles of clothing, little things for the boy, leaving coins on the table as they left. There were no visits from the citizenry, and Rebecca didn't expect any. After all, what was one more orphan to the good people of Austin. And the son of a drunk, at that. They hadn't cared about Boone before, why would they now? Whores and waitresses were not that different to Rebecca's way of thinking. Both were just unappreciated servants to those with money to spend.

Though she'd had offers, she never married. At twenty eight, she doubted she ever would. The men admired her figure, her hair and pretty face, but somehow she could never bring herself to trust them. She'd known too many women who, after the wedding, just became something to poke and beat on.

Rebecca longed for a man to love her, to protect her, but she wanted him to be the right man. So far she hadn't met him. Her fear of men outweighed her loneliness. Having Boone in her home made her happy, and there was little enough happiness in the world.

She dipped the plate in the rinse water, handing it to Boone to dry. He looked so sad, she nearly burst into tears. Rebecca knew Eddie Roberts. She saw him two or three times a week at the cafe. He never ordered a meal, just coffee and pie. She'd engaged in many conversations with him, and sometimes he would mention Boone.

His feelings for the boy were plain enough, just as Boone's feelings were for Eddie. The old Ranger told her of Boone's hard luck, and when Harley brought him in that morning, she instantly fell in love with him. Something about the boy captured her heart. It wasn't just that he was an orphan and needed someone to love him. There was something proud in his eyes. Proud, but sad, too.

The Day Hunters

Even now that he'd come to live with her, she sometimes thought of him as a little man instead of a boy. He carried himself differently than the other boys his age. Mostly, he was the one they followed.

"Did you like your supper, handsome?" she said.

"Yes ma'am. I always like chicken and dumplin's. My mama used to make it. She was a good cooker."

Rebecca smiled. Her heart broke at the same time, the tears rolling down her cheeks.

"Are you sad, ma'am? Why are you cryin'?" Boone didn't like to see anyone cry. He knew that he'd start crying himself, and a promise was a promise.

"Oh, I'm sad and happy, too. It's kind of hard to explain."

Boone feared the worst. "Do you want me to go live somewhere else?"

Rebecca gasped and fell to her knees. She threw her arms around the boy, and cried hard for several minutes. So did Boone.

"No, honey, I don't want you to live somewhere else," she said, trying to regain her composure. "I want you to stay here with me as long as you want to."

"Thank you, ma'am." Boone found it hard to shut off the tears. His own composure did not return so quickly.

"And you don't have to call me ma'am all the time."

"What should I call you then?"

"Well, you could call me Miss Becky. How's that?" Her tears came like a flood again. Rebecca walked to her rocking chair, sat down and cradled her head in her hands.

Boone approached her, trying to be brave. He cautiously put his hand on her shoulder. "You don't have to cry, Miss Becky. I'll look out for you. I promise."

#

Cole and Eli spent the night six miles from Fort Washita. They'd walked their horses most of the day, but the animals could go no farther. Cole hoped he could find suitable mounts at the fort. There was no telling how much ground Lean Wolf made since his escape. He'd ride his horse to death and steal another if need be. But the Rangers could catch him if they had remounts. At least, that was the theory.

Eli made a meal of canned meat and potatoes, a product conceived during the Civil War. Cole felt most of the canned goods he'd consumed tasted like they were made before the battle of Fort Sumpter, though he did have a fondness for the peaches.

Camping close to the fort, they expected no trouble, so they each got a fair night's sleep. Mid-morning found them at the Fort Washita livery. An angry looking man sat at the desk. He ignored the Rangers until Cole spoke up.

"Cole Ellsworth, Texas Rangers. I need to buy some horses."

"Heard of you. I ain't got none for sale," the proprietor growled. His name was Jubal Maine and he was already drunk, though early in the day.

"Looks like you've got some to me. There's nine in the pen."

"All for rent."

"Fine, I'll rent five. How much?"

"The hell you will, Ranger. Get outta here now!"

Pulling his pistol, he jumped out of the chair. It was the wrong thing to do. Cole kicked him in the chin as he drew his own weapon. As Maine fell backwards, his pistol discharged, the bullet shattering the window. The shot brought Eli Plummer on the run.

"Eli, find the guards!" Cole shouted.

His adversary rose to his feet, gun still in hand. Cole fired one round, breaking the man's right shoulder. The impact slammed him into a large post in the middle of the room. The post enabled him to keep his feet. Dropping his weapon, his gun arm hanging useless, Maine pulled a knife from behind his back. He came at Cole with murder in his eye. As he thrust the knife, Cole stepped to the right. Putting his weight into the stroke, he bashed the man in the head with his pistol. Maine hit the floor face first

The Day Hunters

and broke his nose. His flopping arm spilled a filthy spittoon across the floor.

Cole cautiously knelt beside the man to be sure he was still alive. He was in that position when he heard the rifles cock. Standing in the doorway were two very nervous young privates, each with a rifle trained on him.

"Don't shoot, boys. I'm Captain Ellsworth, Texas Rangers."

"And I am Major Faulkenberry," declared the post commander. "What happened here?" He stepped into the room brushing past the guards with an air of superior authority. His British accent put Cole off.

"I tried to buy horses from this man and he attacked me, unprovoked, with both pistol and knife. I have no idea why."

"Maybe I do," the major stated. "Just over a year ago, one of your Rangers came through here. He cleaned this man out at the poker table, then compromised his wife. Maine's been drunk and surly ever since. A tall, handsome chap. Bass Reed, I believe."

Bass Reed. The sound of the man's name cut Cole to the bone. For some reason he wanted to kill Jubal Maine.

"I'm not responsible for Bass Reed's actions, or any other man's," Cole said. "I came here to buy horses, and I'm in a hurry. We're trailin' Lean Wolf and his bunch. They're gainin' ground every minute."

"Then horses you shall have, sir. Lower your weapons, troopers. Get this man to the infirmary. If you will follow me, Captain?"

With a sigh, Cole fell in beside the major, wondering if he would ever be able to forgive himself for the deaths of Bass Reed and the boys. He should have known the boys were too green, but then it was always the young who fought the wars. Too many painful memories—too hard to deal with. Well, no time for that now. They needed fresh horses to resume the search for Lean Wolf. That was enough to think about.

"You look exhausted, Captain," Major Faulkenberry said. "May I offer you and your man breakfast?"

The Day Hunters

Eli perked up at the major's suggestion, but Cole declined. "We ain't got time. My men are waitin' at the Canadian."

"We have heard of the massacre," the major said. "Some of the settlers have moved into the fort because of it, though we have no place to put them. I am sorry about your Rangers."

"Bass Reed was one of 'em."

"Well, again, I am sorry. I am not authorized to sell you horses, Captain. But as temporary post commander, in lieu of Colonel Bedoe's death, I might be able to displace the mount roster for a while. You would be doing us a great favor by capturing this renegade."

"What happened to your Colonel?" Eli asked.

"He contracted syphilis from one of the camp whores. Went crazy and hung himself. Good riddance, I say. The mongrel."

Cole was impressed with the quality of the horse flesh. Though the army didn't enjoy the Rangers' reputation as fighters, he had to concede that they were always better mounted. Major Faulkenberry ordered his men to cut out five good ones.

"I appreciate the help, Major. I'll get 'em back as quick as I can," Cole said. "I give you my word. We'll pay for any we lose."

"Good luck, Captain. Good luck and be careful."

Cole and Eli rode out of Fort Washita better mounted than they'd ever been. The ride to the Canadian River would be an easy trip for such spirited animals. Cole only hoped that Harley wouldn't find the outlaws and kill them all before he got back.

The Day Hunters

chapter 9

Delgado pulled rein nearly a mile from the mouth of the stronghold, which was actually no more than a deep crevice leading into the canyon. Nature had somehow formed the crevice into a series of switchbacks, so narrow in some places that only a single horse could pass through. The entrance was not hidden, but naturally camouflaged with rock and overgrown mesquite. The crevice could hardly be seen at all unless its location was known, and if discovered, would normally be taken for a large washout—a dangerous place to explore. The few who had discovered it, never lived to tell its whereabouts. In this lonely, isolated place Merejildo Zendejaz reigned like a king.

Delgado searched the horizon in all directions. When he was sure he wasn't being followed, he approached the entrance. Making his way through the switchbacks, he came to the guard post, where he was quickly waved through, and informed that Zendejaz was anxious to see him. The narrow passageway opened to a huge canyon with water, grass, and plenty of shade. A perfect hideout in Delgado's opinion. A large horse herd dotted the landscape, along with many lodges. They all looked like typical outlaw hovels, with the exception of the large, decorative tent at the far end.

The tent was of the Bedouin type, the floor covered with colorful rugs and pillows. A large canopy on the south side shaded the stall where Zendejaz housed his keen arabian stallion. His love for the breed stemmed from tales he'd been told by a captive held long ago. The man claimed to have been to Morocco, where he saw "the finest horses the human mind can fathom. Horses with such beauty, speed and incredible endurance, no other breed can compare." When Zendejaz heard of an arabian stallion on a ranch near Santa Fe, he and Delgado, with the captive in tow, went there to steal the horse. Zendejaz was so pleased with the stallion, he freed the captive, and even gave him twenty dollars to travel on.

The wretched women of the camp ran to Delgado like

93

The Day Hunters

beggars, as he threw the dead woman's clothes to them. They put them on over their own filthy rags, then began to dance like giddy school girls, until one of them saw that Delgado led a limping horse. At her single word, the women stopped the dancing, led the horse away, and cut his throat. They each drew a knife and began to butcher the animal, meticulously trying to save every morsel. Their arms and new clothes covered with blood, they laughed and talked, nibbling on the guts as they worked. The sight repulsed Delgado, but he was accustomed to seeing such things. There were few ladies in the stronghold. What ladies there were lived in the tent with Zendejaz. When he had his fill of them, they became community property. They usually didn't last long after that. They either lived an ugly life, or they died an ugly death.

Stepping down from his horse, Delgado passed the reins to a buck toothed young boy and shouted his arrival to the tent flap.

"*Jefe!* It is Delgado with news of the Rangers!"

The casual giggles told him the women inside were dressing. Soon the tent flap opened, and he was ushered inside by the two women. One Mexican, one white, both drunk. A woman called Big Iris was also in the tent. She was a very large woman, about six feet tall, maybe two hundred pounds or more, with an ample bosom she loved to show off.

Big Iris lost her husband and three children in a swollen river crossing. Shortly thereafter, she lost her mind. She would cackle, then cry, then cackle again, sometimes running wild through the camp. But despite such bizarre behavior, Zendejaz kept her because she could read. An oddity for a woman on the frontier. When Big Iris read to him, she became quiet and calm, losing herself in the stories. Sometimes she'd continue reading long after he'd fallen asleep. But today Big Iris read to herself, while Zendejaz had his way with the women.

"Sit, *amigo*. Tell me the news," Zendejaz said. "*Mujeres*, bring whiskey."

"Ellsworth is alive, *Jefe*. He has mounted a troop to catch Lean Wolf. Lean Wolf killed the Rangers that followed him on the llano."

The Day Hunters

The news stunned Zendejaz. He'd heard nothing of the killings in his remote desert kingdom.

"Macon?"

"*Sí*, Macon is alive too."

The Mexican woman served Delgado three fingers of whiskey, while Zendejaz sat back in his chair and closed his eyes. His eyeballs rolled frantically beneath the lids. His breathing became increasingly heavy.

"Ellsworth asked for volunteers," Delgado continued.

"Only two young boys joined him. That makes just six men. I left town before they did, but they were in a hurry. Austin is crying for vengeance."

Zendejaz sprang to his feet, turning his chair over backwards. "*Chingada!*" he shouted. "I thought the bastard was dead. When did you leave Austin?"

"Seven days ago." Delgado emptied his glass and held it out for a refill, enjoying the dust-cutting burn of the whiskey.

"The Rangers planned to leave the next day. Like I said, they were in a hurry."

"Six days on the trail. They may have found Lean Wolf's camp on the Red River by now."

"If they catch him, he can tell them where the stronghold is, *eh?*"

Zendejaz turned quickly. "I know that!" he shouted. He walked to the stall and stroked the stallion's muzzle, until he'd regained his composure. "Forgive me, *amigo*. I must be alone to think."

Delgado started to rise from the chair, but Zendejaz stopped him. "No. You have ridden a long way. *Mujeres*, make a bath. *Chico!*"

The buck toothed boy stuck his head through the flap.

"*Si, Jefe?*"

"Saddle my sorrel. *Vayate.*"

Zendejaz strapped on his bone handled pistols, checked the loads and stepped outside. He turned back to the tent instructing the women, "Take very good care of my friend."

The Day Hunters

Delgado paid particular attention to the white woman hauling water for his bath. She put him in mind of the rancher's dead wife. Zendejaz had a big tub, big enough for both him and the women to get in. While the white woman hauled water, the Mexican stripped him, then led him to the bathtub. Big Iris, in her fantasy world, giggled at something she read.

#

The Rangers huddled close to the fire in the growing darkness, on the south bank of the Canadian River. They had been there in the drizzling rain most of the day, waiting for Captain Ellsworth and Eli to catch up with fresh horses. Far to the west a fierce lightning storm lit up the sky. Violent storms were not unusual for this time of year, but they could play hell with a river crossing.

Moody and Stone Horse slept soundly, though Milo hadn't relaxed since joining the troop—if it could still be called a troop. His young eyes darted to and fro, continually looking for danger. Harley chuckled, remembering that he'd been no different on his first patrol. Every sight, every sound, every smell, meant Comanches.

"Lean Wolf's across the river, son. You'd better get some sleep. You'll need it when Cole shows up," Harley said.

"When do you think he'll get here?"

"Tomorrow, I expect, barrin' any trouble. He'll travel as fast as he can."

"Do you think he'll send me back to Austin?"

"No, he won't send you back. If he was gonna do that, he'd never let you come this far. But listen close, boy. If Captain Ellsworth tells you to stay put, then, by God, you'd better stay put. Cole won't tolerate disobedience."

"Yes, sir."

"Why'd you really come out here, Milo? You didn't ride all the way to the Red River just to tell us about Eddie."

The Day Hunters

"No, sir, I didn't. Truth is, I felt like a coward when you all rode out. I sure didn't like it, so I come to find you. I didn't want to miss a chance to ride with you and Captain Ellsworth."

Brave, but foolish, thought Harley. "Roll up in them blankets. I don't sleep much anyway. I'll wake you if we go to war."

"Yes, sir. Goodnight."

"Goodnight, son."

Harley worried about the foul weather to the west. It must be raining hard up river for the Canadian to be this high. If they were stuck here very long, they'd never catch up to Lean Wolf. He may already be out of reach, a thought Harley couldn't accept. When they crossed the Canadian, they'd be in country the Rangers had never seen before, though Harley was sure Lean Wolf would know it well. He raided and murdered all over this country, by all the reports they'd received.

Harley had killed many a man since becoming a Texas Ranger, not to mention what he'd done in the war. Some died in combat, some by the rope, every one in the name of justice. But what he felt now had little to do with justice. Hatred, shame, anger beyond description, the same feelings the Comanche and the Kiowa held for the white man. Revenge, that's what he wanted. He was sure Cole felt the same.

Lean Wolf was a killer. They could expect no less from him. He'd done nothing to the Ranger troop that he hadn't done to any number of settlers and wagon trains. He simply rode down on his enemies and killed them. Harley and Cole had done the same thing many times, on their raids into hostile camps. It would be no different when they caught up to Lean Wolf. But they would have to move soon, if they were going to catch him. The threatening weather would make things more difficult.

Moody cut a big fart while under his blankets. He had to stick his head out in the drizzle to save himself.

"What time is it, Mistuh Harley?"

"Why, it's night time, Moody. Can't you see that? I'm hungry. Let's get to cookin'."

The Day Hunters

Moody crawled out of his cozy blankets, then set about frying strips of bacon and warming up the beans. Earlier he'd added some wild onions that Stone Horse found somewhere on his scout. The onions couldn't do the beans any harm.

"If the storms quit tonight, maybe we can cross tomorrow," Harley said.

"Yessuh. What about the Captain?"

"If he gets here in time, fine. If not, we'll leave a man here to wait for him. That'll be you, Moody. We can't leave Milo. He's too green."

Moody feared the idea of dividing the troop again. They were in the heart of Indian territory, already shorthanded, and with a green kid to boot. Mr. Harley was a more than capable Indian fighter, but Milo had never been in a skirmish before, and Lean Wolf was no ordinary foe. On top of that, Moody didn't want to wait there alone. Dividing the troop had started all this. Moody had already buried too many friends. He didn't want to dig any more graves.

"Cole better come a'ridin'," Harley said. "We can't wait much longer."

#

The warm glow of the light shining through the cabin window might have served as a beacon on such a wet, miserable night, but the long haired stranger felt something was wrong. Things were just too quiet. He'd been watching the cabin from a distance for quite a while. He heard not a sound over the pouring rain. No shadows passed the window. No dogs barked to warn of his presence. The smoke from the chimney promised dry clothes and hot food, both of which he needed. But still he hesitated to ride in. His life on the frontier had taught him patience and restraint. This was not the first night he'd sat out in the rain, but he saw no point in waiting any longer.

He approached the cabin, taking his time, waiting to hear the nicker of a horse. But he didn't hear it, not even from his own

The Day Hunters

mount. The heavy rain could drown out his hoofbeats, but it was hard to sneak up on a horse. The hair on the stranger's neck stood up. Something was out of order here.

He rode a circle around the back of the place, to get a better look at the stable. There were no horses there at all. Maybe everyone was gone. It was Saturday. Maybe there was a dance close by, though anyone who would travel in this weather surely had more on their mind than dancing. The rain had washed out every track. He could not read a single sign. Then he found the dog.

The mutt had been roped and hung by the neck, likely the quietest way to kill him. Now there was no doubt. He dreaded to think what he might find in the cabin.

Well, he thought, it was now or never. "Hello the cabin!" No answer. In a much louder voice he tried again. *"Hello the cabin!"* Still no answer. The stranger dismounted, pistol at the ready. With great caution, he stepped onto the porch. He rapped on the door and quickly stepped to the side. No response. Dammit. He took a deep breath, swung the door wide and stepped into the cabin. There before him was a sight far worse than he'd imagined.

Dead on the floor lay a young, naked couple, the man atop the woman, covered with blood. A closer inspection revealed multiple stab wounds in the young man's back, the butcher knife still protruding from one of them. He also had two bullets in him, one in his chest, and one in his back. The girl's skull had been brutally crushed. She had a single knife wound to her thigh. The bodies were positioned in a ghoulish embrace, their lips pressed together for one final kiss.

The stranger walked out into the rain, closing the door behind him. He led his horse to the stable, where he stripped the tired beast of his heavy saddle, and forked him a good ration of hay. Stalling, he searched for a bit of grain, but the feed bin was empty. There was none to be found. "Well, Pal," he said to his horse, "where do you suppose he keeps his shovel?"

The Day Hunters

"I'm startin' to think we're crazy drivin' these mules into the territory," Bullock said. "What if the Indians won't buy 'em? What if they just kill us and take 'em?"

"They'll buy 'em, then we'll take the money and head for Mexico, just like I said," Teague argued. "I told you the Indians pay good money for mules. I've had enough of the army and this country. There's too damn much law here for me."

Bullock grew more and more dissatisfied with the situation. As it turned out, Teague was not the leader he claimed to be. Daniels was getting spookier, and meaner, all the time. And Bullock himself began to doubt his own motive and courage. He'd been nervous and scared since leaving Fort Riley. Like everyone on the western plains, he'd heard much about Lean Wolf, none of it good. He had a bad feeling about the whole thing, but he couldn't change it now.

They were watering the mules at a little creek, waiting for Daniels to catch up. He'd ridden toward the settlements to see if he could buy some food, but Bullock was getting worried. He knew Sergeant Teague was, too. The boy had been gone overnight, which in itself posed many possibilities. But mostly Bullock was worried because he thought Daniels was a fool. The things he said and did, made a man wonder what he might do next. Bullock had seen the look on his face when Sergeant Teague recently mentioned the Lakota girl. Bullock thought he could be traveling with a murderer.

The weather was awful—drizzle, then rain, then more drizzle.

"Dern, I hate ridin' wet," Bullock said.

"Well, you know the sayin', 'It don't rain *in* the army, it rains *on* the army.' I guess that's why they issued you a slicker."

"I wish Daniels would show up with some food. I'm starvin'. I wouldn't mind a dry place to spend the night neither."

"We won't wait much longer. That boob might've run off.

The Day Hunters

It's gonna get dark early tonight, what with all this rain."

Another hour crawled by before the deserters heard the sound of three horses approaching at the trot. It was Daniels. He never slowed down as he ponied the horses across the creek.

"Come on. Hurry up. I've got the grub. Let's go!"

Teague and Bullock mounted quickly, driving the mules into the fast flowing water. Teague shouted, "What the hell's your hurry, boy?"

"I stole these horses. Come on. Let's get outta here!"

"Are you bein' chased?"

"I don't know, but I ain't waitin' around to find out!"

"Damn it," Teague said . "I knew it was a mistake sendin' that fool. Now it's not just the army after us, but probably the law to boot."

Having made the crossing, the men pushed the mules into a high lope, many of them slipping, stumbling in the ankle deep mud. The thunder crashed like cannon fire. The rain fell harder still, as the deserters began a desperate race for the Cimarron River.

#

The renegades waited out the rain in a small, abandoned cabin that Lean Wolf had used as a refuge before. The cabin wasn't much, but it was dry. And he was quickly tiring of Emmett spitting blood all over the place.

Emmett had a difficult time enjoying the roasted venison, since half of his teeth were buried in mud back on the trail. His sharp, broken teeth cut into his mouth so that it never had stopped bleeding, giving him even more of an ugly, savage appearance.

"You stinkin' pig. I'm sick of you," Lean Wolf shouted.

"If I see you spit again, I'll kill you, and leave you for the flies."

Both Fast Elk and Emmett were weary of living with Lean Wolf's constant threatening. They felt they had done nothing to warrant such abuse, but knew all too well what would happen if

The Day Hunters

they complained, or tried to leave.

Blood Hawk felt the same. What a foolish thing he had done, joining up with Lean Wolf again. He had succeeded in escaping the man once before, and that was once more than anyone else. All others had died in the attempt. Now, he wondered if Lean Wolf intended to fight the Rangers, or if he was just going to keep running.

Lean Wolf or one of the others, watched him closely since the ambush. Even when he went to relieve himself, someone went with him. Blood Hawk tried to figure what Lean Wolf would do if he caught him in a lie. He only knew it would be something bad. He had not given up hope of killing Lean Wolf, but now he thought mostly of escape—a thing he doubted he could accomplish again.

"Will we try another ambush, or are we going to keep running?"

"You'll do as you're told, so shut your damned mouth," Lean Wolf snapped. "The Rangers are stuck south of the Canadian, but we can do what we please. Right now, it pleases me to get some sleep, so shut up. Fast Elk, take the first watch."

Lean Wolf lay down with his back to the wall, a cocked pistol in his hand for comfort. Each man found a spot on the floor and rolled up into his blankets. In no time, the outlaws fell to heavy breathing, at last getting some much needed sleep.

Fast Elk knew what would please *him*. A woman, or even another farm boy, but he had neither. Once a man got the feeling, it was hard to shake it, and Fast Elk had the feeling. If they traveled east, they would soon reach the Osage land. A land with fresh, young women, but also savage fighting men. If they made for the stronghold to the west, they would have the filthy, broken slave women of the Comancheros. He didn't much care for either choice. Maybe Lean Wolf would consent to a raid on one of the Cherokee settlements. The people there lived in fear of him. It should be easy to take some of their women.

The Day Hunters

Fast Elk felt a night of drinking and raping was just what the renegades needed to take the edge off. They'd been running for nearly a hundred and fifty miles, and it was beginning to tell on the men. The fact that they crossed the Canadian before it flooded was the only reason they stopped here to rest. But Fast Elk knew the swollen river would not stop the Rangers for long. Ellsworth would see to that.

The Day Hunters

Rebecca and Boone returned home from church, to find Isabella waiting on the porch with a nice basket of vegetables. Boone ran to her and hugged her legs. Isabella kissed him on the forehead. "Have you been minding Rebecca, Mister?"

"Yes, ma'am."

"It's a good thing. If you don't, me and the girls are gonna come over here and tickle you 'til you wet your pants."

The tickling was a common threat among the women his mother knew from the saloon. Boone dismissed it with a laugh, though he sure wouldn't want to wet his pants in front of a bunch of women.

"Come in," Rebecca said, "I'll make some tea."

Isabella set the basket on the kitchen table and sat down to shuck the corn. "Mr. Bailey sent the vegetables over. His garden's doing well this year, what with an endless supply of horse manure on Main Street."

Boone changed out of his scratchy blue coat as fast as he possibly could. The summer sun was far too hot for such attire, and besides, it made him itch all over. He returned to the kitchen in bib overalls, without any shoes or shirt.

"Are you planning on leaving when we have company?" Rebecca asked.

Boone shuffled from one foot to the other, staring intently at his black toenail. Ol' Dan had stepped on his big toe one day, while Boone tried to pick out the horse's feet.

"Can me and Toad go swimmin'? Whew! It sure is hot out there."

The ladies attempted to stifle their amusement, but soon they had to give in. To Boone, their laughter was a joyous sound.

"All right," Rebecca said. "But you don't go down to Rankin Bridge. It's too deep down there."

Boone hugged them both and ran out the door, leaving it standing open for the flies to come in.

The Day Hunters

"How's it working out?" Isabella asked.

Rebecca crossed the room to close the door. "He's a hand full. He really misses Eddie. All he talks about are horses, guns, and Texas Rangers. I declare, he thinks Captain Ellsworth hung the moon."

"Well, so do half the people in Texas. Boone had to know how his mother felt about the Captain. She loved him, though I'm not sure he knew it himself. You could do a lot worse."

"I wouldn't want a man who was off getting shot at all the time. How did Louise handle it?"

"She didn't have any choice. You can't help who you fall in love with."

"No, I suppose not. Have you ever been in love, Isabella?"

"Sure. I've been in love, but none of them were. They came to get what they wanted and left. That's the nature of my business, honey. But I can tell you this. If Cole Ellsworth took a shine to me, I'd never let him out of the house. I hear he has a big foot."

The ladies had a hearty laugh, while Rebecca got up to pour the tea.

#

Moody was the first to see the horses approaching. He thought he counted seven, though they were still afar off. Indians? Maybe Lean Wolf had gotten behind them somehow. He was just about to warn the men, when he recognized the lead rider.

"Hooray!" he shouted. "The Captain!"

Though still a fair distance, he could make out two riders, leading five horses. There was no question that one of the riders was the Captain. Rarely did one see a man sit a horse better than Captain Ellsworth. Or Mr. Harley either, for that matter. They rode as if born to the saddle.

As the riders closed the gap, Moody could see the high quality of the horses they led. He felt hope rise inside him. It would be hard to outrun horses like these. Maybe this time they

The Day Hunters

would catch Lean Wolf, a man he looked forward to hanging.

The troop had just finished their noon meal when they heard the cheer go up. Immediately a sense of relief came over the men, particularly Milo. But Harley had to admit, he felt it too. In the pursuit of any foe, Comanche, Kiowa, or otherwise, there was no man he would rather have beside him than Cole Ellsworth. The man's fight and determination were legendary, though when consumed by them, he was damned hard to stop. Harley didn't think he would even try to stop him when they caught up to Lean Wolf.

Cole and Eli rode into the camp to the oohs and aahs of the men.

"By God, Cole, I've never seen you better mounted," Harley said, offering his hand to his partner.

Cole's face bore the smile he reserved only for the very best horses. "They're Kentucky bred, all of 'em. The army loaned 'em to us. Can you believe it? If we bring 'em back sound, we don't have to pay."

"No, I don't believe it. Hell, we'd've whipped the Comanches ten years ago on horses like these. Any trouble?"

"Yeah. Bass Reed."

"Bass?"

"Yeah. Cards and women, about a year ago. The woman's husband attacked me. He runs the livery at the fort."

"You kill him?"

"No, but I disabled him."

"He disabled him all right," Eli whispered to Moody. "He near disabled him to death."

A heaviness came over the troop. Harley tried to lift it with a little teasing.

"Fort Washita's a long ride from Austin, for a ladies' man like Bass. I expect he was needin' a poke."

"He didn't have to poke the man's wife," Cole stated.

"Why didn't he go find a whore?"

106

The Day Hunters

"Well, you know Bass. I expect the wife was handy."

The teasing had failed its purpose. Even Harley wished he'd kept his mouth shut. Milo quickly took charge of the horses, while Moody poured coffee and dished up two plates of a fine pheasant stew. Cole and Eli accepted both eagerly.

"Who got the pheasant?" Eli asked.

"Why, Stone Horse, who else?" Harley replied. "He says he got him flyin', but I say the bird was sittin' out the bad weather. What do you think, Cole?"

"I don't care. The river's pretty high."

"Yeah. But it's gone down some and it's not too fast."

"Dang," Cole said, "that is a fine stew. A good shot, flyin' or sittin'."

Stone Horse thanked the Captain with a subtle nod, showing his pride in the long tail feather that now adorned his hair.

"How far to the Cimarron, Horse?"

"It is eighty miles to the Cimarron, Captain. But I think Lean Wolf's rendezvous is at least a hundred miles upriver."

"By God, in this weather? That'll take a week," Harley said. "You think he'll go to the rendezvous?"

"Who knows what Lean Wolf will do. It will be hard to find his track."

"More like impossible," Cole said.

"I do not think Lean Wolf will cross the Cimarron to the north. The salt prairie is there. There is little to eat or drink on the salt prairie. He will go east or west."

"What's to the east?"

"The big timber. Creek and Cherokee settlements. Further north, the Osage. A fierce people. I think the Osage will kill Lean Wolf if he goes there."

"Then we need to make sure he don't get that far. Well, Harley?"

"All right. I say we cross the river and ride one day north. If there's no sign of him, we'll decide then and there."

Cole tossed off his coffee. "Let's pack it up, boys."

Some of the packing was already done. Harley had decided

earlier that he, Stone Horse, and Milo, would make the crossing no later than mid-afternoon, leaving Moody to wait for Captain Ellsworth. Now that the Captain was back, Asa Moody was a happy man.

With the mules packed and ready to go, the men turned their attention to the string of fine thoroughbreds—all of them bays, none of them mean-eyed.

"Ride a horse you know for the crossin'," Cole said. "You can switch your saddle to one of these on the other side. Less chance of a wreck that way. Horse, you ride two miles upriver. Moody, you go down. If you can't find a better crossin', we'll do it right here."

While they waited for the outriders to return, Harley and Cole walked to the river bank. They stared at the far side, each man waiting for the other to speak.

"How's Milo holdin' up?" Cole finally asked.

"He's damned nervous, but I think he's got the stuff. He said he didn't want to miss a chance to ride with us, the young fool."

"Well, he took care o' Boone before he left town. That shows somethin', I guess. He could've just rode off and left him."

"Yeah. The boy's stayin' with a fine lookin' gal, I'll say that. You know Rebecca. Maybe you oughta go see her when this is over. I'll bet Boone's already told her you're ten feet tall."

Cole didn't want to think about Rebecca, or Boone. . . or Louise. He missed the boy's mother despairingly, but he wanted to keep his mind on Lean Wolf, where he might go, what he might do.

"How long's it been since you had your ass whipped, Harley?"

"It's been awhile, so I reckon I'm due. But if you wait awhile longer, I might get killed and save you the trouble."

Moody and Stone Horse returned at the same moment, neither having found a better crossing.

"We ain't gonna get there standin' here," Cole said. "Me n' Harley'll take the mules across first. We'll be ready to gather

The Day Hunters

the horses on the other side. Eli, you n' Moody start 'em after we cross. Horse, you keep an eye on Milo. Let's go."

#

Twenty miles due north of the Rangers' crossing, Old Jackson He-Crow sang his death song, as he helplessly witnessed the rape and torture of his beautiful granddaughter, Lizzie. Hands tied to the wheels of his wagon, his arms spread wide between them, he sat in the very mud the wagon was stuck in. He and Lizzie had been digging the wagon out when the renegades rode up. His legs were spread, staked to the ground, with his ankles in his own game traps. The fat white man with the broken teeth laughed his idiot laugh, as he piled wood and kindling between Old He-Crow's legs.

"Wet as the wood is, this could take a while," Emmett warned. "But that'll give you plenty o' time to watch the show."

Old He-Crow could hardly hear him over his own singing. His spirit was already seeking the safe place. As much as he wanted to, he could not help his granddaughter now. She would have to seek the safe place for herself.

He closed his eyes tight and kept them closed. He did not want to see what the men did to his beautiful girl. Her screams became muffled, as if she were far away. Maybe, he thought, she *was* far away, calling for his spirit to come to her. But Old He-Crow knew it was not true. He knew why her screams were muffled.

Lean Wolf's war cry split the air when he finished his ugly business. He pulled Lizzie's hair and slapped her in the face, before he relinquished his spot to Blood Hawk. Emmett cursed He-Crow for keeping his eyes shut. He punched him hard, again and again, but he would not open his eyes.

"He won't look, huh?" Lean Wolf said.

"No, or shut up neither, dammit." Laughing like a fool, Emmett pulled his pistol and shot his prisoner in one foot, then the

The Day Hunters

other. At the sound of the gunfire, Lizzie went crazy. She screamed a pitiful, horrible scream, but Old He-Crow just sang louder.

"Go away, granddaughter. Go away to the safe place."

"I can make him look," Lean Wolf said. "Get out of the way." He clumsily went to work with his big knife, butchering the first eyelid, slicing the eyeball in the process. Old He-Crow bit down hard against the pain, but never stopped singing. The second eyelid came off with ease, leaving He-Crow with a full view of the proceedings.

The men just kept taking Lizzie, over and over. They were filthy and they smelled like goats, breathing their stinking breath in her face. They kissed her and cursed her, and rode her like a beast, trying their best to make it hurt. Horrified, he now had no choice but to look at the terrible scene, blood running into his good eye, his cut eye leaking out of his head.

Emmett had the fire lit, fanning it with his hat, but with the damp wood, it was mostly thick, blue smoke—a perfect situation for good eyelids, but Old He-Crow had none. The heavy smoke burned his eyeballs, choking him until he threw up. At last, he could no longer hear Lizzie's cries. His granddaughter had fallen into silence.

Blood Hawk and Fast Elk shook themselves at one another, like little boys will do. Satisfied with the damage they'd done, they relieved themselves and prepared to ride again. Lizzie lay motionless, her grandfather still singing, crying her name, when the damp wood finally ignited.

Old He-Crow's screaming death came quickly, even before the outlaws rode away. But for many long hours, poor Lizzie lay in the cool mud, the smell of her grandfather's burning flesh in her nostrils, wishing her spirit could find the safe place.

#

"Whip them mules! Whip 'em!" Teague shouted. The

The Day Hunters

deserters drove the stolen herd into the churning red waters of the Cimarron. The river was neither deep nor wide, but it was moving fast. Mules and soldiers alike took a brief, but hard swim, with one loss. The big paint mare, stolen by Private Daniels, suffered a seizure of some kind while crossing the swift water. One moment she was swimming strong, the next she froze up, screamed, and sank out of sight. And that was that.

Both the mules and the deserters were exhausted. They'd been riding hard since Daniels rejoined them. They drove the mules far into the night, stopping for only short periods. They all needed rest and a chance to recuperate. The mules were dropping flesh rapidly, what with the constant traveling. The horses were no better, maybe worse. If the men weren't careful, they'd soon be afoot.

"Let's rest 'em a while," Bullock suggested, after reaching the southern bank.

"We've been pushin' nearly a hundred miles."

"You're right, kid," Teague said. "Let's get a fire goin', and see what's left to eat."

The mules and stolen horses immediately rolled in the dirt, to dry themselves of the river water. Many of them chose to lay on their bellies to graze. The soldiers' mounts had no chance to roll. They hadn't been unsaddled since leaving Fort Riley.

The camp came together quickly, as there was little to do, and even less to do it with. The men had eaten all but one loaf of bread. The coffee was nearly gone. Just a small slab of bacon was all that remained of the meat. A worrisome thing to three hungry men, but not nearly all they had to worry about.

"I think we crossed too far east, Sarge," Daniels said.

"Well, I didn't want to cross that salt grass to the west. I don't know how far across it is."

Corporal Bullock wished he was somewhere else. What on earth had he been thinking to agree with such a foolhardy plan? There were plenty of Indians in the territory who would think nothing of killing them, and taking the mules. Lean Wolf would never even know it. Hell, Lean Wolf himself might kill them.

The Day Hunters

Why would he pay for what he could steal? That didn't sound like the Lean Wolf he'd heard about. They didn't know where his rendezvous was for sure, anyway, only that it was along the south bank of the Cimarron River. That could be anywhere for hundreds of miles.

His warm, dry bunk at Fort Riley sounded good, but it was much too late for that. They had become deserters and thieves. Wanted men with a lot of country between them and Mexico. He slowly shook his head in remorse. What would his mama think?

"The rain's quit and the ground's dryin' up. Be easier trackin' now," he said.

"Yeah," Daniels agreed. "And we'll need more grub soon. I'd be glad to go find some."

I'll bet you would, thought Bullock. The fool probably had the law looking for these horses, right now.

"We'll decide after we finish the grub and rest a while," Teague said.

Then, as the coffee pot came around, Teague noticed the blood on Daniels' hands. There was also a button missing off the bloody cuff of his blouse. He kept quiet until they'd finished eating, then spoke to Corporal Bullock.

"Go ride a circle. See if you can spot a cabin or somethin'. Some place we can get some food."

"Why don't Daniels go? I'm a corporal, and he's just a private."

"You'll do as you're told, and do it now!"

Grudgingly, Bullock mounted and loped out of camp, tired of the saddle, and tired of the whole damned mess. If not for the Indians, he'd ride off alone. To hell with these fools.

"You cut yourself, Daniels?" Sergeant Teague asked.

Daniels tried to think of something to say, but quick thought was not his strength. "Nope, but I had to whip that gent to get his horses. He put up quite a fight."

Teague couldn't see a mark on him. "I can't see that he landed a blow. That's a lotta blood for a whippin'."

In a flash, Daniels blew up. "Dammit, I said I whipped

112

him. You callin' me a liar?"

"No, I ain't callin' you a liar. I'm just sayin' that's a lotta blood."

Daniels only shrugged and leaned back on his bedroll, pulling his cap down over his face. But just as he did, they heard the sound of a galloping horse approaching from the west.

"Indians!" Bullock shouted. "Painted Indians. And they ain't comin' to trade!"

"Grab our gear. Shoot some of them mules," Teague ordered. "Leave 'em some meat. Let's git!"

Swinging into their saddles, the men shot seven mules, driving the rest due south at the gallop. Crouched over his horse's neck, Teague looked back to see maybe a dozen Indians racing in their direction. God, he hoped the meat would satisfy them.

#

The renegades continued north, their recent brutality the subject of much laughter and debate. Fast Elk talked of going back to get the girl. He didn't know why they hadn't brought her along in the first place. She was young and pretty, and fought it hard. That was just the way he liked them. Emmett contended she was probably dead already. They had worked her over pretty good. Blood Hawk was just glad to have released the pressure living with Lean Wolf brought on.

Lean Wolf rode at the rear of the group, checking his back trail often. His spirit told him that ambushing the Rangers had done nothing more than inflame their persistence. He didn't understand how it all came to be, but he was sure Blood Hawk was behind it. Maybe Blood Hawk was just getting even for the loss of the ear. Lean Wolf intended to see that he lost more than that. The men had stopped to wait for him. He rode up to the usual sound of Emmett grumbling.

"I could sure use somethin' to eat. And a drink o' whiskey to wash it down with."

The Day Hunters

"I'm sick of your damned whining," Lean Wolf said. "Get the hell away from me, or I'll kill you right now."

Angry, Emmett started to speak, but Fast Elk shut him up with a seething glare.

"We will go to the rendezvous," Fast Elk said. "We will be there if you want us."

"Why would I want you? I'm running you off, ain't I? You're worthless. Ride off, dammit!"

Fast Elk did not know why Lean Wolf thought them so worthless. In the years they had ridden with him, they had always done as they were told. Neither of them were brave enough or foolish enough to go against Lean Wolf. But still he was running them off. Maybe this was their chance to escape him altogether.

The two men turned their horses northwest and left at a high lope, each hoping never to see Lean Wolf again, not to mention Ellsworth and Macon. Blood Hawk turned to follow them, but stopped at the sight of Lean Wolf's pistol, pointed at his chest.

"You're comin' with me, traitor." His spirit was speaking louder, now. He was certain Blood Hawk planned to kill him. "I will let you keep your weapons. You can grab one any time you want."

At first, Blood Hawk feared a bullet in the back, as captor and captive rode off to the east, but decided there was no point worrying about it. He would not be that lucky. He would do better to prepare himself for the long, torturous death he knew was coming. He had waited too long to kill Lean Wolf, and now, he was sure Lean Wolf would take a long time killing him.

The Day Hunters

Four well-armed men rode out of the canyon, a look of grim determination on their leader's face. Merejildo Zendejaz was a wealthy man, and he intended to keep it that way. His success greatly depended on the secrecy of his stronghold's location, and the anonymity of his suppliers. Both would be in jeopardy if Lean Wolf was captured. If Zendejaz had to kill him to keep him quiet, he would.

The New Mexico gentry supplied the rifles, their reward being that the hostiles would hold back the wave of settlers and miners flooding the west. New Mexicans wanted to keep their gold and silver. They needed time to get them out of the ground.

Zendejaz would then haul the guns to Lean Wolf's rendezvous, to make the trade for horses and mules. Lean Wolf would distribute the weapons among the hostiles, who supplied the stolen livestock, making his profit on that end. Zendejaz made his as the middle man, being paid by the gentry to deliver the rifles, selling the horses and mules back to New Mexicans. They always needed a steady supply, as the Apaches regularly stole them. It was a fine deal. Zendejaz would not let Lean Wolf destroy it.

The fool. Now that he'd killed the Rangers, Ellsworth would track Lean Wolf to the ends of the earth. Zendejaz planned to find one or the other of them before that happened.

He traveled northeast, his destination the site of Lean Wolf's rendezvous. It was as good a place as any to start. Riding with him were Delgado, Ruiz, and Ugly John. A pack of cold killers if ever there was one. They'd filled their saddlebags with no more than they needed—jerky, tortillas, coffee, whiskey, and bullets. Zendejaz did not want a pack horse to slow him down.

"I wish I knew how many men are with Ellsworth," Ugly John said. "Him and Macon are quite a few by themselves. Maybe they picked up a few more after Delgado left town."

"*Si*," Ruiz said, "but they don't know we're coming."

"You tryin' to encourage us or yourself?"

The Day Hunters

"Me as much as anyone else, I guess. I, too, wish we had enlisted a few more men. But, they'll stop a bullet just like any other man. This time we'd better make sure he's dead."

Zendejaz did not like the implication. He had been so sure his bullet killed Ellsworth, but he was wrong. When they caught up to the Rangers, he wouldn't make the same mistake twice.

"We'll take him this time," he said. "I wonder if Lean Wolf knows the Rangers are looking for him? Maybe he'll kill them himself."

"Or maybe the whole thing is already done," Delgado said. "Maybe Ellsworth is headed straight for us, right now."

Zendejaz pulled up, turning angrily on his men. "Am I leading a bunch of women?" he shouted. "Are you afraid of the Rangers? Are you cowards? I tell you, we're going to kill the Rangers, or find Lean Wolf and his cutthroats before this thing is over. Let's hope we find Lean Wolf first, then we can go after the Rangers together."

Zendejaz kicked his horse into a lope. He knew the men had every right to worry. Macon and Ellsworth were two of the most dangerous men in Texas, maybe in the whole Southwest. But he, Merejildo Zendejaz, had not lived this long. . .had not built an outlaw empire, by being easily taken. He feared neither the Texas Rangers nor the devil himself, but didn't really want to meet either one.

Now that Lean Wolf had five Rangers to his credit, Zendejaz had no doubt that he was walking tall. Though a vicious fighter, Lean Wolf sometimes became careless in his arrogance. A kill often made him too brave for his own good.

But mostly, Zendejaz feared Emmett the Idiot. Emmett was a man with a big mouth. If captured, he would surely talk to save himself, though talking was unlikely to save him from Ellsworth's rope. If all went well, they would find Lean Wolf at the rendezvous. They should reach the place day after tomorrow.

#

The Day Hunters

The pace maintained by the Kentucky thoroughbreds astounded Harley. Never had he dreamed of being so well mounted, and, as was normal for Harley, he was more than willing to discuss it.

"I swear, Cole, I can hardly feel his feet touch the ground, he travels so light. I'll bet all our horses put together ain't worth one o' these. Maybe we oughta get a few mares to breed when this is all over. With your vast knowledge of all things equine, and my natural leadership qualities, we'd likely be famous horse breeders in a few years."

"Right now, I'd rather think about Lean Wolf."

"Hell, don't you wanna be famous?"

"We're already famous in Texas, and there's more people wantin' to shoot us all the time!"

"Well, that can't last forever. Some day, when the shootin's over, we're gonna need somethin' to do. What *will* we do when we don't have anybody to chase? A damned cow outfit ain't gonna keep us busy. That sounds like watchin' grass grow to me."

"Maybe you could do some real work for once in your life."

"The Lord puts us all in our place, Cole. Some of us are doers, and some of us are thinkers. Now, I have no doubt that you could out work any two men. But without me to keep everything straight, why, you'd be bankrupt in no time. I think a man oughta go with his strong suit, don't you?"

"I think you oughta take a breath."

Stone Horse appeared atop a low hill. He was plainly in a hurry, his tough little paint stumbling once from exhaustion.

"Damn, this don't look good," Harley said.

"Milo, bring up a fresh mount for Stone Horse!" Cole shouted.

Stone Horse slid his mount to a stop, quickly passing his reins to Milo, who just as quickly began transferring the tracker's saddle to the grulla mare.

"We are on Lean Wolf's trail, Captain. I have found two of

his victims one half mile from here. The young girl is still alive."
Looking the Captain in the eye, he added, "I think Milo should stay
with the horses."

Milo protested. "Do I have to, Captain?"

"Yeah, you have to, son. We'll take the mules with us.
When you hear two quick shots, come on. Let's go, boys."

Stone Horse swung into the saddle, the grulla just a few
strides behind the others, leaving Milo all alone. He relieved
himself as he watched the men ride away. The big, empty country
made him feel lonely and afraid. He'd come to like the Rangers'
company. They were the kind of men he wanted to be. He'd
ridden out of Austin without much thought, but now the danger
was clear. He only hoped he had what it took, when the time came
to be brave.

#

Stone Horse left the unconscious girl wrapped in a blanket
he found in the wagon. He placed her so she could not see her
grandfather, but knew better than to disturb the scene. Awakened
at the sound of the galloping horses, the poor thing went into
hysterics. Trying to run, she lost her blanket and fell naked in the
mud. She tried to scream, but had no voice. She had already
screamed it away.

Moody dismounted, his horse slowing to a trot. He
retrieved the blanket, and quickly subdued the terrified girl. He
wrapped her up and held her tight, as she fought hard to get away.

"You all right now, missy," he said. "Everything's all
right. We Texas Rangers. You all right, now. Ain't nobody
gonna hurt you."

Harley stared at the corpse in disbelief.

"By God, I've never seen a melted man before."

"No," Cole said, "nor do I want to again." He didn't think
he could ever see anything worse than he'd seen on the llano. And
half of that was the work of coyotes and buzzards. But here it was
before him. "Dammit, Harley, we've gotta stop this maniac.

The Day Hunters

Horse, go find us some tracks. Eli, let's get to work."

Harley had to vomit twice before he could free the corpse from its bonds. The man's face was completely gone, the torso burned to the bone—a sight too gruesome to look at. His hands and feet were the only way to identify his gender. Cole and Eli worked steadily on the grave, neither man having anything to say.

Harley removed the tarp from one of the pack mules, and wrapped the body in it. He then fired two shots to summon Milo. He didn't want the boy to see such a gory sight.

The shots frightened the girl, but at last she stopped fighting. She began to sob deep racking sobs. Moody gently rocked her in his arms. He spoke to the girl about all sorts of things, the weather, the horses, a doll his little sister had as a child. He sang to her and held her close, quoting some Bible verses he'd been taught as a boy. Eventually, she began to quiet down.

Stone Horse rejoined them shortly. He'd followed the renegades' tracks for two miles, then returned to make his report.

"They have not changed direction, Captain. They are still going north."

"Still four of 'em?"

"Yes."

"I wonder why they left the donkey harnessed up like this," Eli asked. "Looks like Lean Wolf would've killed him out of meanness."

"He likely thought it meaner to let him starve," Harley said.

The poor beast had no doubt been terrified by the fire, but with the load of wood the wagon carried, he had not been able to pull it out of the mud. It was a wonder he hadn't hurt himself trying to get free, but seemed none the worse for the experience.

Milo arrived with the horses, just as Harley began unloading the wood to free the wagon. The strain on the boy's face was evident.

"Give me a hand here, will you, son?" Harley said.

"Yes, sir." Milo tied the horses and went to work. He never once looked at the girl. Harley noticed pieces of the youngster's bandana, stuck into his ears. A trick he no doubt

The Day Hunters

learned from Eddie.

"You can take them rags outta your ears," he said. "I think she's all screamed out."

With the wood unloaded, Harley whipped up the donkey and freed the wagon easily. The donkey calmly dropped his head to graze, as if nothing at all had happened.

Cole and Eli lowered the body into the narrow grave, and began to fill it in. But before they could make much headway, Moody came forward carrying the girl.

"She gave up," he said. "Might as well put her in there, too."

"Sorry, Moody. She say anything?" Harley asked.

"Yessuh. Her last breath . . . she say her name is Lizzie."

Harley looked beneath the blanket, and saw a pretty girl's face, frozen in fear.

"Murderin' bastards," he said.

"I ain't ever had somebody die in my arms, Mistuh Harley. 'Specially not a little girl. What kind o' men would do such a thing?"

"The crazy kind, I expect. Turn the donkey loose, Milo. Let's get this done."

"We'll take care o' this, Moody. You go on," Cole said.

"No, suh. I'd rather help, if it's all the same to you."

The job was quickly finished, though Moody worked with a heavy heart. The troop gathered around the grave, wringing their hats in their hands. Stone Horse offered a prayer to the winds, then mounted his horse and left.

"Lord," Harley said, "we didn't know these folks. But we know they didn't deserve what they got. And we ask . . . that you give us opportunity . . . to send you the villains that done it. Amen."

While the men tightened their cinches and prepared to travel, Harley took pencil and paper from his saddlebag. He spent the next few seconds meticulously writing something, then walked over and showed it to Moody.

"This word says Lizzie," Harley told him. "Now, you go

120

The Day Hunters

gather some stones, and put 'em on the grave just like this, in case somebody comes lookin' for her. You take your time. Catch up when you're done."

"Yessuh. Thank you, suh."

"Let's go, boys. We ain't gonna catch him sittin' here," Cole said.

As the troop rode away at the gallop, Harley glanced back to see Moody kneeling at the graveside, studying the paper, carefully placing the stones.

#

The Rangers traveled into the evening, Milo horrified by the death of the girl. He hadn't seen the corpse of the old man, and was glad he'd missed it from what he'd heard. But he did get a glimpse of the girl when Harley looked under the blanket. The only dead bodies Milo had ever seen, with the exception of Eddie Roberts, had all been in coffins, a quiet, peaceful expression on their faces. Even Eddie appeared rather content in his astonishment. But Lizzie didn't look content. She looked tortured.

She couldn't have been more than fifteen or sixteen. About the same age as some of his cousins back home. The thought that something like this could happen to them was more than Milo could bear. He began to tremble, trying to hide his face. Eli took notice and spoke to the youngster.

"When you sign on to be a Ranger, you're never ready for what you'll see. None of us feel any different than you do. We've just seen it all before. You never get used to it. You just learn to deal with it."

"I don't know how. How can you deal with somethin' like that?"

"They'll pay for it, Milo. That's how you deal with it. Knowin' that someday they'll pay for it."

After three hours in the saddle, Harley spotted Stone Horse just before sundown, sitting on a fallen tree, trying to count the legs on a centipede.

The Day Hunters

"Horse, what in the hell are you doin'?" he said.

"I caught this bug inside the tree. I want to see how many legs it has."

"Why, everybody knows a centipede has a hundred legs."

"How do you know? Have you ever counted them?"

"No, but . . . forget it. You found anything?"

"Ahead, in a small pocket, there are three soldiers with a herd of mules. All the mules are branded U.S. They look like they have been traveling hard. They do not have a fire."

"Sounds like a herd o' *stolen* mules to me," Cole said. "What about Lean Wolf? You seen anything o' him?"

"No. Lean Wolf's track is lost in the pocket. The mules have wiped it out. Tomorrow, I will try to find it on the other side."

Cole's heart sank when Stone Horse gave him the news. The same news he'd been hearing for years. Lean Wolf was gone without a trace.

"Let's have a look, Harley. We'll camp here, boys. But no fire 'til we get back," Cole said. "Keep an eye out for Moody. He can't be far behind."

The three men crawled on their bellies to the rim of the pocket, where Cole surveyed the scene with his spyglass. "They're U.S., all right," he said, passing the glass to Stone Horse.

The long glass was a fascination for Stone Horse. He hoped someday to have one of his own, but the Captain did not need it to see the mules were U.S.. Hadn't he already told him that?

"The army wouldn't send these mules through the territory," Harley said.

"They're lookin' to trade with the Comancheros. Maybe Lean Wolf himself. I guess they ain't seen him yet, since they're all still alive."

"Why ain't they seen him?" Cole asked. "Looks to me like they'd run right into him. Dammit, he must've broke off somewhere."

The Day Hunters

"Well, in the mornin', why don't we take our U.S. stock on down there and join 'em? Maybe they know somethin'."

"Yeah, maybe."

#

The stranger crossed the Cimarron at the break of dawn, the river now barely deep enough to swim. But from the looks of the weather to the west, it could be running full again very soon. A bloated paint mare had washed up in the bend. By the smell, she was about ready to burst. Once across, he found seven dead mules, each expertly butchered. The monotonous drone of the flies made the only sound on the empty prairie.

He rode a big circle, east to west, studying the tracks. They were as clear to him as newspaper print. The Indians had ridden down on them from the west. The deserters shot the mules and ran, then a rider was sent to get the women to do the butchering. Ten or twelve horseback, about the same number of women.

"Good move, Teague. You ain't as dumb as they said you were. What do you think, Pal?"

The fine black morgan did not respond.

"I wish you'd say somethin' once in a while. I've got ears, y'know."

The black continued to stomp at the flies, prancing in anticipation of leaving them behind.

"We'll catch up today. They can't be too far ahead."

His name was James Butler Hickok, known on the frontier as "Wild Bill." Since the war, where he served as a civilian spy for the Union, he'd done many jobs throughout Kansas—deputy marshal, dispatch rider, guide, and army scout. At present, he was charged with apprehending three deserters from Fort Riley, along with the forty mules they had stolen. And now, he was sure, at least one of them was a murderer.

Hickok buried the young couple behind the cabin, and rode into the nearest settlement to tell the law when and how he found the bodies, and how he could be reached if need be. He well knew

123

The Day Hunters

how brutal life on the frontier could be, but nobody deserved to die like that, except maybe the man who did the killing. Wheeling his horse, he rode south at the gallop, the high spirited morgan running a hole in the wind.

The Day Hunters

Chapter 12

There was the definite smell of rain in the air, as Captain Ellsworth kicked out the morning fire. The men busied themselves saddling, and packing, checking their guns—things they had long since learned to do without thinking. Stone Horse had been gone for hours. Moody saw him off well before sunrise, with no more than a cup of last night's coffee to go on.

The chancy weather made the horses nervous, particularly the high strung thoroughbreds. They stomped, and kicked, and wrung their tails, in expectation of the day's activities. Moody and Eli spent the previous evening teaching Milo to braid rope hobbles, for all the additional stock they were now traveling with. Clearly the boy had done a good job, as the horses were certainly putting his work to the test.

Cole could see that Milo was as nervous as the horses. The boy had checked the load in his pistol no less than four times in the last thirty minutes. Twice since awakening, he'd gone off to empty his bowels. Cole sensed the tension in the other men as well. He knew it wasn't fear, but the silence told him of their anxiety. It was common among most all men before a confrontation. All men except Harley Macon, of course. Harley had already seen too much violence to be anxious, even under fire.

"Well, Cole, you ready?" he asked.

"I reckon. You boys swing around to the west and spread out. Keep Milo between you."

Milo felt a wave of relief upon hearing the Captain's order.

"Stay out of sight, away from the rim," Cole continued.

"But keep your seat in case they try to run. Don't show yourselves unless we signal you. Remember, we want information, not bloodshed. Any questions?"

Moody and Eli shook their heads. They'd asked everything they needed to ask years ago. But Milo's nerves got the best of him. He blurted out his question.

"What should I do if the shootin' starts?"

The Day Hunters

"Stay outta the way," Cole said. "Don't draw your weapon until you need it. You wouldn't be the first man to drop his gun in battle. Let's go, boys. Good luck."

Harley and Cole rode away leading the horses, with no more pretense than if they were bound for a church social. Moody and Eli spoke between themselves, then mounted and headed for the rim. Milo still didn't think he was ready. But he checked the thong on his holster again, and rode off to catch the two Rangers.

#

After spending a long, cool night with no fire, the mood in the deserters camp was foul, each man sullen and withdrawn. They had eaten what little food was left throughout the night. Now they waited for daylight to build a fire, and boil the last of the coffee.

"I thought we were tryin' to find Lean Wolf, not hide from him," Daniels said. "How long do you want these mules to slow us down? This is a hell of a plan you've got, Teague. It's a good thing Lee surrendered when he did, if this is the best you Rebs can do."

"You son of a bitch!" Teague rolled from his blanket, pistol in hand.

"Wait a minute," Bullock said. "Look there."

At a distance of only a hundred yards sat two well-armed, well-mounted, tough looking riders. One led a string of fine thoroughbreds, no doubt army stock. The other rested the butt of a Henry repeater on his thigh. Teague didn't think they had come to exchange formalities.

"Who are you?" he shouted. "What do you want?"

"I'm Dick Turpin," Harley echoed, secure in the belief that the average mule rustler knew nothing of British folklore, "and this here is Mr. Boone."

Cole seethed at the reference to the boy. "Damn you, Harley. Can't you be serious? We may have to kill these men."

126

The Day Hunters

"Well, even if we do, they won't care who done it.

"Looks like we may be huntin' the same man," Harley shouted. "Can we come a little closer?"

Teague didn't know what to do. He knew his men had lost confidence in him, but he didn't want to appear weak. "Fifty yards and no more!" he said. Turning to his men he told them to spread out, flank the riders, and be ready to shoot. "Let's see if we can all get out of this alive."

The riders approached with caution, but seemed unruffled by the gravity of the situation. Apparently, they had been in such predicaments before.

"We heard a man could do some tradin' up this way," Harley said. "Looks like you boys heard the same thing."

"Maybe so," Teague said.

The rider holding the rifle did all the talking, but somehow the quiet one worried Teague even more. Something about the look on his face reminded him of men he had known in the war. Men so hardened by all the killings, that a few more wouldn't make any difference.

Cole rode close beside his companion, concealing the pistol he held in the same hand as the lead rope. He could simply drop the rope and open fire, if it all came down to that. He thought the sergeant looked pretty salty, but the other two were plainly scared. And none had an eye for distance, as the Rangers had closed the gap to thirty yards before the soldiers even noticed.

"That's far enough," Teague shouted.

"We've got some grub and coffee, if you boys can risk a fire," Harley said.

That struck a chord with the cold, hungry men. They hadn't eaten or felt the comfort of a warm fire, in quite a while.

"Let 'em come in," Bullock pleaded. "Hell, Sarge, I'm starvin'."

Teague wanted the men to keep riding. He'd been in enough trouble to know what it felt like, but his empty stomach

The Day Hunters

finally won out.

"Scabbard that rifle and come in, nice n' easy!"

Harley complied and the two rode in slowly, each deciding who they'd take down first, if the soldiers chose to start the music.

The hair on the back of Sergeant Teague's neck told him these were very dangerous men, not the least bit concerned with the soldiers' one man advantage. Somehow he doubted it would matter if they were five against these two. If there were only two.

"Why don't you have them boys come on in?" Harley said. "We don't bite."

Just ten feet from where the sergeant stood, Harley turned his horse to the left, and Cole turned his to the right, forming a wedge. Each man dismounted to the inside, protecting themselves from a flank shot, while Cole covered the dumbstruck sergeant with his pistol. It had all been just that easy.

"Are we gonna talk or open the ball?" Harley asked.

"Why, let's talk," Teague replied. The business end of a .44 Colt, always put him in a more sociable mood.

"Good. We're huntin' a man called Lean Wolf. We heard he's a wide open market for horseflesh. We'd like to show him a sample of what we can deliver. Looks like maybe we're in the same business. You heard of him?"

"Yeah, I've heard of him. We're lookin' for him, too."

"Then that's settled," Harley said. "Now, let's get that fire goin'."

Teague called for his men to come in to the fire. Hungry as he was, Bullock couldn't get there fast enough, but Daniels chose to hold his position at the flank. He was suspicious of the riders, thinking maybe they had come from the north. It was unlikely, but anything was possible. Daniels was sure Teague suspected something, but mostly he didn't like the way the quiet rider kept watching him.

Daniels didn't know why he'd killed the young couple. He

The Day Hunters

didn't have to kill them. He just lost his head in the passion of the moment. As he watched them through the window, making love on the floor in front of the fire, he became so excited he couldn't stop himself. He came through the door threatening them, brandishing his pistol. He held the young man at gun point, while he took what he wanted from the girl. At some point, when he was lost in it all, the young man made his play. The fireplace poker came down hard on the back of Daniels' neck, stunning him as the young man ran to the kitchen.

Daniels shot him in the back, then clubbed the girl with his pistol as she fought to escape his embrace. He clubbed her until she stopped moving, then finished what he started, just as the young man attacked from the kitchen with a knife. Daniels fired again, this time a fatal shot to the chest. The young man fell on top of the dead girl, driving the knife into her thigh. In a fit of anger, Daniels pulled the knife from the girl's leg, plunging it repeatedly into the young man's back. He then laid the bodies in the position he'd first seen them, and began to search the cabin. Gathering what food could be found, he walked out and never looked back. He had stolen the horses on a whim.

Now there were two hard strangers in the camp, and he thought he might have seen a little dust to the northeast. Maybe there were more than just these two men. Maybe it was the army, or Indians, or the law.

Daniels didn't like the way it was shaping up. He was glad his horse was close to hand. Yes, now he was sure he saw dust, much closer, moving fast. Daniels stepped toward his horse, the animal sensing the tension. Then he saw the rider. "Oh God," he whispered. "It's Hickok."

Daniels swung into the saddle and charged to the west, crouching over his horse's neck. He fired his pistol to scatter the mules as he made his way to the rim. The deserters panicked and reached for their guns.

"Texas Rangers!" Cole shouted, but it was already too late.

Cole's bullet struck Bullock a perfect kill shot, straight through the heart at close range. The trooper had pulled his

The Day Hunters

weapon with his trigger finger still looped in his coffee cup.

Teague whirled to face Harley Macon. For a split second he looked into his eyes. What he read there was plain. It was the bullet or the rope. He raised his pistol, and Harley put a bullet through his forehead. As Daniels cleared the top of the rim, two shots echoed, one of them a rifle, then all fell quiet. Sergeant Teague lay on the ground and shook. He tried to embrace something invisible in the air, but died before Harley had to shoot him again.

"What the hell set that off?" Cole asked.

"Damned if I know. We'd better go check on the boys."

Before they took a step, they heard Moody call from atop the rim.

"It's Milo, Cap'n. He been shot."

"Dammit!" The men mounted quickly and rushed to the scene. They found Milo with a big hole in his left side, the shooter lying close by. Cole went to check the body of the dead soldier, while Harley hurried to the wounded boy's side.

"Milo, what happened?"

"I heard the mules runnin', then the shootin'," Milo said.

"I'd just drawn my pistol when he came over the rim and shot me. I don't know who shot him. I didn't. Damn, that bullet's hot!"

"It ain't the bullet that's hot. The bullet went clean through," Moody said. "It don't look too bad, but he ain't gonna ride for a while."

"Didn't Captain Ellsworth tell you to stay out of the way?" Harley chuckled, trying to calm the boy's fears. Moody worked steadily, cleaning the wound, a process Milo seemed to be taking in stride.

"The private took one rifle slug through the spine," Cole said. "He didn't feel it. How's Milo?"

"He all right," Moody pronounced. "Young and tough."

"Now, this is just fine," Harley said. "We've got a bunch o' dead men and a shot up kid, and we don't know any more than we did when we got here."

The Day Hunters

"Who shot this soldier? That's what I'd like to know," Cole said. "Where's Eli?"

"He on the other side o' the rim," Moody said. "I think the same direction that soldier came from. Maybe Mistuh Eli got him."

Harley surveyed the distance. "It'd be a hell of a shot, if he did. Ain't many could make a shot like that. And hit a movin' target? I doubt it was Eli."

"Then who was it?" Cole asked. "We'd better ride around and have a look. Moody, keep your gun cocked."

Harley and Cole prepared to mount, then they heard the rider approaching.

"Hello! I'm comin' in and I've got your man. Don't shoot me."

Harley thought he recognized the voice that came over the ridge. In fact, he was sure he recognized it.

Hickok rode in with Eli Plummer leading the way on foot. Hickok led the Ranger's horse. Eli held his hands on the top of his head, his face a picture of embarrassment. Cole fumed at the sight of one of his men held captive, but Harley, as usual, began to laugh.

"What's so damn funny?" Cole asked.

"That black look familiar to you?"

"Why, yes. That's your morgan gelding. I remember that snip on his nose. Is that Hickok?"

"Yeah, that's him. Howdy, Bill."

Hickok looked puzzled, then broke into a smile.

"Well, I declare. Harley Macon. About a year ago in Galveston."

"Right, at Mamie's. As I recall, yours was the ugly one."

"She weren't much to look at, I'll give you that. But she could do things that are hard to describe." Hickok dismounted the weary morgan, shaking his legs to get the blood moving.

"Bill, that's a fine horse you're ridin'," Harley said.

"Yes, sir. He tells me everyday how much he misses you."

Their meeting in Galveston at first had been tense, each

131

The Day Hunters

knowing the other by reputation—Macon, the Confederate hero, Hickok, the Union spy. They spent the evening at the poker table, the clinking chips and flowing whiskey gradually putting things in a softer light. The following morning, to Harley's chagrin, he was informed by Mamie herself that he'd lost the morgan to Hickok in the card game. Hickok held a king high straight, Harley nines and fours. There were no hard feelings between the men, but Harley surely liked that morgan.

Offering Hickok his hand, Harley made the introductions.

"Cole Ellsworth, Bill Hickok."

The two shook hands, but under duress. It was plain that Cole didn't like the man. But then, Cole didn't take to most folks right off, and especially not to men so well dressed.

"You can put your hands down, Eli. He ain't gonna shoot you now," Harley said.

"Bill, this is Eli Plummer. When he finds himself in situations where he thinks he might be killed, Eli feels it best to take his time."

"What're you doin' up this way, Harley? Not enough to do in Texas?"

"Lean Wolf. He massacred five of our men and we aim to hang him. You heard anything?"

"No. I've been trackin' these deserters from Fort Riley. And I'm lookin' for a jacket with a missing button." Stepping over to check Daniels' body, Hickok saw where the button had been torn off the sleeve. He had found it clenched in the dead girl's hand.

"I guess that's your bullet in him?"

"Yeah. At least one of 'em murdered a young couple back in Kansas. I found 'em a while back. You get the others?"

"Yeah, we got 'em."

"Get a fire goin'. We'll camp here," Cole said. "Get Milo set up to stay a few days. Moody, you stay with him. Where you takin' these mules, Mr. Hickok?"

"I don't know as I can take 'em anywhere by myself," he said, annoyed by the Captain's demanding tone. "I'd hoped these

men would come in peaceable, though I doubted it.   Camp
Chicoine, I guess. It's the closest. I suppose I'd better take their
horses, too."

Hickok could never handle all the stock alone.   Driving
them would have been a big job, even for the three men that drove
them here. But Cole didn't want to send Eli. Milo's wound had
cost him two men already, as Moody would have to stay and care
for the boy. He didn't think he could spare another. But what
really worried him was splitting the troop yet again. Eli was a
good man, and careful, but he would be making the return trip
alone through new country. Indian country. Moody could be
trusted in any situation, but now he had a wounded kid to worry
about. And a lot of damned horses. The kind of men that traveled
this country would cut Moody and Milo into pieces for a string of
horses like that. Cole knew he'd be forever haunted by the mistake
he'd made on the llano. He didn't want to make another one.

"I think I'll take a walk," Harley said.

"Yeah," Cole said. "I think I'll join you."

Harley lowered his voice as the two walked away.

"Well, here we are again, Cole. What now?"

"I hate to send Eli with Hickok. I'd rather leave him with
Moody, if we have to do without him ourselves."

"Yeah . But we can't leave a man in a bind like that. It
ain't right."

"Hell, he said himself he doubted them soldiers would
come in alive. And why would they? So they could drive the
mules back to Fort Riley, and get hung for desertion? That's takin'
a lot for granted, if you ask me. The army should've sent a man
with him."

"But they didn't. Look, we can travel faster, just the two of
us and Stone Horse. We ain't got many choices, Cole. Lean
Wolf's gainin' ground every day."

Cole nodded in agreement, but said nothing. He just turned
and walked back to the men.

The Day Hunters

"Eli, you go with Mr. Hickok. Keep your nose open," Cole said. "There's a lotta injuns around. When you're done, hightail it back here and wait for us. When Stone Horse gets back, me n' Harley'll take two of the remounts and go after Lean Wolf. We'll leave the rest of the horses here with you, Moody. You can handle it, can't you?"

"Yessuh. I can handle it."

"Good man. Let's break out the shovels."

#

Stone Horse had to ride far to the north to find the tracks of the renegades. It had taken him nearly all day to decipher them. When he made his big circle, he found that they had split up. Two went east, and two went west. The question was, which way did Lean Wolf go? When the renegades split, the herd of mules passed between them, traveling south, wiping out the trail. Whatever direction Lean Wolf chose, it was plain he had a good lead. This news would not set well with the Captain, but Stone Horse could only report what he knew.

Earlier, he had seen a long haired white man on a fine black horse, also riding south along the trail of the mules. His buckskin jacket was adorned like some kind of chief. He thought it could be the man the whites called Hickok, but he did not know. Whether it was Hickok or not, Stone Horse thought he would like to take that handsome scalp, himself.

He maintained a rapid pace, keeping the paint horse at a lope. He wanted to find the Rangers before dark. He assumed they would be at the soldiers' camp. At least, that was the place to start looking.

On arrival, Stone Horse saw that the soldiers' camp had been moved to the western ridge. The ridge was timbered, so he could not see clearly who was there. He saw three graves to the south of the camp, and the fine black horse tied to the picket line. Who had been killed, he could only guess. And who was the rider of the black horse? He skirted the ridge from a distance, until he heard Moody call the men to supper. Judging by the sounds from the camp, everything was normal.

Stone Horse rode up to the fire unannounced, startling everyone. All but Milo laid hand to a gun. Hickok jumped to his feet, drawing two pistols, a wild, crazy look in his eyes.

"Whoa, Bill! That's our scout," Harley said. "I swear, sometimes I think he wants to get shot. Dammit, Horse, can't you give a man a little warning before you ride in here? This is the legendary 'Wild Bill' we're entertainin'."

"You go to Hell," Hickok said.

Cole didn't care about entertaining the great "Wild Bill". He wanted to know about Lean Wolf. "Where is he, Horse?"

"Lean Wolf and his men have split up, Captain. Two have gone east, and two west. I think Lean Wolf has gone east, but I do not know."

"Why do you think he went east?" Harley asked.

"The idiot man is heavy. His horse leaves a deep track. That horse has gone west. Fast Elk usually travels with the idiot man."

"That ain't much to go on," Cole said.

Stone Horse shrugged as Eli poured him a cup of coffee.

"Is Milo dying?" he asked.

"No, just sleepin'," Eli said. "Moody says he'll be all right."

"What happened to the soldiers?"

"They got what they deserved," Harley said, to no one in particular. "Bill says they stole these mules and murdered a young couple in Kansas. Not to mention they were deserters, the damned rabble. If I'd known that, I'd've hung 'em."

"Ain't you forgettin'? The war's over," Hickok said.

"Not out here. There's plenty o' fightin' to do out here on the plains, and they're the ones gettin' paid to do it. You sign on, you do the job. You know that, Bill."

"Yeah, I know. I signed on to get 'em. Sorry you boys got caught in the middle, but I appreciate the help."

The Day Hunters

"The worst is, we didn't learn anything about Lean Wolf," Cole said. "How far to find his track, Horse?"

"Ten miles, and a bit."

"Well, it'll be dark before we get started. We'll leave in the mornin'. Moody, you better get somethin' to eat. I'll keep an eye on the boy. Eli, you take the first watch. I'll relieve you in three hours."

"Yessir, Cap'n."

"Bill," Harley said, "you got any cards?"

The Day Hunters

Chapter 13

Blood Hawk, at some point in the ride, realized he was not as brave as he thought he was. He had wantonly terrorized captives, and enjoyed watching them squirm. Nearly all of them promised anything they had for their freedom. Now, he realized their fear. His thoughts raced with plans of escape, combat, and suicide. Lean Wolf had been true to his word, in allowing him to keep his weapons. But Blood Hawk could not summon the courage to reach for one. Maybe, if he waited, a chance to escape would present itself. If the chance didn't come soon, it would be too late.

He often thought of riding off, and taking the bullet in the back. But what if Lean Wolf only wounded him, or shot his horse? His captor would not stand for any delay. He would torture him, or murder him brutally, then and there. Death always sounded better when it happened to someone else. But if it had to be, he would rather it happen quick.

The renegades reached the timberline in the early evening. Blood Hawk was surprised, but thankful they were stopping, as Lean Wolf was not known to stop often. Blood Hawk's bladder felt as big as his head. He knew if he did not dismount soon, he would wet his saddle again.

"Keep your seat," Lean Wolf said. Pistol in hand, he stood close to his captive's horse, and relieved himself, long and slow. The sight of Lean Wolf spattering the ground tortured Blood Hawk until he could stand no more.

"Why don't you just shoot me, you bastard?"

"Shut up, and get off that horse."

Blood Hawk stepped down, desperately trying to find the courage to attack. But the coward in him was too strong.

Pressing his pistol into Blood Hawk's back, Lean Wolf marched him forward under a large red oak.

"This is the tree I will hang you from, traitor."

Lean Wolf struck him hard behind the ear with his pistol. Blood Hawk went to his knees, unconscious from the blow.

The Day Hunters

Banging his head on the tree trunk, he fell on his face, the earth between his legs turning to mud. Lean Wolf had to laugh at the sight of Blood Hawk's breechclout darkening, like a little boy's when he wets himself. The Kiowa even had a little boy look on his face, as if his mother might be mad at him. Lean Wolf drew his knife and cut off the breechclout, exposing Blood Hawk's backside to the air.

"Now it's your turn, *boy,*" he said, cocking and un-cocking his pistol.

#

Harley caught Cole about a mile out of camp, having to lope his horse the full mile to do it. He knew what it would be from here on out, as his partner had set the pace at a long trot. "The most efficient pace. Easier on the horse," Cole was known to say, and Cole Ellsworth knew horses. Harley couldn't say the same for the man's social graces.

"I swear, for a man who disapproves of rude behavior, I expect you could write a book on the subject," Harley said.

"What?"

"Why, hell, Cole, you could've at least said goodbye. Bill's a fine companion, and a good poker player. And what about the boys?"

"I gave them their orders last night. I saw no reason to hinder pursuit just to say goodbye to 'Wild Bill'. We need to find those tracks before the weather catches us. It's bound to start rainin' soon."

"Well, you still could've said goodbye."

"Goodbye!" Cole spurred his horse into a lope, leaving Harley to catch up again.

"Damn you, Cole. They were my men, too!"

Cole pulled his horse to a stop, and turned on his friend.

"Bass was the only *man* among 'em, Harley. Dammit, the rest were just boys."

"They were Texas Rangers! They hired on to Ranger, and

got killed for their trouble. We were just boys when we started. It could've been us just as easy."

"Or Milo," Cole railed. "Why the hell did he come out here? You told him to stay in Austin. He disobeyed orders, and now he's shot."

"But he ain't dead. Moody'll pull him through. Don't forget that we'd all be dead if he hadn'ta come. Eli's with Hickok. He couldn't be much safer. It ain't about the boys now, Cole, nor all the mistakes we've made. It's about Lean Wolf. You, and me, and Lean Wolf."

Cole knew Harley was right. No need to keep beating a dead horse. What's done was done. He could do nothing to change it.

"We can't worry about the boys now," Harley said.

"We've gotta think about the task at hand. Lean Wolf's bound to know we're on his trail. Why else would they split up?"

"I just hope we're trailin' the right man. What if Lean Wolf went west, and we're trailin' the flunkies?"

"We'll catch 'em, and hang 'em, then head west. Sooner or later, he'll make a mistake, and we'll be there. We'll get him, Cole. As God is my witness, we'll get him."

Cole smooched his horse back into the trot. As the drizzle fell, the two hard riders headed northeast at the most efficient pace.

#

The brewing storm promised to be a big one, as was evident by the naked man Stone Horse found blowing in the rising wind. The man had been emasculated. He had eleven arrows shot into him from every angle. The bear trap around the dead man's neck was secured to the limb by a heavy chain. The neck was nearly cut in two, the head hanging down the back of the corpse. The dead man danced in the gusty wind, banging into the tree trunk, breaking some of the arrows off, driving others clear through. Stone Horse allowed that Lean Wolf always came up with the most interesting ways to kill a man.

The thunderclouds threatened a heavy downpour, but the drizzle was not yet strong enough to wipe out any tracks. The signs told Stone Horse that Lean Wolf had ridden northeast with the dead man's horse in tow, making no attempt to conceal his trail nor to pick up his pace. The tracks showed an easy trot, the outlaw having left just hours ago. But the corpse had been hanging since the night before. Stone Horse could plainly see where Lean Wolf slept throughout the night, as the body of his victim swayed in the breeze just a few feet away. He had probably fallen asleep to the sound of the creaking limb.

#

Stone Horse left a trail a child could follow. Cole took this as a lack of confidence in the Rangers' tracking skills, but well understood its purpose. What good would it do if Stone Horse found Lean Wolf, but the Rangers couldn't find *him*?

They followed the tracker's lead due east across a tall grass prairie. At some distance, they could see the timberline looming even darker than the storm clouds. The men had donned their rain slickers, but soon were so hot they took them off, rather choosing the cool drizzle. It looked as though Lean Wolf was heading straight for the timber. Now the tracking would be even harder.

"Aww, hell," Cole said. "Look there."

The Rangers saw Stone Horse signaling them, the corpse spinning circles in the wind. They approached at an easy lope, not seeing any point in galloping to a funeral.

"By God, Cole, ol' Lean Wolf's creative, I'll give him that," Harley said.

"Do you know him, Horse?" Cole asked.

"Yes, I know him. He is Blood Hawk, the Kiowa half-breed. His mother was Comanche. I do not know why he is with Lean Wolf. Lean Wolf cut his ear off a long time ago. These are his own arrows. Lean Wolf does not carry a bow. He only likes guns."

The Day Hunters

"Well, he's done more than cut his ear off this time," Harley said. "I expect he got the trap from the woodcutter."

"I wonder how he got him up there?" Cole asked.

"Now, that's one for the engineers. How the hell do we get him down? That's a better question. I guess we oughta bury him."

"I could hold your horse while you climb up there and get him."

"I got the last one as I recall," Harley said. "I'll hold your horse."

"Maybe if I stand in my saddle, and you lift him up, I can get the chain off. Horse, hold my mount."

Cole's horse was on the verge of panic, what with a man standing on his back, and a dead body hanging just inches away. Stone Horse did his best to calm the animal, but his horsemanship was less than required, only adding to the problem.

Harley took hold and lifted the body by the legs. Cole reached for the chain just as the bullet struck Blood Hawk full in the chest. The concussion knocked Cole off his horse and sent him rolling. Drawing his pistol, he scrambled for cover.

Harley dropped the body and lay flat in the mud. When he did, the force tore Blood Hawk's head clean off. The corpse hit the ground hard, rolling under Cole's mount. The frightened horse bolted, with Stone Horse holding on tight to the reins, frantically trying to get the animal to safety. Blood Hawk's head rolled across the ground, coming to rest upright on the severed neck, as if his body had been buried standing up.

"Well, that's twice now," Harley said. "If this son of a bitch ever learns to shoot, we may join the singin' with the Cameron boys."

"By God, he's gotta be the luckiest man I've ever heard of," Cole said.

"Oh, I don't know. I'd say we're pretty damn lucky, too. We're still alive."

"Yeah, well so is he."

The Rangers hunkered low, trying to see where the shot came from, but there were no more shots—only a Comanche war

The Day Hunters

cry, and the drum of fleeting hoof beats in the rain.

#

Lean Wolf raced through the downpour, thoroughly disgusted with himself. Why hadn't he picked a better spot to hang Blood Hawk? He had not been able to get a clear shot from anywhere in the area. Exactly the kind of mistake his father would have beaten him for. "You are stupid, like the Mexicans," the old warrior would say. "If you can not act like a Comanche, I will kill you."

Try as he might, Lean Wolf did not fit with either the Comanches or the Mexicans. The Comanches hated his Mexican blood, the Mexicans hated the Comanche. He was lucky his father hadn't killed him, but he had not been so lucky killing Ellsworth and Macon. He'd set two traps for them, and both had failed. Why hadn't he just shot the horse? He'd had a much better shot at the animal. A wounded horse would at least slow them down. Now, he would have to keep running.

Lean Wolf had never known Ellsworth to leave a body unburied, which is why he hung Blood Hawk in plain view for the Rangers to find. He was sure Ellsworth would stop to bury him, and Macon would speak to his lord—a weakness in all the whites. If their God was so powerful, why didn't more whites live like he said?

Now that the Rangers were so close, he wondered if Ellsworth would stay to bury the body, or if they were already on his trail. He would not wait to find out. Whether they did or they didn't, Stone Horse was probably right behind him.

He could pick up the Osage Trail in a few miles. From there he would make better time. The rivers would flood quickly in a rain like this. If he could cross the Arkansas, he might escape. But if the Rangers found the trail, they could make better time too. He hoped they would wait to bury Blood Hawk, and give him the head start he needed. If he had to fight, he would rather fight

The Day Hunters

Stone Horse. Lean Wolf savagely whipped his horse, and ran for the Arkansas River.

#

"By God, there's a lotta creeks n' rivers in this country. We'd better catch up soon," Harley yelled, the wind and rain so loud he could hardly hear himself think.

"He can't be far ahead," Cole shouted. "But now I fear we'll lose him in this damn weather. If we ain't careful, we'll lose our tracker."

Even the ancient oaks were straining against the powerful wind. The rain fell in sheets, making it hard for the proud thoroughbreds to maintain their rapid pace. Cole knew their horses wouldn't last long in weather like this. The wind would soon exhaust them. He glanced across his horse's rump to see his own tracks disappearing, almost as fast as he made them. How the hell would they ever find Lean Wolf's tracks?

"It don't look good, does it?" Harley shouted.

"No, it don't. Maybe it'll rain itself out soon. Surely it can't keep this up very long."

"Like hell. Forty days and forty nights holds the record."

The horses began to fight the bit in a effort to lower their heads, trying to keep the rain out of their ears. They broke stride in the awful wind, requiring the riders to drive them even harder.

"There," Harley yelled, "a notch in that tree." Stone Horse had barked the tree to mark a path for the Rangers. The white of the trunk showed clearly in the darkened timber. "Well, at least we ain't lost."

Cole's horse snorted and jumped to the side. The sudden leap left him fighting to keep his seat. There beside the trail lay their tracker's paint, with a large, bloody hole in his chest.

"Captain! Over here, Captain!" Stone Horse shouted and waved his arms, to get the attention of the Rangers. He crouched under a small rock shelf, trying to keep from getting any wetter, though Harley didn't see how that was possible.

The Day Hunters

"Damn, Horse, I've taken baths, and didn't get as wet as you. Are we close?"

"Close enough for Lean Wolf to shoot my horse. I have marked a path for you. In one half mile you will reach the Osage Trail. Lean Wolf is on the trail one mile ahead of you. He is running to the Arkansas River. I cannot keep up in this weather on foot. You will have to go on without me."

Cole had no doubt what Stone Horse meant. If Lean Wolf reached the river, he might get across, leaving them stranded on the wrong side again.

"Thank you, Horse. You take care," Cole said, offering his hand. "Wait for us here. We'll be back to get you as soon as we can." Reluctant to leave a good man with no mount, the Rangers turned and rode out of sight.

Stone Horse wished he had a warm fire, but there was not a dry stick to be found. He thought he would take a long, well deserved nap under the shelter of the rock ledge. Though the ledge didn't offer him much protection, he was glad to have it. He knew that, miles away, the rain beat down unmercifully on the only body Captain Ellsworth had ever left unburied.

#

Lean Wolf didn't think the crossing could be much farther, but it was becoming harder to maintain his course, even on the marked trail. He had already missed the trail twice. He picked it up again purely by luck, but he had lost precious time. To make things worse, the rain had turned to sleet. The horses were more and more difficult to control. Blood Hawk's horse did not want to follow. Lean Wolf thought of turning him loose, but it was always good to have a fresh horse when Ellsworth and Macon were behind you.

He didn't know where the Rangers were, but they were close. He could feel it. He thought of stopping to switch horses, but didn't want to take the chance. What if he lost control of the

144

The Day Hunters

animals once he dismounted? What if he lost them both? They would run wild in this storm. He would never catch them. The last thing he wanted was to be left afoot.

Between the cracks of thunder, Lean Wolf heard the Rangers behind him, shouting in the distance. They sounded even closer than he'd thought. Lean Wolf beat his horse harder and harder, but the horse was worn out. He had to do something fast, or he'd soon be dangling from a tree limb.

When Lean Wolf was a boy, before he and his father began to hate each other, the old warrior would often brag on his son's horsemanship. He had learned all the daring tricks that were so commonplace to a young Comanche brave. One trick was to mount a running horse from the back of another running horse. Lean Wolf was just desperate enough to try it, though conditions would make it far more dangerous. Thunder, lightning, wind, rain, sleet, and mud, and still the Rangers kept coming.

Lean Wolf positioned the heaving animals in preparation to make the jump. Now, grab the horse's mane . . . left foot in the saddle . . . push . . . swing—then he felt the horse stumble.

The rifle slug tore into the horse's ribcage, knocking him broadside into Blood Hawk's horse, both of them going to the ground. Lean Wolf was thrown out of danger, but a long way from safety. *He had to reach that horse!* He lay on the ground a few seconds more. Several bullets whizzed over his head. He then ran to the horse, mounting almost before the horse could stand, brutally whipping the animal with his reins. Another shot burned Lean Wolf across the back as he disappeared into the storm.

Cole put a well-placed bullet through the wounded horse's brain, as he passed by in full pursuit. Conditions couldn't have been much worse. The heavy mud made it nearly impossible to maintain any speed. But Lean Wolf couldn't travel any faster than the Rangers. At times they caught a glimpse of him, though he still held a commanding lead. At least a quarter mile in Cole's estimation.

"I think he's off the trail," he yelled to his partner. The sleet had once again turned to rain. The ice on the ground would hold the tracks longer than the mud. Following would be easier, but the river was close and Cole knew it.

#

"Godammit!" Lean Wolf shouted. He was completely off the trail, and on the wrong river. He viewed the rushing Cimarron from atop a high bluff, at least a mile west of the fork. The river was much higher and faster than he had anticipated. He was trapped. The Rangers were almost within rifle range, but Lean Wolf had no rifle. He lost it when his horse went down, so he did the only thing he could do. What his father would have done. He drew his pistol and charged the Rangers, with the war cry they had heard so many times.

"By God, Cole, look at this lunatic," Harley said.

Cole spurred his horse to the gallop and raced to meet his enemy. Lean Wolf crouched over his horse's neck and fired his pistol, but he was well out of range. He was only making noise.

Harley tried hard to steady his mount, to line up the shot that would end it all. But Lean Wolf whirled and fired his last round, purposely burning the hip of his own horse. The wounded animal jumped, running wild at a maddening pace. Lean Wolf kicked his feet from the stirrups. He whipped and whipped, the horse struggling for traction in the slimy mud. Then with a leap and a defiant scream, he and his horse disappeared over the bluff.

Stunned at what they'd just seen, the Rangers pulled to a stop near the edge of the bluff, staring in amazement at the flooded, racing river.

"I swear, that's gotta be forty feet," Harley said.

Searching the river, they could see no sign of Lean Wolf or his horse. Common sense told them he could never survive such a

The Day Hunters

fall, but still they waited. They didn't have to wait long.

The war cry they heard from across the river told them Lean Wolf was alive. He had escaped justice once again. His raping, murdering life would go on. But Cole wasn't willing to quit.

"We'll wait for the river to go down," he said, his threatening tone a mixture of both fury and obsession.

"Oh, hell yes, Cole! And while we're up this way, we'll take after Frank and Jesse. That damn river won't go down for days. He'll be in Canada before we can cross. No. We lost him. We'll just have to live with it."

"I ain't sure I can."

"Well, you'll have to. Maybe the Osage'll get him, or Hickok. He's a capable man."

"Yes, I expect he is."

The two sat in gloomy silence as the rain decreased to drizzle, then finally stopped altogether. The thunder rolled for what seemed like forever, almost as if mocking the Rangers.

"Hell, let's go to Mexico," Harley said. "Maybe we'll feel better after we've hung a few bandits."

"I doubt it," Cole replied.

The Day Hunters

Chapter 14

Lean Wolf lost a good horse in the river, not to mention his weapons, his shirt, and one moccasin. But he was alive. He had some broken ribs, he was sure of that much. He recognized the pain, as he'd broken them before when he was a boy. He knew he was in for a rough time. The ribs were so painful, he barely noticed the burn of the Ranger's bullet across his back. He wished he could examine the wound, but it didn't seem bad enough to worry about. He'd certainly had worse wounds than this one.

Moving gingerly, Lean Wolf searched the timber for cover. He wanted someplace dry he could lie down and rest, but could see no such place. The timber was soaked. He couldn't light a fire, even if he had the means.

Dammit, why hadn't he just shot it out with the Rangers? That would have been a better death than he was facing now. Those with broken ribs often died of pneumonia lying beside a warm fire. How long would he last, lying in the mud?

Lean Wolf knew he was on the edge of the Osage land—a dangerous place to be. The Osage didn't like strangers, especially not renegades with Lean Wolf's reputation. If they found him, they would kill him. If they learned his identity, he might be tortured to death. Fear of capture gripped Lean Wolf's heart, even more than the fear of death. He needed a place to hide, but since there was no such place in sight, he would walk until he found one. That could prove to be a long walk.

He headed west between the Cimarron and Arkansas rivers, hoping to find something to help him survive. It was a long way back to the rendezvous. He knew there would be little in between. Maybe if he was lucky, he would come across a traveler, or better yet, a hunter. But he had to be careful if he did see someone. He was in no condition for a fight. A horse is what he needed most. A Comanche without a horse was not a Comanche at all, though he knew if he had one, it would be a long, painful ride.

Lean Wolf trudged on through the timber, sinking to his

148

ankles in the cool, sticky mud. The sky grew dark and threatening. It was just starting to rain again. Within minutes, he found himself in another terrible storm.

A frightful wind blew through the timber, breaking large limbs off the trees. The rain poured like a waterfall. Lean Wolf lay flat on the ground, his face in the mud. Tree limbs popped and snapped all around him. Thunder, like cannon fire, echoed across the sky. Lightning struck a tree close by, with a crack so loud it made his ears ring. Then, as quickly as it started, it was over.

Lean Wolf struggled to his knees and witnessed the damage of the storm. He thought of the wonderful fire he could build, with so many broken limbs. But there was no need to spend time on that. If he didn't find shelter soon, he was sure he would die. But at least he would die a free man, not at the end of Ellsworth's rope.

He thought he had covered about two miles, when he saw the giant old elm tree with the hollow trunk. The tree would provide a little shelter, though he would not be able to stretch out. Lean Wolf crawled inside on his hands and knees, wincing at the pain in his ribs. He couldn't lie down, but it didn't matter. He could sit up and most of him would be inside. The old tree wasn't much, but it was something. And there were plenty of bugs inside. Lean Wolf had eaten worse. But first he needed to sleep. He leaned back on the trunk and closed his eyes, trying to get comfortable with his feet sticking out in the rain.

Zendejaz and his killers plodded through the heavy mud, hoping for the rain to stop. They were just a few miles from Lean Wolf's rendezvous, but five days on the trail, much of it soaked to the skin, had put the men in a harsh mood. Had they been just miles from the stronghold, the mood would have been much different. There were women and whiskey at the stronghold. There would be gambling, big fires, music, and good food. At the stronghold, they would have all a man could want on a rainy day.

The Day Hunters

But the rendezvous would be different. It would be a mud hole in this weather. The few tattered lodges would not keep out the rain. There was probably not a dry spot to lie down anywhere. If Lean Wolf was not there, they might never find him, what with all the heavy rain. But someone was there.

Three horses stood tied at the picket line. Their noses nearly touched the ground, as they tried to escape the rain.

"Who you reckon?" Ugly John asked.

"I think that is Fast Elk's horse," Delgado replied, "and Emmett's, too. I don't know the other."

The Indian standing watch saw the riders at three hundred yards. He fired his pistol to raise a warning. Two men quickly emerged from the lodges. Both came brandishing weapons.

"*Sí*. It is Fast Elk and the idiot," Zendejaz said.

Drawing his pistol, he fired two shots in the air. He heard the same come from the camp—a call to ride in. No one recognized the man standing guard, but if he knew of the rendezvous, he deserved watching.

"Spread out," Zendejaz said. "We don't know if others are in the lodges, or what they might do. Get ready. Ride in from all sides."

The outlaws drew arms and circled the camp. The three men there, stood waiting. While the others chose their ground, Zendejaz rode straight up to the men.

"Is Lean Wolf here?" he asked.

"No," Fast Elk answered. "Ellsworth came looking for us, but our ambush failed. I don't know where the Rangers, or Lean Wolf are."

The outlaws slowly drifted through the camp. There appeared to be no one else around.

"Who is this man?" Ruiz asked, pointing to the Indian standing guard.

"We don't know," Fast Elk said. "He speaks with sign. He has no tongue. Someone cut it out."

"But what he *does* have is a white woman captive," Emmett said. "He's sellin' pokes for two rifle bullets."

The Day Hunters

"Ah, a woman," Delgado sighed. "Where is she?"

"In that lodge over yonder. We took a lotta the fight out of her."

Wheeling his horse, Delgado leveled his pistol and shot the guard twice in the chest. The man hit the ground dead, sliding from his rocky post like a lizard with no backbone.

"I think he will accept two pistol bullets instead," Delgado laughed.

"Drag him in to one of the lodges, close to the picket," Zendejaz ordered.

Emmett and Fast Elk did as they were told. The outlaws dismounted, and tied up at the picket line.

"What the hell are we doin' this for?" Emmett asked.

"I don't know," Fast Elk said. "All I know is there are four of them and only two of us. I wish now we'd took the woman and run."

"Place him on his knees with his face on the ground," Zendejaz said. When it was done, he entered the lodge and placed his fine saddle on the man's back, to keep it out of the mud.

"Now we will go see the woman," he said. "Tomorrow you will lead me to where you last saw Lean Wolf."

"Yes," Fast Elk said. "We will take you there."

The three men walked across the muddy clearing to where the outlaws were gathered around the ratty lodge, smoking cigarettes and drinking whiskey. They dearly wanted to get at the woman, but none dared go in before Zendejaz, lest they provoke his anger.

Zendejaz poked his head inside the lodge. Taking notice of the woman's poor condition, he declined to enter. He preferred a woman in a little better shape than this one.

"She looks like a rat. How long has she been here?"

"They were here when we got here," Fast Elk said. "That was two days ago."

"It's a good thing you come along when you did," Emmett said, grinning his broken tooth grin. "I was purt'near outta rifle bullets."

151

The Day Hunters

"You can have your bullets back. The Indian won't be needing them, now. Use her if you want," Zendejaz said. "But don't kill her. We will take her with us. If we put a little meat on her bones, we can sell her. Or kill her later, if she becomes too much trouble."

Zendejaz turned and walked away. He heard the woman gasp as the pack of killers entered the shabby lodge.

#

The Rangers backtracked from the river to pick up Stone Horse, and make their way to the camp where Milo and Moody were waiting. Harley's horse had come up lame, though he didn't think it was anything serious. The horse probably just put his foot wrong. Harley recommended twenty-four hours rest. When they found the large rock shelf, big enough to shelter horses and men alike, Cole ordered a stop, as they were all exhausted. The shelf made a perfect camp, with plenty of dry wood beneath the overhang, allowing the men to build a good fire and finally dry their clothes. The rain started again, shortly after they put up for the night, but now it mattered little. They were safe, warm, and soon would be dry. The rock shelf would dissipate the smoke from their fire. It was unlikely the camp would be seen.

Cole stripped off his wet clothes and hung them over his saddle, close to the fire. He put on a pot of coffee and thought of Louise, while he waited for it to boil. He was embarrassed that just the thought of her could still bring his impulse to life. He turned away hoping the men hadn't seen.

Louise was gone. He could think about her all he wanted, but he'd never see her again. Cole had known plenty of women, but Louise was the only one he'd ever really cared about. On her good days, she could make him laugh. On her bad days, he'd make her feel safe, when he was around, which wasn't often. Now he wished he'd been there more, but he was a Captain of the Texas Rangers. He had to go where the job took him. Louise respected

The Day Hunters

that. Cole knew he would miss her forever.

Harley snored loud enough to wake the dead. He didn't sleep very much, but when he did, no one else could. Stone Horse was peeved at Harley's snoring. After all, didn't he and the Captain need sleep, too?

"Just leave it alone," Cole said. "He'll only sleep a few hours, then we'll get our turn. He likely won't sleep again for two days."

"How can he keep going with so little sleep?"

"The war done it to him, though he's always been restless. Hell, somebody's been shootin' at him most of his life. How can a man relax like that?"

"How do you relax, Captain? They shoot at you, too."

Cole merely shrugged. "They won't be shootin' at us for awhile, I guess. When we get the troop gathered up, we'll be headin' back to Austin. We'll be lucky if the governor don't fire us for losin' Lean Wolf again."

"So what if he does?" Harley said. He awoke with a start, as he always did, joining whatever conversation was taking place, as if he'd been listening to every word. "We were plannin' on quittin' anyway, remember?"

"Oh, I remember, all right. I remember you tellin' the governor we'd take the border after this was all over, too."

"Well, maybe he didn't take me serious."

"Generally, I find governors to be serious people, Harley."

The rain slowed to a drizzle. Stone Horse thought maybe he could find some game sitting tight through the bad weather, so without a word he left to go hunting. Whether talking or snoring, Harley made it difficult to sleep.

"I'll tell you what I'd like," Harley said. "A big pot o' cafe coffee, and a plateful o' sugar doughnuts. Damn, that sounds good to me."

"I doubt that's what Stone Horse brings back."

"If we were at the cafe in Austin, we could get 'em. And see that good lookin' Rebecca, too."

"I wonder how Boone's makin' out."

153

The Day Hunters

"Boone's gonna be fine. I'd be more concerned with how Rebecca's makin' out. A fine lookin' gal like her hadn't oughta be alone. I expect she needs a hero, and Boone's still a little too young."

Cole scoffed. "Why don't you go be her hero then?"

"Because there ain't but one woman I'd hero for, and she lives in Tennessee."

"I ain't heard you speak of Abigail in awhile. Thought maybe you forgot about her."

"That's because you ain't ever seen her, Cole. A man never forgets a woman like Abigail. She was a hell of a good cook, too."

"We'll rest up here awhile, then go get the boys. I expect Milo's pretty nervous, by now. When we get back to Austin, maybe we'll all go get some doughnuts. I swear, that does sound good."

#

Lean Wolf hadn't seen the sun in so long, that it startled him when he woke with the light shining on his legs. He'd awakened many times throughout the night, wishing he could change positions and get comfortable. But there was no comfortable position when you had broken ribs. The burn across his back was scabbing over, cracking a little each time he moved.

Starving, Lean Wolf ate as many bugs as he could stand before crawling out of the old elm tree. He did not want to bend down to crawl back in. Once outside, he limped to the river, grimacing as he lay down to drink. The water tasted good and cold, helping to revive him for the long journey to come.

The birds of the forest apparently cared nothing for Lean Wolf's plight. They sang and rejoiced at the morning sunlight, shining through the trees. Lean Wolf wished they would just shut up.

Though he could locate no other wounds, today he hurt all over. Hitting the water from such a height had been quite a concussion. He believed he landed on his saddle horn, accounting for the broken ribs. He dreaded the thought of traveling, but he could not stay here. He had nothing—no food, no weapons, and most important of all, no horse.

Lean Wolf had to rethink his situation. He thought his best chance to find a horse was to backtrack to the east toward the settlements. But he would have to cross the Arkansas River. He also knew the Osage were in that direction. If he continued west, he might end up walking all the way to the rendezvous. Neither choice appealed to him, but he had to do something. Ellsworth was so determined, he might be looking for a place to cross the river right now. Hell, maybe he had crossed already.

Lean Wolf knew it would be several days before the river went down. He didn't think Ellsworth would risk drowning to catch him. But he had survived the fall, and the swim. If Ellsworth could find a decent crossing, maybe he would try it, though Lean Wolf knew there was no need. Sooner or later he would have to go south again, and when he did, Ellsworth or Macon would be there waiting. Dammit, if Zendejaz had killed the man, he wouldn't have this problem.

Lean Wolf dunked his head in the river and rose to all fours, shaking like a dog. He gasped as the movement shot pain through his body. Carefully getting to his feet, he decided to play it safe and head west. Maybe his luck was still with him. He would follow the Cimarron, and hope to find a horse somewhere. By the time he reached the rendezvous, crossing the river should be easy, horse or no horse, providing it didn't rain anymore. If he made it to the rendezvous, someone would show up sooner or later. Fast Elk and Emmett said they were going there. Maybe they were still there, though why anyone would stay at the rendezvous was a mystery to Lean Wolf.

It was just a spot to trade guns and horses. Hardly the kind of place anyone would want to live, though it *was* a good place to rob people. Occasional passers-by would see the ragged lodges and stop for the night, often ending up robbed and dead. Setting his jaw, Lean Wolf started west. He wished he, at least, had a walking stick.

#

Boone Randall had a roping arm that itched all the way to his shoulder. He'd practiced and practiced, and gotten pretty handy, but what was the purpose of having a rope, if you never got to rope anything but the hitching post, or the sheriff's old dog, Barney? Such were Boone's thoughts as he watched the small bunch of cows being driven down Austin's Main Street. A local farmer drove them in to sell or trade for goods and supplies, or maybe pay his bills around town. He drove three cows, each with a calf at her side. One of the calves was a mottled red heifer. Boone licked his lips and fingered the strands of his rope.

The cattle were still a ways off, but Boone knew they would pass right in front of the sheriff's office, where he stood watching with his friend, Toad Phinney.

"I dare you," Toad said.

"You're crazy. I'd get a lickin'."

"I double-dare you."

To back down from a double-dare was a serious thing. Maybe more serious than getting a licking for roping the calf, Boone didn't know for sure. The licking would only last a short while, but Toad wouldn't let him forget that he'd backed down. Not only that, but he'd probably tell every kid in town. Boone wondered how long a double-dare back-down could be held against you.

"You won't get a lickin' if you miss," Toad added. "And you will, I bet."

Boone recoiled, hurt that his friend thought he couldn't rope the calf. "You ain't got anything to bet."

Toad reached into his pocket and pulled out three peppermints that had melted into one ugly clump. The candy had sand and lint stuck on it, but Boone considered this a minor inconvenience.

"How many loops?" he asked.

The Day Hunters

"Two, but you gotta pull your slack."

Boone was skeptical. "I don't know," he said. But even as he said it, he knew he would try to rope the mottled heifer.

"You better make up your mind. They're almost here."

Boone stepped behind the sheriff's horse standing tied at the hitch rail, and shook out his loop. The cattle were close. He could smell the dust they kicked up. The first cow came into view, the mottled heifer jogging along between Boone and her mother. He could almost taste that peppermint. Boone tossed his loop, easily catching the heifer around the neck, as she was no more than five feet away.

In his shining moment, Boone forgot to jerk his slack. But the heifer didn't. She bolted, running wild down the street, yanking Boone off his feet, and dragging him through the dust. The sudden commotion spooked the farmer's horse, which soundly bucked the farmer off and disappeared around the corner.

All down Main Street tied horses pulled back, breaking reins, ropes, and even one hitch rail. The horse was seen leaving town at the gallop, dragging the hitch rail behind him. Dogs barked and chased the calf, while the other cows bellowed and chased the dogs. Boone ate dirt, and refused to let go of the rope. People on the street laughed and cussed, and tried to control their horses. Toad ran behind his friend, yelling at him to let go.

The heifer had weakened quite a bit by the time Sheriff Pence got to her. He flanked the calf with the skill of an old cowhand, slipped the rope from her neck, and let her up. Bucking and bawling, she ran to her mama.

Sheriff Pence wanted a word with Boone, but the boy was coughing and sneezing so bad, he turned his gaze on Toad Phinney. "What happened here, son?"

Toad knew it was time to talk fast. "Well, sir, the whole thing started when Boone roped the calf . . ."

The farmer stomped toward them, more than a little put out.

"What the hell's got into these kids?" he shouted.

"I'll handle this, mister," the sheriff said. "Your calf ain't hurt, so just go on about your business."

The Day Hunters

"Oh my God! Boone, are you all right?" Rebecca shrieked, gasping for her breath. She had run all the way from the cafe, watching Boone plow up the street. "Come on. I'll get you home and clean you up."

"Afraid you can't do that, ma'am," the sheriff said.

"Boone was on the clock, workin' for me when this happened. I'm afraid I'll have to take him down to the jail."

Sheriff Pence answered Rebecca's cold stare with a wink, out of Boone's eyesight—which wasn't hard to do since Boone's eyes were full of dirt. The boy looked like he'd fallen head first into a barrel of brown sugar. Toad Phinney had already run for it.

"Well," Rebecca said, "if that's what you have to do." She kissed the boy on his dirty cheek, and with one more hug, started back to the cafe, leaving Boone on his own with the law.

Sheriff Pence took Boone by the ear and marched him down the street to the jail. Boone didn't know what to think. He wondered if the sheriff would give him the licking, or if he'd get one from Miss Becky when he got home. Or if he still had a home. Boone was afraid of going to jail. But he was more afraid the Captain would never let him be a Ranger, now.

The Day Hunters

Chapter 15

Rebecca puttered around the house, fixing this, cleaning that, while she waited for Boone to come home. She knew Sheriff Pence wouldn't lock him up, but she worried with the boy being so late. She'd come home from the cafe a few minutes after seven, her usual time, and now it was seven-thirty. Charlie Dean, who owned the cafe, had been sending home leftovers since Boone came to live with her. There was no need to cook. She had today's special, beef and noodles, warming on the stove.

Lord, she needed something to do with her hands! She'd never had anyone to worry about before, but since Boone arrived, she seemed to be worried all the time. Was he safe, warm, cold, dry? Was he getting enough to eat? Where was he? She knew Sheriff Pence had the boy's interest at heart, but she hoped he wouldn't work him too hard.

Rebecca was thankful the sheriff had taken an interest in Boone's welfare. She knew a boy needed a man in his life. Since Eddie's death, Boone spent much of his day at the sheriff's office. Sheriff Pence, having no family of his own, was happy to have his company and his help.

But she wondered if she was in over her head. After all, what did she know about raising a child? She was the youngest in her own family. She'd never even been a babysitter. But when she heard of the boy's trouble, she couldn't help but offer her home. He'd wanted to stay at the sheriff's office, but with the constant flow of thugs and drunks, Sheriff Pence didn't want him there at night. He had to live somewhere, or run wild in the streets.

The kitchen door opened slowly. Boone stepped inside, evidently unsure of what his reception might be. He looked exhausted, his hands beet red. The legs of his trousers were wet, with the marks of soap stains all over them. He had the look of a young boy who had just learned what work was all about.

"Hello, handsome. Did you have a nice day at the jail?" Rebecca asked, a little upset, but relieved he was home.

"No, ma'am. Sheriff Pence made me n' Toad scrub the

The Day Hunters

whole jailhouse. I never knew how dirty it was before.

"Toad got mad and cried about five o'clock," he added.

"I suppose you won't have to wash up for supper. Your hands look clean enough."

"No, ma'am. It sure smells good, and I'm hungry."

Boone looked so tired, Rebecca wondered if he could stay awake long enough to eat. But she filled his plate to overflowing and got him started. The boy pitched in and ate like a thrasher, cleaning nearly half his plate before Rebecca sat down with her own supper.

"I suppose you'll know better than to rope another man's calf in the future."

"Yes, ma'am. I didn't mean to make trouble. Are you mad at me?"

"No, I'm not mad at you, honey. But you could have been hurt. You know that, don't you?"

"Yes, ma'am. I'm sorry."

Boone obviously had something else on his mind.

"What is it?" Rebecca asked.

"Do you think Captain Ellsworth'll be mad at me?"

"Well, I don't know. From what I hear about Captain Ellsworth, he's a pretty strict man. But he was a boy once, too. I'll bet he's done at least one foolish thing in his life. Do you want some more noodles?"

"No, ma'am. I'm gettin' sleepy." The boy had completely cleaned his plate, and was rapidly losing consciousness.

"Take your wet clothes off and get into bed. I'll come in when you're covered up."

Boone wasn't yet comfortable with Rebecca seeing him undressed. He stepped behind the hanging blanket that formed the wall of his room and stripped off his clothes, crawling into the bed the whores of Austin bought for him. He was almost asleep when Rebecca came in.

"Tomorrow's another day," she said, stroking the boy's hair, tucking the blankets close around him. "We can always try to do better tomorrow."

The Day Hunters

"Yes, ma'am. Do you think I'll still get to be a Ranger?"

Rebecca smiled. The boy had a one track mind. "I suppose you'd have to do something worse than rope a calf, to be rejected by the Texas Rangers. Goodnight, honey. I'll see you in the morning."

"Goodnight, Miss Becky."

Rebecca picked up his wet clothes and stepped out into the kitchen. Boone listened a few moments to the pleasant sounds she made, as she cleaned up the supper dishes. He'd heard his mother make the same sounds in her kitchen. And Opal, too. He wondered if the two of them were together, wherever they were. But then he remembered that Opal's husband Wesley was there too, so Opal was likely with him. Boone didn't like to think his mother was alone. Maybe she was with his pa now.

Boone didn't know much about his pa. His mother rarely talked about him after she started drinking, and that was when he was just a toddler. But his mother did tell him that his pa was a rare gentleman, and that he was tall and handsome, like Captain Ellsworth.

The boy burrowed deep into the covers, drifting off to dream almost instantly. He dreamed that Captain Ellsworth and the troop had returned safely to Austin. And that he would soon be riding with them to the border.

#

Lean Wolf had been walking for what seemed like forever, when he saw the campfire flickering in the distance. It looked to be a rather small fire, suggesting the camp's inhabitants were Indians. The whites would never build such an unimpressive little fire, even in the heat of summer—one of the reasons they were easy to find and kill. The whites liked to build big, roaring blazes, and spend their time sitting around talking and looking at them, hindering themselves of any ability to see in the dark. The whites

161

The Day Hunters

also liked to sit close to the light, making themselves perfect targets for an ambush. But this was not a white man's camp.

Lean Wolf could see no one near the fire, nor anywhere around for that matter. No movement, no sound, nothing. There was no lodge near the fire. Maybe the fire builder was just traveling. Out of the corner of his eye, he saw a splash of white on a paint horse, tied a short distance from the camp. He thought maybe he saw another horse standing alongside the paint. He could not be sure. But there was one horse, and that was all he needed.

He would have to get closer to get the lay of things, but he was apprehensive, almost fearful. His ribs had not healed much in the few days he had been walking. He did not feel up to a fight. Also, he had no weapons, though he had found a suitable walking stick just the day before. The walking stick was heavy. It could be used as a club in an emergency, but Lean Wolf wanted something more substantial. Maybe he could circle around to where the horse stood tied, and steal it quietly before anyone knew. But he was not a great horse thief, like some of the men he had known. Killing a man and stealing his horse was one thing. Sneaking into a camp like a ghost and stealing horses, relying only on stealth and courage, was quite another.

Lean Wolf had once known a man who caught a hawk with his bare hands by simply walking slowly, talking to the bird, until finally, when he was close enough, the man reached out and caught the hawk by the legs. Catching the hawk had given him great power, but such men were rare. Lean Wolf did not think he could catch a hawk, though he would happily eat one if he could.

The camp was still. Lean Wolf thought whoever was there might be sleeping, though it had just turned fully dark. He skirted around the camp as quietly as possible, making his way to the paint horse. The horse turned his head to look at him, but to Lean Wolf's surprise, seemed to think little of a man approaching in the dark. Probably a warrior's horse, trained to accept such things. Also, his eyes had not tricked him. There was another horse standing beside the paint. The second horse, a small brown pony,

162

The Day Hunters

pulled a travois bearing a lodge and camp gear.

As Lean Wolf drew near to the horses, he heard faint, muffled sounds coming from the darkness. The sounds of passion and encouragement. The woman's voice sounded very young, the man's a little older. She squealed and giggled like it was her first time, while the man told her just how to move. Lean Wolf assumed the couple had gone off from the main camp to become man and wife. They must have been in too big a hurry to set up the lodge. He knew it was not a rape, as he would have recognized the sounds more clearly. He knew much more about rape than he did about being man and wife. Still, the sounds enticed him. He had to think hard to keep his mind on his business.

With the couple so engaged, Lean Wolf decided to take both horses and avoid any chance of pursuit. He wished he could steal a weapon, but the man would keep his weapons close by, more than likely within arm's reach. He needed food. Surely there was some in the camp gear. But he could live another day without food if he had to. The travois would only slow him down. He untied the bindings and quietly lowered it to the ground. Lean Wolf freed the horses, leading them far from the camp before mounting. As he did, he heard the couple shouting in confusion, searching for their lost animals.

#

The sun had not yet shown itself, when Zendejaz ordered his men to horse. The cloudless sky and pink horizon received a hearty welcome from the outlaws, though they wished the clear weather had come sooner. Maybe they wouldn't have had to sleep in the mud again.

The men spent most of the night trying to stay dry in the ragged lodges, but they provided little shelter. When the rain fell hard, they might as well have been outside. The men could not escape the mud, no matter where they were.

The woman, having been repeatedly raped and beaten throughout the night, had slipped into a catatonic stupor. Her vacant stare and apparent indifference seemed comedic to her captors. They shook themselves at her and blew her kisses, teasing her to no avail.

"Get her on a horse," Zendejaz said. "I think she will be very sore by the time we camp tonight. We're going to ride hard today."

"I'd say she's pretty sore right now," Emmett laughed, "after all the sweet love we made last night." He saddled the dead guard's horse for her. The very horse she'd ridden in on as the Indian's captive.

Her strawberry hair was caked with mud, as was every stitch of her clothing. Both her green eyes were black and blue, one of them swollen clear shut. Her nose was bent a little to the left. Not an inch of her exposed skin was clear of bite marks and scratches. All the bite marks were made by sharp, broken teeth.

"Damn, Emmett," Ugly John said, "were you tryin' to eat her?"

The outlaws laughed, but Zendejaz didn't. He wasn't happy about the biting, but he hadn't told them not to bite her, only not to kill her.

"Get her on her horse," he shouted. "*Vamonos!*"

Emmett grabbed her by the length of her hair and dragged her through the mud. He tossed her onto the horse's back. The hard saddle made her cry out. Once the woman's wrists had been tied securely to the saddle horn, Emmett ran his filthy hand up what was left of her skirt, and pinched her where it would hurt the most. She responded by kicking Emmett in the mouth with the heel of her shoe, causing him to lose yet another tooth. Emmett spit out tooth and blood, to the amusement of his cohorts. The woman turned her head away, afraid that Emmett might hit her. But she didn't make a sound.

Ruiz laughed. "When you get the rest of those sharp teeth knocked out, maybe we'll find another use for you."

Emmett turned on the woman, his eyes burning with anger. He pulled her shoes off and threw them in the mud. "You bitch," he snarled, making obscene gestures with the handle of his

The Day Hunters

tomahawk. "You'll pay for that when we camp tonight."

"Leave her alone," Zendejaz shouted. "I told you we're not going to kill her." Zendejaz spurred his horse and ran over Emmett, knocking him to the ground to make sure he'd made his point. Emmett hit the soupy mud, face down with a splash.

"If you don't want that tomahawk used on you, put it away and mount up. We have more important things to do than torture this woman. There will be plenty of time for that later."

Emmett rose to one knee, slowly getting to his feet, as the rest of the outlaws rode away with the woman. He wiped the mud from his face, mounted and rode after them, his anger approaching the killing point. Fast Elk had ridden off without ever looking back at him and they had been riding together a long time. Had Fast Elk abandoned him? Would they still fight together if it came to that?

Zendejaz would pay, thought Emmett, just like the woman. He was tired of being treated like "Emmett, the idiot." Lean Wolf had run him off, now Zendejaz spoke to him like a dog. What gave that bastard the right to talk to him that way? Maybe Zendejaz would suffer the tomahawk, before Emmett used it to cut his head off.

#

Milo Simms could hardly believe his own good fortune. He had faced the enemy as a Texas Ranger, and lived to tell the tale. The feeling he'd had when the soldier came over the rim was one of both fear and exuberance. Of course, if he had been the one to shoot the deserter, that would have been even better. Or at least he thought so. Both Harley and the Captain had killed one, and Mr. Hickok, too. None of them seemed to take any particular pleasure in it. Milo guessed he should be satisfied not being hurt any worse than he was.

The gunshot wound was not serious. Under Moody's care he was healing quickly, with no sign of any infection. According to Moody, it was the shot of whiskey he poured into the bullet hole

The Day Hunters

three times a day that kept the infection in check. Moody also gave him several drinks every day, to help keep him settled and still. Milo thought he'd be ready to ride in just another day or two, so excellent was the black man's care.

Though firewood was abundant, the nearest water was a little creek three miles away. Moody made the trip alone, several times daily, leading small bunches of horses and mules each time he went. While the stock watered, he would fill and refill every bottle and canteen available. Much of the water was used specifically to bathe Milo's wound. Milo doubted his own mother could have done more for him. He intended to make it up to Moody the first chance he got.

Milo's only chore was to keep the fire burning. Moody had laid everything out, so he could toss the wood into the fire from where he lay recuperating. But now he was on his feet a little more every day, so he had taken up stirring the pot occasionally. While gathering wood the evening before, Moody ran down and clubbed a fat, young possum. The possum had been simmering overnight, along with a few potatoes, carrots, and onions. The smell made Milo ravenous. He lowered the pot a little closer to the fire.

The horses sporadically rolled in the mud, enjoying the warm morning sun. Something they hadn't seen in a while. They all abruptly raised their heads when they saw Moody approaching, leading four of their own number. A few of the horses began to whinny as the rider drew close. A sound that, to Milo, seemed ten times louder in Indian country. Moody dismounted and tied his horse, hobbling the others, as he turned them loose. In a few hours he would make the same trip again.

"Any trouble?" Milo asked.

"Nope, no trouble. How you feelin'?"

"Not bad, but it itches like crazy."

"Lie down. I'll take a look."

Milo did as he was told, though he wished he hadn't when, after removing the bandage, Moody stuck his bony finger into the bullet hole up to the first knuckle. Withdrawing the finger, he

166

The Day Hunters

wiped the blood on Milo's pants.

"Healin' pretty good. I was goin' in a lot deeper a couple days ago, but you was asleep then."

Milo was glad he'd missed the examination.

"Roll over. Let me see your back."

"I'm sure it's just fine."

"Roll over." Moody repeated the finger assault on the exit wound and reported the same as before. "You'll be all right. Close up in a few days."

"When do you think we'll see somebody?"

"Mistuh Eli should be back in a day or two."

"What about Harley and the Captain?"

"Don't know what to tell you, there. The Cap'n's a hard man to shake on the trail. He'll chase Lean Wolf clear to Hell, if there's a way to get there. But you can't predict them things. With all this rain, and so much high water...well, it's hard to say."

"How long can we wait?" At that very moment, Milo seemed to have grasped the grim situation.

"Cap'n say, if he ain't back, strike for Austin while we still got food enough to get there. Got taters and the like for about eight days. Maybe that little gray you was leadin' when you found us. He looks poorly. I think the hard trip did him in."

Milo didn't look forward to eating the gray. He'd been a steady mount, though maybe too old for such a hard ride. Milo had mistakenly picked the horse due to his lack of experience at such things. Now faced with the prospect of eating his horse, he vowed to do better if there was a next time. As far as he could tell, nothing lived very long on the frontier. It sure wasn't like this in Cleveland.

The Day Hunters

Chapter 16

Lean Wolf rode ten miles from the couples' camp, before stopping to get some rest. The riding gave him an awful pain in his side. Hunger had badly weakened him. He built no fire, as he had nothing to build it with and nothing to cook if he did. The fire would be too easily seen anyway.

He needed rest more than anything else. Now that he had the horses, he would not have to travel for such long stretches. He slept hard throughout the night, waking only occasionally to the sound of the horses munching grass.

By daylight he rode upriver, wishing he had some way to catch a fish, or a bird, or anything to eat. He was still two days from the rendezvous. He wondered if he would make it. He had no guarantee that anyone was there, and if someone was, they might take advantage of his weakened condition and kill him.

Anger built inside him as he traveled. Some day, he thought, he would find Ellsworth. He would kill him slowly—and Macon, too. He would bind them together in wet cow hides, and watch the hides crush them as they dried. Such a death would be fitting for the men who tried to crush the power of the Comanche people. He would smear their eyes and ears with honey, and let the ants drive them crazy. Then, he would let the dogs have them.

Lean Wolf stopped to drink from the river. He needed to rest a little while, but he didn't get his chance. The sound he heard brought him quickly to his feet—hoof beats and rattling sabers.

"Indians!" he heard the soldiers shout. Then they were racing toward him.

Lean Wolf swung to the paint's back while running alongside. The running sent a sharp, stabbing pain through his body. He left the other horse behind, but the little horse tried to follow, not knowing what else to do.

Bullets cut the air around him as he galloped across the Cimarron. The soldiers shouted, "kill him, kill him," but the bullets didn't find him. Once across the river, he hooked his leg over the paint's hip and dropped out of sight, hanging to the horse's side. The little brown horse struggled to keep up, but was soon outdistanced by the younger paint. At the whinny of a soldier's horse, he re-crossed the river to join them.

The lieutenant called the troop to a halt at the bank of the river, much to the soldiers' dismay.

"Ain't we goin' after him, sir?" the sergeant asked.

"No. I'm not wearing these horses out to catch one poor beggar. Didn't you see he was nearly naked? He probably stole the horses, but it's not like he was some noted outlaw. Catch that horse. Let's move out."

#

The black man bathing in the slow moving creek was one of Ellsworth's Rangers. Delgado was sure of it. He had seen the man before on his scouting trip to Austin. This was news Zendejaz would want to hear. Maybe Ellsworth himself was close by.

Five horses stood hobbled, grazing on the fresh, sweet grass the recent rains and sunshine had produced. Delgado watched from a safe enough distance that the horses had not announced his arrival. The black's weapons lay close to hand, but he seemed relaxed and content, enjoying the warmth of the afternoon sun.

Delgado scanned the area as far as his eye could see, but saw no sign of a camp, nor of any other Rangers. Maybe the black had been cut off from Ellsworth and the rest of the troop. Maybe they had done battle with Lean Wolf and he was the only one left. If that was the case, Zendejaz would want to see the bodies of the Rangers. It was a safe bet the black knew where Ellsworth was, whether dead or alive.

The Ranger soon stepped out of the creek, drying himself with his shirt before putting his clothes back on. Though obviously a large man, Delgado was especially impressed by his deep chest, his heavily muscled arms and shoulders. This was a powerful man. Delgado had seen such men take incredible

The Day Hunters

punishment, sometimes absorbing several bullets before giving up the fight. He had no reason to believe this man would be any different.

Minutes later, after he had removed all the hobbles, the man mounted his horse and led his string off to the south, searching for any sign of trouble. Delgado followed at a safe distance, also casting a wary eye. Not only did he have the Rangers to think about, but there were plenty of Indians in this country, too. If the Rangers caught him, he might bluff his way out of trouble by posing as a passing *vaquero*. But chances were, he would not bluff the Indians. They would probably kill him and steal his horse. Or worse. The idea of dying, tied to a torture post, did not appeal to Delgado. It would pay to be careful.

Delgado counted two mules and three more horses, when the Rangers' camp came into view. The three horses were all branded army stock. He saw only one more Ranger in the camp. He looked to be a young boy, and walked as if favoring a pain in his side. The two men visited while the black hobbled his string of horses, then turned them loose to graze. They each poured a cup of coffee and disappeared under the tarp they used for shelter. Delgado could see only their feet protruding. This was plainly a two-man camp. No one else was around, nor did it look like they had been. But then Delgado saw the three rocky graves, just a little further south.

Ten head of livestock, three graves, and a wounded Ranger. Maybe his first thought was correct. Maybe Ellsworth and Macon were in those graves. Delgado rode quietly back to the west, to a meeting with Merejildo Zendejaz. The outlaws were probably no more than ten miles behind. They could return to the camp before dark. Maybe this would all be over tonight. They could be back at the stronghold in a few days. Delgado looked forward to the fiesta that always accompanied the return of Zendejaz. Maybe they could steal some fresh women on the way back.

\#

The Day Hunters

The outlaws poked and teased the woman, pestering and cursing her, until she'd become despondent. She hadn't said a word since leaving the rendezvous. But the men didn't care if she talked. They didn't want her for conversation. In fact, the less she talked, the better they liked it, though they did enjoy hearing her whimper when they took her. Her whimpering had become a source of great amusement to the men.

Zendejaz ordered a close watch on her, so she wouldn't get a chance to kill herself. He could see her slipping out of her mind. He didn't do it because he cared about her, only that she might bring a good price when fattened up a little.

"There," Ruiz said. "Delgado."

Zendejaz raised his hand to order a stop. The men looked to their guns as the rider approached.

"I have found the Rangers' camp," Delgado said. "There are two men there. The black is Ellsworth's Ranger. I do not know the other. I think he is just a young boy. There are also three graves just south of the camp. Ten head of horses and mules. Three of them are army horses. I saw no sign of Ellsworth."

"Three graves," Zendejaz repeated. "I wonder who is in them? How many weapons did you see?"

"One rifle in the black's saddle boot. Each man wore a sidearm. But there was a small shelter where there may be more guns. I could not see."

"How far to the camp?"

"Only a few miles. We can be there by dark."

"Three graves, and three army horses," Zendejaz muttered. He booted his fine sorrel into the trot. His men followed readily, talking among themselves, anxious to reach the camp and solve the mystery of the graves and the horses. Fast Elk was anxious to meet the young boy.

#

"We butcherin' the gray tomorrow mornin'," Moody said.

"We leavin' the mornin' after. I hope Mistuh Eli make it

171

The Day Hunters

back, at least."

"Dern, I hate to do it."

"Everything dies, Milo. You just gotta find some reason for bein' here at all. Maybe Ol' Gray's reason is to get us back to Austin. It's just the way o' things. Now, if you'da picked another horse, somethin' mighta happened, and you wouldn'ta found us, then we'd all be dead. Maybe that was your reason. Best not to worry about such things. They just happen."

Moody's calm wisdom was a comfort to Milo. He'd come to think much of the man, his wit and practical approach to life. It was plain to see why the Captain valued him so.

He felt certain that Moody could lead the way back to Austin, but he too wished Eli would get back. Eli and Moody had ridden together a long time. He was known among the troop as a steady man who would fight hard, if it came to that.

He'd also heard Moody say that Eli was the best hunter in the troop, though the horse meat should be enough to see them home. At the moment, home seemed so far away. Milo was doing most of his own doctoring now. He thought he would travel just fine, but it was a long trip. Only time would tell.

The Rangers made one final check of the hobbles before putting up for the night. The shadows crept far across the land when Milo looked west and saw the first rider. An Indian on a hard muscled yellow paint.

"Moody!"

"I see him. And two more off to the right. I wish we was closer to them rifles. We go for 'em now, they'll kill us for sure. Keep a hand close to your pistol, but don't pull 'til I do. They still a ways off. Maybe we can get a shot when they get closer."

Milo's throat tightened. He could barely swallow. His mouth turned dry as dust.

"You take the injun," Moody added. "When the time come to shoot, shoot him where he look the biggest and keep movin'. I'll try for the other two."

As one, both men looked to the south to see four more riders, one of them a woman tied to the saddle, a greasy bandana in

172

The Day Hunters

her mouth. The Rangers were cornered.

"If you reach for your guns, we will shoot you to pieces," Zendejaz shouted. The outlaws were steadily closing in now, no more than seventy yards away. An easy shot with a rifle, which all of them carried openly.

"Drop them pistols and kick 'em away," Emmett shouted. He cocked a round into the chamber, as he leveled his rifle at Moody.

Reluctantly, the Rangers did as they were told. Milo looked to Moody for some answer to it all. Delgado was the first to reach them.

"On your bellies and keep your mouth shut," he said, making a quick survey of the camp. "Two rifles, two pistols," he said to Zendejaz.

"I think we will be safe from these Texas Rangers," Zendejaz said. "They look harmless to me."

The remainder of the men had reached the camp, casually unsaddling for the night. They hobbled horses, added fuel to the fire, and went about the chores as if they'd made the camp themselves. Emmett searched the packs for food. Fast Elk checked the coffee pot.

Milo laid on the ground, terrified, with six killers walking around him kicking dust in his face. They acted, almost, as if he wasn't there at all. He desperately wanted to speak to Moody, but was sure he would be shot if he did.

The woman hit the ground hard, her face just inches from Milo's. When she looked into his eyes, she began to cry. Something she hadn't done in days. Her fear came flooding out. Moaning and crying, she stared at Milo in horror.

Milo had to turn his head. He couldn't bear the sight of the pitiful woman. When he did, he saw Fast Elk looking at him, as a man might look at something he longed for. Milo turned his face to the ground. Good God, how did he get here?

"Where is Ellsworth?" Zendejaz asked.

Neither man answered. Ugly John jumped onto Moody's back, grabbed a handful of hair and bashed his face into the ground.

"You better talk, nigger. It's only gonna get worse." Producing a lash of rawhide from his pocket, he tied Moody's hands good and tight.

"Don't know where the Cap'n is," Moody stated. He had blood running out of his nose.

"You're a goddamn liar!" Ugly John bashed Moody's face again.

Milo knew he would be tied and questioned next, but what should he do? What could he do? If he told them the Captain hadn't returned, the outlaws might wait to ambush him. But what if he never came back? He was afraid if he didn't do something, they'd kill Moody and he'd be alone. Then he remembered the graves.

"The Captain's buried down yonder," he said.

"Milo, don't tell 'em." Moody caught the boy's lie immediately.

Ugly John delivered a vicious kick to Moody's ribs. "Shut up, nigger!" he shouted.

"And Macon?" Zendejaz asked.

"He's down there, too. And another Ranger." Milo took notice that, throughout the interrogation, no one had yet made a move to tie his hands.

"I do not see any soldiers. Why do you have army horses?"

"Don't tell 'em nothin' else, Milo. We said all we gonna say."

Ugly John kicked Moody in the head, which proved to be the last straw for Milo. He attacked Ugly John with a ferocity he had never felt in the boxing ring.

Every man pulled a gun, except Zendejaz, who merely held up his hand to stop them.

Ugly John's first impulse was to draw a weapon, but the effort did him no good. Milo kicked the gun from his hand, with a kick he'd learned from a well traveled Chinaman. He followed it with a straight left hand that broke Ugly John's nose and knocked him to the ground.

The Day Hunters

The outlaws both mocked and cheered Ugly John. He cursed them all, pulling his knife as he came to his feet.

Moody watched in astonishment at Milo's attack. The woman rolled out of danger, but otherwise took little notice of the conflict.

Ugly John attacked with the knife. Milo stepped right, brushing the knife arm aside. He threw a straight right hand to Ugly John's mouth, his lips bursting with blood. Milo walked forward punching hard and fast, swinging with the intent to kill Ugly John. He landed a hard left hook to the chin, driving Ugly John to the ground. This time he rolled through the fire. After a moment to clear his head, the outlaw regained his feet, charging Milo empty handed.

Milo threw a wicked left hook, swinging low, striking the liver. Ugly John gasped and fell to his knees. Milo landed a right hook to the temple. Ugly John dropped to the ground, his arms and legs convulsing, blood running out his ears and mouth. In a few moments, he was dead. Milo was sure he soon would be too, but Zendejaz simply ordered Ugly John removed from the camp.

"You are a good fighter," he said to Milo. "Tomorrow morning, my men will dig up the graves and see who is in them. If I do not find Ellsworth and Macon in the graves, your death, and the death of your friend, will take much longer than Ugly's."

Milo saw a million fingers of light explode, and then, total darkness.

#

Lean Wolf came upon the outlaws' camp, solely by the devil's own luck. Crossing the river that morning had put him right on course to find Zendejaz and his men, sitting around a nice fire sipping whiskey. He saw two men tied together, a woman lying on the ground. There were many horses tied to the picket line, but not so many men. Why was Zendejaz this far east?

"*Aieeyah!*" he shouted.

Every man rolled into the darkness, cocking his rifle as he

The Day Hunters

did. The tied captives tried their best to lie flat.

"It is Lean Wolf, *amigo*! I would like a drink of your whiskey."

"That's him all right," Emmett said. "I'd know that ugly voice anywhere."

"Are you alone, *compadre*?" Zendejaz asked.

"Yes, I am alone. . .and starving."

"Come in, but be careful. These men want to kill someone."

Lean Wolf dismounted and walked into the camp, under the scrutiny of every eye. He knew he would be killed if he made a fast move, no matter who he was. When Zendejaz was sure the visitor was Lean Wolf, he began to laugh.

"You look like you have been to Hell, *compadre*. We thought maybe Ellsworth captured you. But these Rangers say he is dead. Buried in the graves just over there."

"The whites will never catch me, *amigo*. Not ever. Maybe Ellsworth *is* dead. He was alive when I last saw him, but I traveled on foot for days before I found a horse. I can't remember how long. It took a good while to get here."

"Well, we will see tomorrow. Sit down. Tell your story."

Lean Wolf dropped to the ground exhausted. Emmett filled him a plate of potatoes and onions, while Fast Elk handed him a cup of coffee, topped off with a generous portion of whiskey. Ruiz took care of his horse.

As Lean Wolf told of his escape, Moody listened closely to every detail. Though he wasn't sure he believed the part about the cliff, he took comfort in hearing that the Captain and Mr. Harley had not been killed. That meant they were likely on their way back here, but to what? To find he and Milo murdered? To an ambush? He wished there was some way he could warn them, but how? When would they get here? There was no way of knowing. And what about Mr. Eli? Where was he? And Stone Horse? Lean Wolf said he'd been left afoot. Had the Captain found him? Was he

The Day Hunters

alive?

Moody closed his eyes and silently called on the God he'd learned about. He didn't want to think about tomorrow. It would arrive soon enough, and there was nothing he could do about it. If this was to be their fate, so be it. He just hoped the renegades wouldn't chop them up, like they did the boys on the llano.

#

Milo and Moody sat tied back to back, watching the black sky turn to gray. There had been little sleep throughout the night. Neither man spoke, as if somehow putting it off until another time. It was their way of hoping there would be another time. But each man knew that when the graves were opened, they would be killed. It was how they would be killed that worried Milo the most.

He'd awakened from the head blow to see Emmett and Fast Elk watching him closely. The two laughed and talked all evening about other boys they'd captured, rarely taking their eyes off him. He had seen the looks before. There were plenty of greasy old men in the fight game who took young boys for pleasure. Often, due to a life of poverty, the boys would go with them for money. But Milo never had. He was too good a fighter to have to please old men in the alley. But this was a different time, a different place.

Milo took a chance and spoke to Moody, before the camp began to stir.

"How do you think they'll kill us?" he whispered.

"Don't know. Hang us, maybe. Somethin' bad, I reckon. I'm scared too, Milo."

Milo's eyes leaked at the corners. "I ain't sure if I'm afraid of the dyin', or what might happen first." He tried hard to control himself, but fear had the advantage.

"Wait a minute! They don't need us to dig up the graves. Why ain't they already killed us? They coulda killed us last night if they wanted to, no matter who's buried down there." Moody

The Day Hunters

thought maybe this glimmer of hope would strengthen Milo's resolve. But it didn't change the "what happens first" part.

Delgado rose from his blankets and walked off to relieve himself. He was followed by each of the outlaws until they all stood in a line, spattering the ground, groaning from the pains of hard riding.

When they returned to the camp, Zendejaz ordered the captives untied.

"Take them out to make water. If they try to run, shoot them. The rest of you start saddling. Then we will see who is in the graves."

"I'll take the boy," Fast Elk said, rapidly untying the Rangers.

"Leave him alone. We don't have time for that. Let them piss and get these horses saddled."

Fast Elk and Emmett walked the captives just a few yards away, allowing none of them any privacy. The woman had only her ragged skirt to hide herself from their leering eyes. The outlaws took a few moments pleasure cursing and threatening them, before marching them back to camp.

Zendejaz had just finished saddling his horse, when he heard the woman gasp. He'd heard so many sounds come from the woman, that he first thought to dismiss it. But this time, there was something even more desperate in her voice.

Off to the east a few hundred yards, rode a large band of well mounted Indians. Zendejaz pointed them out to his men. Fast Elk identified the tribe.

"Cheyenne warriors. They are hunting trouble, not meat. They have not seen us yet, but they will."

"There are too many to fight," Zendejaz said. He whirled and stared coldly at Milo. "I guess we will not dig up the graves today. But I have a feeling you are lying. Get them on their horses."

The outlaws quickly tied the captives to their saddles, and started drifting the stock northwest. They had covered no distance at all when they heard the war cries behind them. Fast Elk, Ruiz,

The Day Hunters

and Delgado fell to the rear, laying down a field of rifle fire. The rest of the band kicked their horses into the gallop.

The Indians returned fire, but they carried only single shot carbines. They had no chance against the outlaws' Henry repeaters. The Indians fell back, realizing they were out-gunned and that pursuit was futile.

"Damn it, if we had known they had no repeaters, we could have waited and killed them all," Ruiz said. "I think they have some good horses, too."

"We have enough horses to drive already," Delgado said.

"I am glad, for once, the Indians didn't have repeaters."

When the outlaws were sure the Cheyenne were gone, they wheeled their horses and picked up the gallop, toward the stronghold and the big fiesta.

The Day Hunters

From his hiding place in a narrow wash, along the creek a few miles from the Rangers' camp, Eli watched the Indians riding north. He had seen them approaching from nearly a half mile away, allowing himself plenty of time to find cover, but having no idea they would change their course and pass so close to him. He didn't know what tribe they were from, but that mattered little. The scalps tied in their horses' manes told him all he needed to know. This was a raiding party, all well mounted, though they had no captives or booty. All were young warriors, with both rifles and bows. Eli had seen it before. They were just out to do some killing.

The sick feeling in his gut made him wonder if those scalps belonged to his comrades. Judging by the Indians' route, they had likely passed the Rangers' camp. If Milo and Moody were alone when they did, both were probably dead. If the Captain and Harley had returned, it would have been more of a fight, but no man was immune to a bullet or an arrow.

Eli could hear their voices as they approached, though he could not decipher the language. His years as a Texas Ranger had given him a working knowledge of both Comanche and Mexican, with a little Kiowa thrown in. But these were neither Comanche nor Kiowa. He knew little of the tribes this far north of Texas, though he had heard much about the Cheyenne while at Camp Chicoine. Evidently, the Cheyenne were not happy living in the south. They wanted to go back to the far north country, but were being forced to stay on a poor reservation, south of the Arkansas River. Eli never knew an Indian who liked to be forced to do anything.

Hickok had recounted several run-ins with the Cheyennes, calling them fierce, proud warriors, and "some of the handsomest injuns there are." Eli didn't know much about handsome Indians, but he knew plenty about scary Indians. He thought this bunch would fit the bill.

They stopped their horses in the little creek, allowing them

The Day Hunters

time to drink. Two of the horses took the opportunity to stretch out and add water to the creek themselves, inciting a general laughter among the Indians.

Eli kept his head down, his hand over the grulla mare's muzzle. All mares were disposed to nicker at other horses. If she chose this moment to nicker, it would surely be the end of him. He hoped the Indians couldn't hear his heart pounding, they were that close. He hadn't drawn a breath since they stopped to water.

When the horses had taken their fill, the raiding party started north at the gallop. They traveled along the very route Eli had followed to get here only a short time ago. The mare became fidgety when the horses left. Eli had to be extra careful in keeping her quiet, whispering in her ear, gently stroking her muzzle. He removed the bandana from around his neck and placed it over the mare's nose, tying her mouth shut just to be sure.

Now with the party just a short distance away, Eli mounted the nervous mare. He headed straight for the Ranger camp at a quiet, nerve-racking walk, fearing that somehow the Indians might hear him. They had only to look at the ground to see his fresh tracks. Eli hoped they were in too much of a hurry to do so.

Within the half mile, Eli had the mare at full gallop, his mind filled with memories of burned out cabins, murdered settlers, and dead Texas Rangers. He had been with Captain Ellsworth since joining the Rangers, and with Moody nearly as long. He tried to prepare himself for what he might find, but upon arrival at the campsite, he found nothing. Moody and Milo were gone, along with all the stock. Had they returned to Austin? Had they been killed or captured?

In only a moment, he found the tracks heading northwest. Too many tracks even if Harley and the Captain had returned. Besides, Eli didn't think the Captain would ride off without leaving him some kind of sign. That meant Indians or outlaws. The tracks looked fresh, maybe only a few hours old, though Eli, admittedly, was not a skilled tracker.

He dismounted and tied the mare, quickly searching the area for clues. A short distance from the camp, he found the body of a man with what looked like an old gunshot wound to his face. The flies were so thick, they had almost covered him up, but the buzzards hadn't found him yet. The man had no fresh wounds anywhere, though he looked like he had taken quite a beating. The body had been looted and left naked in the sun. Eli saw a few moccasin tracks, a lot of boot tracks, and a few barefoot tracks, too. He thought these tracks may have been made by a woman, though barefoot tracks were especially hard to read.

Ten head of stock had been left with Moody, and maybe tracks for that many more. He couldn't be sure. Too many to go after alone, he was sure of that. Had Stone Horse been there, he not only would have known how many horses, but also if the barefoot tracks belonged to a woman or a child.

When he felt he'd learned all he could, Eli put his rope around the dead man's ankles, took a turn around the saddle horn, and dragged the body down to the gravesite. With his bowie knife, the only tool he had, he began digging a hole in the hard, rocky ground.

#

The Rangers traveled at a brisk trot, the thoroughbreds feeling good and fresh. The noonday sun was not so hot today.

The weather had taken another ugly turn, and kept them at the rock shelf camp longer than expected. Cole was anxious for a cup of Moody's strong coffee. Harley not as much. Mostly they were anxious to see that their men were safe. They'd spoken much about Milo since leaving him in Moody's care. Both agreed he had the makings of a Ranger. They thought he'd get along just fine, but they'd also thought Bass and the boys would. Now they were dead, their murderers still running free.

"Well, maybe it'll do us some good to get off the plains and go to the border," Cole said. "It's safer for the boys in Mexico than it is up here."

"To hell with Mexico," Harley said.

"To hell with Mexico?"

The Day Hunters

"Yeah. *To hell with Mexico*! You said yourself that Pease would likely fire us."

"I thought we settled this."

"We didn't settle anything. We won't hardly get down there 'til election time. If that damn carpetbagger Davis gets elected governor, he's gonna disband the Rangers. He's already made that plain."

"And if he does, that'll be the end of it. But you told Governor Pease we'd take the border. After we gather these men, that's where I'm goin'. You can break your promise if you want to."

"Promise? To a politician? Hell, what's that worth? I'd say about as much as a promise *from* one. They lie for a livin', the sons o' bitches."

Cole found Harley's statement hard to argue with. The legislature had been promising the Rangers better horses and provisions for years. Now that they might be disbanded, they were starting to see improvement. The Indians were daily promised a better life, while actually losing the best life one could ask for. A free life. Cole didn't spend much time trying to out-think the government. To him, it had always been a matter of keeping the settlers safe. Soon there would be so much army intervention, the Rangers wouldn't have any more work on the plains, anyway. They might as well go to Mexico.

The thought that he'd lost Lean Wolf and his band of killers weighed heavy on his mind. He knew Harley felt the same way. He'd all but forgotten about the thirty days the governor gave them to catch Lean Wolf. But it didn't matter now. They lost him, and that was that.

Stone Horse had been traveling on foot since leaving the rock shelf camp. He held the point well ahead of the Rangers, having announced that he'd heard enough of the white man's talk. When the Rangers saw him stop abruptly, then wave them on, they knew there was trouble in the camp. They rode in fast, pistols drawn, to find Eli piling rocks on a freshly dug grave.

"Who is it, Eli?" Harley shouted. He quickly scanned the

183

The Day Hunters

area, but saw no one else around.

"I don't know. I found him this mornin'. The boys are gone, Cap'n. I think they've been captured. Bunch o' tracks goin' northwest. Big bunch."

"Injuns? How many?"

"Boots and moccasins. I don't know how many. There's a lotta tracks. I think one might be a woman."

Stone Horse jogged to the campsite to read the sign, while Harley and Cole dismounted to help Eli finish the grave.

"What happened?" Cole asked.

"I come in this mornin'. Saw a bunch o' injuns ridin' north, but they didn't have our boys. When I got here everybody was gone. I found this fella over yonder."

"What'd he look like?"

"His jaw was broke crooked, and he had an old powder burn. Looked like somebody shot him in the face. He was naked as a jaybird."

"Ring a bell, Harley?" Cole asked.

"Can't say it does. You?"

"No. Maybe Stone Horse knows him."

"He had the hell beat out of him," Eli said. "Somebody worked him over good."

"Maybe Milo," Harley said. "I hear he's handy. If it was, they likely beat hell outta him, too. Or both of 'em."

"You get that breed, Cap'n?"

"No. We lost him."

The Rangers walked to the campsite, a worried, dejected lot. Stone Horse had already read the sign there. He was making his big circle, looking for more. They thought they'd make coffee while they waited. It was about all the provision they had left.

"How far to Camp Chicoine?" Cole asked.

"About forty miles," Eli said.

"We need provisions. And a few more guns if we can find 'em. How many troops there?"

"Likely not more'n fifty or sixty. It's a pretty small outfit. Mostly just a relay station."

The Day Hunters

"You don't think the army's gonna loan you any troops, do you?" Harley said. "Hell, you were damn lucky they loaned you the horses. And now we've lost three o' them. I doubt they'll be happy about that."

"All I know is we'd better get movin', if we're gonna get our boys back," Cole said.

Stone Horse returned and began his report, accepting the coffee Eli offered.

"Seven riders came in from the south and west, and one more from the north. One of them was a woman. They stayed the night and left this morning. A large band of warriors passed by to the east, but there was not a fight. Three rifles held them off from that ridge." Stone Horse gulped the scalding coffee and held out his cup, which Eli quickly refilled.

"Eli says the dead man had a broken jaw, and a powder burn on his face," Cole said. "You know him?"

Stone Horse startled at the description. "Yes. I heard a man like that rides with Zendejaz."

"Zendejaz? What the hell's he doin' down here?" Harley said.

"It don't matter what he's doin'," Cole said. "They've got our boys, and we're goin' after 'em. Let's eat somethin' and get started. Horse, you take the grulla and follow 'em. We'll go to Chicoine for supplies and another horse. Maybe we can get some information. We'll meet you somewhere on the Cimarron."

After sacking a little coffee to take with him, Stone Horse mounted the mare and left to follow the tracks. He would find something to eat on the trail.

"We ain't got anything to eat," Eli said, "except a little jerky and some apples I brought from the fort."

"We can eat that on the way. Let's move."

"Maybe somebody should go with Stone Horse," Harley said.

"No. I ain't lettin' another man outta my sight. They'd have a time catchin' Stone Horse."

"I guess this means we ain't goin' to Mexico?"

185

The Day Hunters

"To hell with Mexico," Cole replied.

#

Stone Horse liked the grulla mare. He was glad to be on her back again, and intended to ask the Captain if he could keep her. After all, hadn't his horse been killed? She had an easy gait and a good disposition, whereas most mares could be disagreeable. But the grulla had proven steady throughout all the time on the trail. He thought of the nice foals she might have, if bred to his brother's good stallion.

He followed the outlaws at a leisurely pace, keeping his distance, holding to cover. He thought one of them might fall out to check their back trail, but so far he had seen no one. They had a four hour head start, but their route merely followed the Cimarron River. A blind man could have tracked them. Zendejaz was in a hurry and it showed.

Stone Horse crossed the river to ride the northern bank. The northward bend of the Cimarron meant he could travel fewer miles than the outlaws, to cover the same distance. If he pushed, he could locate their camp tonight. Then keeping them in sight would be an easy matter, until they reached the caprock.

Zendejaz had superior knowledge of the country. There was no question about that. Not to mention that tracking on the caprock was nearly impossible—the very reason Zendejaz had been in business so long.

His years with the old Apache had served him well. The stronghold must have a good water supply and plenty of forage, to accommodate so many men and horses. And this bunch may not be all of them. Stone Horse was sure finding such a place was not just luck. Zendejaz had probably searched for it long and hard. Maybe he even fought the Comanche for it.

To live in such a harsh country took courage and fortitude. Zendejaz must have plenty of both. The Quahada Comanche lived there, and further west, on land even more harsh, the Apache.

186

The Day Hunters

Stone Horse doubted anything would be too tough for Zendejaz, having grown up with the old outlaw, Golonka.

Though the Apaches would not hesitate to kill a captive, if they chose to let them live they were rarely abused. Stone Horse could imagine how the boy grew up, running wild in New Mexico, tracking, hunting, stealing horses from his own people, the Mexicans. Stone Horse thought it sounded like a good life.

But now the whites were here, and showed no sign of leaving. All the Plains nations would someday fall to the whites. It would only take a little more time. Stone Horse tracked for the Texas Rangers because the Tonkawa had long been at odds with the Comanche. And for the money they gave him. He felt no other need for the white man.

He found their behavior strange and unsettling. When they were given the news that their friend, Eddie, was dead, they stood around the fire telling stories and laughing. Stone Horse did not know how white spirits reacted to such things, but he was sure a Tonkawa spirit would take offense. The sight of Captain Ellsworth laughing was the most disturbing of all, as the Captain rarely did anything out of the ordinary. Harley, on the other hand, was renowned for his peculiar behavior. Maybe he went crazy killing the bluecoats in the east.

Kicking the mare into a gallop, Stone Horse chose a straight line route, abandoning the river to make better time.

#

The summer sun was a long time setting. The renegades used nearly every minute of daylight before stopping to camp for the night. They had paused to water the horses and relieve themselves just twice throughout the day, though water in this country was plentiful.

Stone Horse arrived an hour later. He had pushed the mare to the ends of her endurance, only to find that he wanted her even more. She had all the stamina a man could ask for. An important

The Day Hunters

quality in a place as dangerous as Texas.

He stopped at the edge of the timber to observe the activity in the camp. Zendejaz had chosen a good spot, the river and some sparse timber on one side, a wide empty plain on the other. Approaching the camp without getting killed would be difficult. Stone Horse was under no obligation to sneak into the camp, but he wanted to know how the Rangers fared. There might not be enough left to save.

Tying the mare a mile from the river, Stone Horse advanced on foot. He moved silently through the water, drawing near enough to locate Milo and Moody. Both were bound and hobbled, but seemed to be holding up well. The woman, on the other hand, was not. She looked haggard and withdrawn, defeated. Stone Horse could imagine what she had been through. This looked like a pretty rough bunch. He recognized Fast Elk and "Emmett the idiot", but knew none of the others by name. There was an Indian asleep just out of the firelight. Stone Horse could not see his face. The others were Mexican. Zendejaz was easy to pick out as the man in charge.

Stone Horse dropped back and built a small fire, making a little coffee in his cup. He had nothing to eat, but he did not mind. Being empty made him feel light and fast. He would set some hooks down river tonight, and have a nice fish for breakfast. Later, he would take the mare for a walk, allowing her time to eat her fill.

#

The outlaws, as usual, were ill tempered, having been on short rations of food and whiskey for quite awhile. The only distraction they had was the woman, and now Zendejaz had ordered her off limits.

"You're going to kill her, you dogs. Leave her alone," he said. "The next man to touch her will be sold in her place. You can dig in the mines until you die."

The men knew Zendejaz wasn't bluffing. He'd sold many

The Day Hunters

a captive to the mines in New Mexico. They also knew that cheap gun hands were easy to find. Plenty of men would jump at the chance to ride with Zendejaz. Though they griped and grumbled, soon the camp was quiet. The men fell asleep, one by one, as they were exhausted and had nothing else to do.

The woman sat close to the captured Rangers, the men offering some comfort that she wasn't alone. Occasionally throughout the day, they spoke to her, trying to get a response of any kind. They asked her name, where she lived, was she married, but nothing could bring her out of her hiding place. The blank stare unnerved Milo, but Moody had seen it before.

"She might come back, she might not," Moody whispered.

"It's all up to her. Lizzie was young. She coulda come back, but she didn't want to. I ain't sure this woman wants to, neither. I expect it feels safer where she's at."

"I wish there was somethin' we could do for her. She didn't eat a thing all day."

Zendejaz had held such a rapid pace that Milo nor Moody had eaten either. But watching the woman suffer somehow made them forget that. The outlaws ate only jerky in the saddle. They would have to find some food soon. The few supplies the Rangers had wouldn't hold this bunch for long.

"This damn rawhide's so tight, I can't feel my fingers," Milo said. "I doubt I could do much, even if I could get loose."

"Better just sit tight. You make your move too soon, you end up dead. You wait too long, you end up like her. Then you won't try, at all. Better wait and save your strength. I ain't plannin' on givin' up."

The woman's expression changed when she heard Moody's statement. Her eyes softened, and ever so quietly she began to cry.

"Ma'am," Milo said, "can you hear me?"

She nodded her head, trying hard to keep quiet.

"You be still now. If you wake 'em up, there's no tellin' what they'll do." Milo inched over, moving closer to the woman. He allowed her to rest her head on his shoulder.

189

The Day Hunters

"My name's Rachel," she whispered. "Rachel Whitaker."

"Well, that's just fine, Miss. I'm Asa Moody, and this is Milo. . ."

"Milo Simms, ma'am. We're Texas Rangers."

"I know. I've been listening."

"How long they had you, Miss?" Moody asked.

"Three days. It feels like a lot longer. They killed the Indian that captured me, at a place they called the rendezvous. They took me after that. I think that's where we're going back to."

Rachel stopped talking when one of the outlaws stirred, but he simply rolled over and started snoring again.

"The rendezvous, Miss, you sure?"

"Yes. They were looking for that one, Lean Wolf. But he wasn't there. They came down here looking for him or Captain Ellsworth."

"I wonder where the Captain is?" Milo asked.

"I don't know, but we can't count on anything. We don't know he's alive, just cause that injun said so. We on our own, and we gotta think that way. If the Cap'n's alive, he'll find our tracks, if it don't go to rainin' again."

The thought of the Captain or Harley being killed hadn't entered Milo's head until now. He just assumed, from all he'd heard, that they'd be back no matter what. But now he felt all cold inside, like when he watched the Captain bury the young girl, Lizzie.

"What about Eli? You think he's all right?"

"Them injuns we seen this mornin' was ridin' the same way him and Mistuh Hickok left. I hope he didn't run into 'em comin' back."

"What're they gonna do with us?"

"Keep us for slaves, I expect, or sell us to the mines. But we can't give up. We gotta look for a way out. Don't do anything on your own, just stay ready."

The conversation began to wear on Rachel. She laid down on her side and curled up in a ball.

"That's right, Miss. You try to get some sleep now. We all

The Day Hunters

better get some sleep."

"Good night. . . Rachel," Milo said.

The Day Hunters

Harley crept through the darkness, approaching the sleeping figure on hand and knee. He carried a razor sharp knife between his teeth, and well knew how to use it. The sleeper sat with his back to a tree, completely oblivious to the world. Harley could smell the whiskey on his breath. The man rested a rifle across his lap. He was on the verge of tipping over when Harley lay the blade to his skinny throat.

"If I was a Comanche, you'd be dead, boy," he whispered.

"Oh God!" the sleeper gasped. He woke in a panic, struggling to get to his feet. Harley banged the boy's head against the tree.

"What's your name?"

"Private Lewis. Are you gonna kill me?"

"Nope. But I could have. Lean Wolf wouldn'ta woke you up. You ever heard o' him?"

"Yeah, I heard of him. Who the hell are you?" The private tried to struggle again. Harley pressed the knife a little harder.

"Harley Macon. Texas Rangers. Who's in command here?"

"Major Clayton. Are you gonna turn me in?"

"I ain't decided. Come on in, Cole."

Cole walked silently out of the trees, a disgusted look on his face. Eli followed, leading two very tired horses. Cole couldn't remember ever covering forty miles so fast.

"Private Lewis, this is Captain Ellsworth. I'm sure he has somethin' he'd like to say to you. The gentleman with the horses is Eli Plummer."

"I seen him before. He was here a couple days ago with Wild Bill."

"That's mighty observant of you, son," Harley said. "I guess you wasn't nappin' then. We need a corral. Which way?"

"All the pens are full. 'Cause of all them mules him and Wild Bill brought in. There's a few empty stalls in the stable, north end of the street. There's another guard up there."

192

The Day Hunters

"Hell, what difference would that make? He's likely asleep like you. Hickok still around?"

"In the canteen playin' cards. He'll probably be there 'til sunrise."

"Let's get these horses put up, Eli. Cole, you know where to find me."

Cole let the boy sweat awhile before he said anything to him. The whole incident scared Private Lewis half to death, but Cole could still see some pride in his eyes. His pride was the only defense he had, against the shame of being caught so unaware.

"Well, are you gonna turn me in?"

"I ought to. A man that falls asleep on guard could get a lotta people killed in this country. There's men out here that'll cut you to pieces for fun. We just buried five of our boys, not long ago. There wasn't much left of 'em."

"Major Clayton, he'll put me in the stockade if he finds out."

"Might do you some good. Besides, that seems like a light punishment for endangerin' this whole camp. If you'd been in Harley Macon's outfit, he'd've hung you. You're a damn disappointment, son."

Cole turned and walked away, toward the stable at the north end of the street. A soft bed of straw sounded good to him. He would see Major Clayton about a horse in the morning, but for now he looked forward to a few hours sleep. Private Lewis looked as though he'd been thunderstruck, but he was certainly wide awake.

#

Harley stood in the doorway of the canteen, taking note of the surroundings before he stepped inside. Hickok leaned on the rough plank bar, retelling the Dave Tutt story for the umpteenth time. Throughout the story, at just the right moment, he would stop speaking and another free drink would appear on the bar.

Free drinks and adulation had become part of daily life for

The Day Hunters

Wild Bill Hickok. His covert adventures in the Civil War were now legend throughout the west. The McCanles killing in Rock Creek, Nebraska, and his gunfight with Dave Tutt in Springfield, Missouri, had even reached the papers back east. The young soldiers worshipped him, while the more seasoned troops saw him as a blowhard and a dandy, though they would never say it to his face. Wild Bill Hickok was a man you spoke softly to.

Harley was amused by what he saw. He knew from experience how easily things could be blown out of proportion. Hickok's prowess with a gun was well known, along with his willingness to use it. But Harley no longer put stock in heroes, or knights in shining armor. He too had suffered the hero treatment, throughout most of the war and after. He felt little of it was justified. Often the difference between dead man and hero was no more than where the man happened to be standing when the shooting started. So far, Hickok had always been standing in the right place. Harley could say the same thing for himself. Hickok saw him when he came through the door, but continued telling the story.

The canteen was no more than a board shed, with a few ratty tables and a dirt floor. The bar was just planks on whiskey barrels, with any number of names carved in them. On the wall behind the bar hung a picture of a plump, naked woman, a bullet hole through each nipple. Harley crossed the dimly lit room and dropped two dollars on the planks. He requested a bottle of whiskey and two glasses, then retreated to a corner table, where Hickok joined him at the end of his tale.

"Bill, I swear, you oughta run for president," Harley said, filling the gunman's glass.

"No thanks. You know what happened to Mr. Lincoln. One round in the back of the head? I don't care to go that way."

"Hell, it don't matter how you go, just so it don't hurt too bad, or take too long."

"Yeah. What're you doin' here?"

"Moody and the wounded boy have been captured. All the stock stolen. We need supplies and another horse. Our tracker's on their trail."

"Damn! You boys plain run outta luck."

"Stone Horse thinks it's Zendejaz. They've got a woman with 'em. Captive, I expect."

"Any idea where they're headed?"

"To his stronghold on the llano, I reckon. We were tryin' to find the place when our boys got killed. You know anything about it?"

"Just that it's never been found."

"How about you joinin' up with us? You got anything pressin' you?"

"Yeah. I'm goin' to Hays City, now that I've been paid. They need a sheriff in Ellis County. They think I'm the man for the job."

"You? A sheriff, Bill?"

"Yeah. Kinda funny, ain't it?"

"Any gun hands hangin' around? We might need some extra help."

"Nothin' but the dregs around here. Nobody I'd trust. You've got a good man in Plummer, though. I like him. I guess he made it back all right."

"Yeah, he's a good man. But we've got two more good men in big trouble. And one of 'em green as grass. Sure I can't talk you into it?"

"I already wired 'em in Hays and told 'em I'd be there. I'm leavin' tomorrow."

"Too bad. We'll see what we can turn up in the mornin'. I expect you've already fleeced the flock?"

"Fact is, I'm down a little. Some of 'em have been fleecin' me."

"Barkeep!" Harley shouted. "Bring us a deck o' cards. Now let's see if we can get your money back."

#

The Day Hunters

Daylight found Cole and Eli loading provisions on a pack horse so ugly that Eli was afraid of him. The horse had one eye, and a broken ear that flopped up and down every time he moved his head. The beast kicked and tried to bite at every opportunity. The Rangers began to look at the floppy ear as a warning that the horse was about to react. Major Clayton refused the loan of a saddle horse, but was happy to give up the pack animal, as he'd broken one trooper's leg and bit fingers off two other men. But he was said to be sound and a hard traveler.

When Cole asked why the army kept the horse, the major replied, "To keep these fools on their toes. Nothing like a vicious equine to keep a man alert. I think they've learned their lesson." Cole could hardly argue with that.

"What're we gonna do for another horse?" Eli asked.

"I expect we'll have to buy one from a civilian, though I don't see many around I'd rely on. We've got a long, hard ride ahead of us."

As if in answer to Eli's question, Harley came trotting up the street on the black morgan, an ear-to-ear grin on his face.

"Well, Cole, once again I've solved the problem. Looks like I done better'n you. Where'd you get that nag?"

"He's all they'd give us. The major says he's game. How'd you get your horse back, as if I didn't know?"

"Three jacks. Ol' Bill can't bluff like he used to. I even got his saddle. Maybe I oughta take up poker for a livin'."

"Maybe you should, if you don't mind trailin' some outlaws first. You got anything else you need to do?"

"Nope. I already done it. I doubt she'll ever forget me."

"Uh- huh. I'm gonna send the governor a telegram before we go. Let him know what we're doin'."

"Well," Harley said, "let's go, then."

Before the Rangers reached the telegraph office, they had to stop and tie Flop-ear's mouth shut. He'd already bitten Eli twice on the leg. Cole rode ahead to send the telegram, leaving Harley and Eli to take their chances with the pack horse. Eli held a grip on the nag's good ear, while Harley tried to tie his mouth.

The Day Hunters

Flop-ear reared and struck with both feet, at one point catching Harley on the toe. Harley was hopping around on one foot, holding the other, threatening to shoot the horse, when Hickok rode up laughing.

"By God, that serves you right for beatin' me outta my morgan."

"That's my morgan now," Harley said, laughing just as hard at Hickok's mount. "I swear, this ain't no place for horse tradin'. You think that bag o' guts is gonna get you to Hays?"

"He'll have to. These boys are stingy with their good stock. I hope I don't run into any speedy injuns."

"Why, just the sight o' that ugly bastard oughta send 'em runnin' for home."

Hickok held out his hand. "It was good seein' you, Harley. I'd better get goin'. No tellin' how long I'll be gettin' there. Good luck to you boys."

"Thanks. Keep your back to the wall, Bill."

"I always do."

#

Before the sun rose again, the outlaws were on the trail. A drink of whiskey and a piece of jerky, was all any of them had before leaving. The captives, again, had nothing. Stone Horse followed, feeling full and rested. He'd caught a nice perch on one of his hooks. The fish made a fine breakfast, along with the good, hot coffee. The mare felt strong beneath him. Maybe not as fresh as yesterday, but well fed and ready to travel. The outlaws rode with a sense of purpose, though Stone Horse didn't believe he had been seen. Besides, why would they run from him when they could just come back and kill him? He let the mare have her head. They rode northwest at an easy lope, enjoying the colors of the dawn.

#

Zendejaz drove his men hard through the morning,

The Day Hunters

stopping only that they might relieve themselves. By midday, the horses needed a real breather. The outlaws took a long break in a cool stand of timber, along a creek that flowed into the Cimarron. Delgado rode ahead as he always did.

Lean Wolf and the captives fell asleep the moment they dismounted, but the rest of the men were hungry, bored, and mean. They wanted something to eat, and the woman. And they wanted them both right now. Fast Elk and Emmett would have been just as happy with the boy. Zendejaz still held that they not be molested, but the men were becoming hard to control.

"I told you to leave them alone," he said. "They will be sold at the next trade. I want them in good shape."

"They ain't gonna be in any shape at all, if they don't get some grub," Emmett said. "And neither are we."

"You don't look like you're starving to me," Ruiz said. "So shut up."

"Why don't you shut me up, *cabron*!"

A heavy stillness overtook the camp. The two faced off, each man waiting on the other to draw. While they waited, Zendejaz calmly drew his own pistol.

"I will shoot the first man to touch a gun," he said. "We will be back at the rendezvous tonight. The old gray horse should make it that far. We will eat him then."

The gray, indeed, was in bad shape. The hard riding had just about finished him.

"Maybe we will rest for a day when we get there," Zendejaz added.

"Hell, if we got time to rest, I don't know why we didn't go back and dig up them graves," Emmett said. "If Ellsworth's dead, I'd like to see it."

"You don't have to know. I can find many men to ride with me, *idiota*. I do not need you. If you want to live, shut your mouth and get some rest. We will leave in two hours."

#

The Day Hunters

Delgado amused himself watching the rickety little wagon cross the plains. One man drove the wagon, while another rode alongside. There was a second saddle horse tied to the tailgate.

The decrepit mule that pulled the wagon looked like he might die if they didn't reach their destination soon. Who would be driving a wagon through this country, and such a ragged one at that? Around here a man needed a fast horse and an equally fast gun, just to survive. Their horses didn't look very fast. Only time would tell about their guns.

The wagon's erratic course made Delgado think the driver was drunk. The rider seemed a little wobbly, too. A wagon load of whiskey, maybe? Now that would interest his *compañeros*. The rider carried a Sharps .50 caliber. Hunters? A wagon full of hides? Delgado doubted that. There were few buffalo left this far south, though other game was plentiful. So what then? He decided there was only one way to know. Delgado checked the loads in his pistols, and rode out to meet the travelers.

Had it not been for the wariness of the animals, Delgado could have simply ridden up and shot the men. They were both about to pass out from drunkenness. Their greasy buckskins stank to high heaven. The wagon driver had wet his pants. Delgado saw this as a perfect time to have a little fun. He pulled his bandana up over his nose, drew his pistol and fired a shot in the air.

"Stand and deliver, *Señores*! Drop your weapons, or I will kill you both."

"Bandits, Cooney. Bandits!" the driver yelled. He tried to whip the mule into action, but the beast decided he'd gone far enough. He just stood flat footed, craned his neck, and looked back at the driver. The rider tried to heft his rifle, but lost his balance and fell off his horse. The big Sharps went off and shot the mule in the foot, causing him to rear and fall, turning the wagon over. Out of the wagon came the driver, ten jugs of whiskey, three of them broken, assorted food and camp gear, a freshly killed antelope, and five Spencer carbines. The saddle horse tied to the wagon broke his rein, but only ran a few yards before dropping his head to graze.

199

The Day Hunters

"Drop your weapons and step away, *Señores*. If you try anything foolish, I will kill you."

The men obeyed, stumbling back from the wagon. Delgado smiled behind his bandana. Maybe these idiots were Emmett's brothers. He fired one round, putting the thrashing mule out of his misery.

"*Señores,* you are in dangerous country. But I see you have plenty of weapons. Where did you get them?"

"Poker game. Won 'em off some hunters down south," the driver said.

"Tell me your names."

"I'm Dukes, and this here is Cooney Bob."

Delgado knew Dukes was lying. There would be no hunters further south. All the buffalo had gone north. Besides, buffalo hunters carried Sharps, not Spencers. He didn't believe five hunters would gamble with their guns, anyway. Dukes held his hands high, struggling to keep his balance. Cooney Bob gave up and sat down in the dirt. He stared at the dead mule, trying to get his eyes to focus. The stain down the front of his shirt showed he'd thrown up recently.

Delgado thought them a sorry pair, but they had things the renegades needed. Food, lots of whiskey, guns, and maybe some money, too. He knew Zendejaz would want all they had. He made up his mind to kill them and take it.

"Set the wagon right. Hook up one of your horses to pull it. Hurry up."

"You gonna leave us out here, or kill us?" Dukes asked.

"I would never leave you out here, *Señor*."

The men unhooked the wagon and set it back on its wheels. Cooney Bob pitched in with the loading, while Dukes attempted to strip the harness from the mule. Soon they were both wringing with sweat from the whiskey. Their faces grew red, then turned pale gray. Their breathing became heavy and ragged.

With the wagon loaded, Cooney Bob came forward to help his partner with the harness—a difficult chore, what with a dead mule lying on it. He dropped the beaded parfleche he carried over his shoulder, then removed his stinking buckskin. The bag fell open when it hit the ground. Delgado saw the scalps inside.

"Ahh, you are scalpers. Now I know how you got the guns. If they are Mexican scalps, I *will* leave you out here."

"They ain't Mexicans," Dukes said, putting his hands in the air again. "Honest, mister. Don't leave us out here. They're Kiowa scalps. All of 'em."

"I don't care about the Kiowa. I hate them. But how did you take so many?"

"We poisoned their whiskey," Cooney Bob laughed. "We got 'em in a trade, then poisoned 'em."

"*Bueno*. I think maybe my *jefe* could use two smart men like you. Hurry. Hitch the wagon. I will take you to meet him. We will have a good time drinking your whiskey."

The men stripped the harness and quickly hitched the wagon. Their swollen pride gave them a newfound strength. As they creaked along toward the rendezvous, Delgado could only imagine what tortures Lean Wolf would inflict on the scalpers.

#

Governor Pease had just sat down to lunch at the cafe, when Boone came in with Mr. Olson to deliver the telegram. Boone had delivered many telegrams to Sheriff Pence, but this was the first one he'd carried to the Governor of Texas. A task so important, Mr. Olson from the telegraph office, thought he'd tag along. After all, he had to eat anyway.

Boone couldn't have been more proud of his mission, but when he saw the governor drinking his coffee, his big adam's apple bobbing up and down, he got so nervous, he froze in his tracks. Soon everyone in the cafe was staring at him, including the governor. It dawned on Boone that he didn't even know how to address the man. Governor? Mr. Governor? Your Honor? Harley called him a potentate, but Boone didn't know what a potentate was.

The Day Hunters

Smiling at the boy's dilemma, Rebecca finally broke the silence.

"Boone? What is it? Are you hungry?"

"No, ma'am. I got a telegram for. . . dern it."

Mr. Olson winked at Rebecca and took a seat by the window. Boone walked to the table, his head hung low, and handed the envelope to Governor Pease.

"Why, thank you, son. Why don't you sit up here and join me? I'll bet you'd like a piece of pie."

Boone was astonished at the governor's offer. He looked to Rebecca to see if it was all right.

"Go on," she said. "I'll get your pie."

Boone climbed into the chair, sitting straighter than he ever had, being quieter than he'd ever been. He noticed that everyone in the room fell silent, waiting for the governor to open the telegram. When he did, the sound of the tearing paper was almost deafening.

The governor's face took on a stern, worried look as he read the news. Boone guessed it must be something serious. But then, he supposed everything the governor did was serious. Rebecca set the pie down in front of him. Boone wasted no time getting started.

Governor Pease sipped his coffee and locked eyes with Rebecca. "Could we have some privacy, Miss?"

Rebecca quietly caught her breath. "Boone," she said, "why don't you take your pie out on the sidewalk. Leave the plate on the bench when you're done. I'll get it later."

"Yes, ma'am. Thank you for the pie, sir."

Boone took his pie and went outside. He dropped a single cherry on the dusty sidewalk, but quickly picked it up and ate it, hoping no one would see. The cherry couldn't have been very dirty, no longer than it was down there.

"What is it, sir?" Rebecca asked.

Every ear in the cafe was listening, so the governor just handed her the telegram.

It read: Governor Pease.

The Day Hunters

Lost Lean Wolf at the Cimarron. Moody and Milo
captured.
We think it's Zendejaz. In pursuit.
P.S. Please let Boone Randall and Rebecca Tate
know that we're all right.
Capt. C. Ellsworth

Rebecca passed the telegram back, wiping her hands on her
apron. Governor Pease put it in his coat pocket, and returned to his
lunch without a word. Rebecca made a quick check of her tables,
then went outside to talk to Boone.

"How's the pie, handsome?"

"It's good, but it might be better with some chocolate on
it."

"No chocolate today. Maybe next time."

Rebecca was hesitant to tell Boone about Milo and Moody.
She knew neither of them, though Boone had mentioned them
often, as he did all the Rangers. She decided to leave that part out.

"The telegram was from Captain Ellsworth. He said to tell
you they're all doing fine."

"He did?" Boone could hardly believe the Captain would
send him a message.

"Did Harley say anything to me?"

"No, honey, just the Captain."

"If they're all right, how come the governor looked so
worried?"

Rebecca chuckled in her lie. "He mostly feels bad for the
outlaws. He figures there won't be an outlaw left in north Texas,
by the time the Rangers get back."

"Shoot," Boone said, "I coulda told him that."

The Day Hunters

Chapter 19

Milo was sickened by the treatment of the gray horse. Zendejaz assigned the chore to Dukes and Cooney Bob, who were both so drunk by the time they started, they had to shoot the horse three times before it died. He thrashed and kicked and bit the air, in an effort to hold on to life. Milo wished he could cover his ears to muffle the sound of the horse's screams.

The butchering went no better. The fools chopped and hacked with no idea what they were doing. Before long they were covered with blood and guts, having ruined much of the meat. Milo was surprised Zendejaz would allow such waste, but it seemed not to bother him at all.

Fast Elk, on the other hand, went about his task like a master butcher. He skinned and cut up the antelope, almost with a reverence for the animal. While the meat roasted over the fire, Fast Elk took great pains to preserve the hide, scraping away every bit of meat and flesh, before rolling it into a tight bundle to keep it clean. When he finished the job, he hit the whiskey hard. Most of the renegades were already drunk, their mood vicious and mean. Zendejaz only sipped the whiskey. Milo had never seen him drunk. Zendejaz liked to be in control.

Milo felt his fear rising again. Who knew what these drunken animals might do? Zendejaz was only one man. He could never control this bunch alone, if they decided to rebel against him. Rachel was terrified. Milo could see it in her eyes, and why not? These men were accustomed to having whatever they wanted. Zendejaz had deprived them of that for days now. Milo knew he was in just as much danger. Fast Elk and Emmett were just biding their time, licking their chops. Moody sat and watched, carefully analyzing each man, each movement, waiting.

Emmett disappeared into one of the lodges. He came out dragging the stinking corpse of an Indian several days dead. The men hung the corpse from the limb of a tree and used it for a target, to practice their knife throwing skills. A knife stuck in the

204

The Day Hunters

body, won a bullet from each of the other men. Soon the rotten corpse was torn to pieces, and Delgado had won a lot of bullets. Lean Wolf took the moccasins off the Indian and put them on his sore feet. Ugly John's boots didn't fit very good. They had rubbed big blisters on his toes.

"That's the man who captured me," Rachel said. "They shot him down like a dog."

"I'd say he got off easy," Moody said. "This is the worst bunch I ever seen."

Zendejaz untied the captives' hands, allowing them some circulation. Returning to the fire, he cut them each a generous portion of the antelope, which they devoured like starving wolves. They hadn't eaten a thing in two days.

"I think you will do well in the mines," he told Moody.

"You look very strong. I'm surprised you haven't tried to fight us."

"Don't know nothin' about minin'," Moody said, talking with his mouth full.

"Mostly I know about growin' things, vegetables and the like. 'Course, the last few years, I *have* learned a lot about killin' folks."

"Ahh, you haven't lost your spirit. That's good. You will need it when you can no longer see the sun. The young one, I don't think he will last as long. He is a good fighter, but there are many *locos* in the mines. But then, maybe he will not go to the mines. Fast Elk has offered me fifty dollars for him."

Milo looked across the camp to see Fast Elk watching closely.

"Don't worry. Fast Elk doesn't have the money now, but he wants you. He will find a way to get it. I think the traders will offer more for you than fifty dollars. We will see what happens when the time comes."

When the captives had finished eating, Zendejaz retied their hands and gave them each a cup of coffee, the first they'd had since being taken prisoner. The coffee tasted so good, it brought a faint smile to Rachel's face. Her bruises had faded somewhat, now more yellow than blue. Milo thought she looked much younger than before.

"Nice to see your smile, Rachel. Can I call you Rachel?"

"Why, yes. I'd prefer it if you did."

In his eighteen years, Milo hadn't banked much experience with women. But being with Rachel made him feel good. Like when he was a boy, hoeing corn with his cousin Hannah and her skirt blew up. He saw her bare thighs, and as a result was befuddled for a week. Rachel's skirt being in such poor condition, her bare legs and feet were exposed all the time, the sun turning them the color of honey. Even in such an awful fix, Milo could think of little else. But his daydream was cut short by the sound of cursing and threatening from across the camp.

"I told you they was Kiowa, not Mexican," Dukes shouted.

"You said you hated Kiowas."

"I do," Delgado said, "but Lean Wolf doesn't."

"Tie them to the trees," Lean Wolf said.

"Wait a minute," Cooney Bob pleaded. "You sons o' bitches. Wait a minute!"

The renegades subdued Dukes and Cooney Bob in just moments. Both were so drunk they could hardly resist. They stripped the men naked, and tied them with their hands behind the trees. Dukes tried to kick them and fight them off, but he was knocked down hard for his trouble. Cooney Bob cried and begged for his life.

"Anything," he said. "I'll do anything. Please don't kill me. I didn't scalp 'em, he did. He poisoned 'em, too. I didn't do it. Please don't kill me. Please?"

"Shut up, you snivelin' bastard," Dukes said. "He'll do anything, all right. I been on the trail with him for a year. He'll do anything you want him to."

The renegades knocked Cooney Bob to his knees. They laughed and mocked him, as they stripped off their gun belts. Lean Wolf was more interested in torturing the scalpers. He placed Ugly John's knife in the coals of the fire.

While he waited for the knife to glow, Lean Wolf took

The Day Hunters

Dukes' own knife, dull as it was, and scalped him, laughing all the while the man screamed. Dukes cursed and screamed, but he didn't beg, showing far more courage than his partner. Lean Wolf raised the thin scalp high, blood running down his arm. He split the night air with the shrill Comanche war cry.

Rachel pulled her knees up and buried her face beneath her arms. She tried to cover her ears with her shoulders, to shut out the screams of the tortured scalper, but it didn't work. She hated the sounds the men made with Cooney Bob—the same sounds they made when they mounted her. They grunted and groaned, and laughed like boys, while the poor man begged for his life. She began to sob, trying her best to keep quiet. God, how she wished she could die!

"Stay strong," Moody whispered. "I think they forgot about us for a while. Stay strong now."

"I'll make 'em kill me before I'll let 'em do that to me," Milo said. "They're crazy."

"Yeah. Try to think about somethin' else, but be ready for anything."

Moody knew he would have to shoot Rachel first, if he could get his hands on a gun. He and Milo together couldn't take all the outlaws. He knew the outlaws would kill them, then torture Rachel because they'd resisted. The thought of killing a white woman didn't set well with him, but he could see no other way. It would have to be done, and he would have to do it. Such a job was too much to expect from Milo.

Zendejaz cut himself a nice piece of the antelope, and sat back to enjoy his meal. Moody waited, looking for any chance at all to get his hands on a weapon. But the chance didn't come. Zendejaz kept a close eye on him, as if maybe he suspected something would happen. The gruesome activities taking place around them barely held his attention, though he was getting tired of Dukes' screaming.

"Can't you shut him up, Wolf? I'm tired of listening to him cry."

Lean Wolf pulled the knife from the fire, held Dukes' nose shut until he opened his mouth, then lay the red hot blade on his tongue. Dukes screamed an awful scream, his body contorting in pain. His tongue dried quickly, bursting to flame. Lean Wolf yanked the knife out, tearing the skin from the tongue, then plunged it into Dukes' heart. The blood sizzled as it ran the length of the blade. Dukes died instantly, smoke and blue flame rising from his mouth.

"I think he will be quiet now, *amigo*," Lean Wolf laughed.

"*Gracias*. I like more quiet when I am eating."

The outlaws had given Cooney Bob about all he could take. He begged the men to stop, but they wouldn't. When finally he tried to fight back, Fast Elk cut off his privates and threw them in the fire. To the whoops of the others, Ruiz shot him in the head, and the camp was quiet again.

The captives sat in terror of what they'd just witnessed. Moody knew such things happened, but had never actually seen them. The scene only confirmed what he'd always believed. There were a lot of things worse than dying.

"Sit down everyone," Zendejaz said. "Have some food. Then you can drag them away. I'm getting sleepy. I don't want to wake up and see them in the morning."

#

Stone Horse held his rifle at the ready, in the event one of the renegades would attempt to harm the captives. He knew he couldn't take them all, but with the element of surprise on his side, he might take two, maybe three, if he was lucky. Of course, shooting the captives themselves would be much easier. They sat close together, all in a row, and they were bound. If he had to, he could shoot them all, and be gone before the renegades could

The Day Hunters

saddle up to come after him. If he shot at the renegades, someone would kill the captives, anyway. Stone Horse hoped he wouldn't have to shoot at all.

He was clearly able to recognize the second Indian now. Lean Wolf. The lame horse and bad weather had slowed the Rangers down too long. Lean Wolf had rejoined the renegades before the Rangers even got back to the camp. Maybe the stories about Lean Wolf were true. Maybe he was part demon, after all.

Stone Horse wretched a little when he saw Lean Wolf put the glowing knife in the white man's mouth. He was sure the white man's spirit must have been begging for death, by then. To be scalped with a sharp knife was bad enough. To have it done with a knife so dull the scalp had to be sawed and pulled away, should have been enough to kill the man. But he was tough and stubborn. He took the scorching knife in his mouth, then Lean Wolf stabbed him in the chest. After one final shot, the renegades came to the fire to eat, then dragged the bodies away.

Stone Horse wished he could sneak through the darkness and kill a few of them, but it would only serve to warn the others. They might kill the captives so they could travel faster, then Captain Ellsworth might kill *him*. He could do nothing but wait until morning. The whites had done a terrible job butchering the gray horse. Maybe Zendejaz planned to stay a while and save the meat. The camp did not look well provisioned. Stone Horse doubted they would ride off and leave so much meat on the ground. But if they did, he would have plenty.

As the activity in the camp seemed to be dying down, Stone Horse made his way back to the mare. She was lonesome for company and glad to see him. He stroked her muzzle and walked her out to graze.

#

Morning proved Stone Horse correct. The renegades showed no intention of leaving. He watched as Fast Elk and Emmett worked on the gray horse, cutting the meat into strips.

209

The Day Hunters

They hung the strips on the old wagon to dry. Two at a time, the outlaws bathed in the Cimarron, leaving two others to stand guard and watch over the prisoners. When every man among them had taken their turn in the river, the prisoners got their chance.

The guards observed intently as Rachel washed herself. They each cradled a rifle in their arms, but at times seemed too distracted to use them. Rachel kept her dress on, though it made little difference. The sight of her firm bosom, encased in the wet dress, was difficult to ignore. Stone Horse had a hard time ignoring it himself. Moody kept his back turned, but Milo couldn't. He took peek after peek, trying to appear inconspicuous.

"Well," Moody said, "I'm ready to get out. Guess I'm clean as can be."

"I can't right now," Milo said.

"Why not?"

"I just can't, that's all!" Milo blushed like a schoolboy. "I'm glad she can't see under water."

Rachel and Moody stepped out of the river together. Moody placed his shirt over her shoulders, to help cover up the wet dress. They looked around for Rachel's shoes, but they must have been carried away by some varmint.

While the leering guards were momentarily distracted, Milo looked across the river and saw Stone Horse watching from behind a knoll. His first instinct was to swim across, but Stone Horse quickly disappeared. Milo's heart beat uncontrollably. Were the Rangers close? Were they already here? The excitement of watching Rachel bathe, subsided with the excitement of seeing Stone Horse.

Milo made his way back to the bank, trying to be calm. He hoped the outlaws wouldn't see his bare chest pounding. He would wait for the moment when he could let Moody know. If he didn't know already. Moody might have seen Stone Horse, too. It was hard to read the man.

Upon arrival at the fire, Milo found Moody and Rachel

already bound. He too was quickly tied and pushed to the ground. Each of the captives was given a piece of the horse meat, which to Milo's liking could have been cooked a little longer. But at least now they were being fed. Milo felt a little stronger than before. The food and rest were doing him good. His spirits were high. Any minute the Rangers might ride in and rescue them. He wanted to talk to Moody, but he would just have to bide his time.

#

"I swear, Cole," Harley said. "That major saw you comin' when he saddled you with this knot head."

He rode well behind the cantankerous pack horse, occasionally pitching his rope to keep the beast moving. The horse kicked every time the rope hit him in the hip. When Flop-ear felt like traveling, he traveled hard and fast. But if he felt like stopping, he stopped just as hard, and just as fast, at one point planting his feet, jerking Eli clear out of the saddle. While Eli lay on the ground taking inventory of himself, Flop-ear tried to bite him, even with his mouth tied shut.

"That's all we need," Harley continued, "to get a man hurt out here. I say we split the pack and shoot the son of a bitch."

"He's all we've got, Harley. If he don't straighten up by the time we find Stone Horse, I'll give you the pleasure of shootin' him."

"I'll cut an X in the bullet, just to make sure."

All in all, the Rangers were making pretty good time, holding a generally steady trot. According to the information he'd received at the fort, Cole didn't think the Cimarron could be much farther. He felt sure they would reach the river before sundown. Though his troop had never been so well mounted, they still were no closer to catching their adversary. And now that adversary held two of his men captive, if they hadn't already been killed. If Zendejaz made it to his stronghold, Cole felt certain they'd never find him. The country was just too big, and there was too little

The Day Hunters

water. He'd put Stone Horse up against any tracker in the west, but still, in all these years they'd never found the place.

The Rangers had been just north of the Brazos when they shot it out with Zendejaz. When the outlaws rode out, they continued riding to the north. There had to be water someplace between the Brazos and the Red, but the Rangers had never found any that far west. Cole was sure the stronghold must be north of the Red River, maybe even north of the Canadian. If that were the case, the Rangers would have access to more water traveling the route they traveled now. Even so, he knew it was a long shot.

"Look there," he said. "Plovers. The Cimarron must be close."

"Good hour o' daylight left," Harley said. "Let's keep pushin'. I doubt Zendejaz is more than a day ahead of us. Maybe we'll catch up to Stone Horse."

"Let's just hope they're stayin' with the river. There's a lotta water in this country. They might've cut off somewhere."

"Well, if they did, Stone Horse'll leave a sign."

"Harley, I've been thinkin'. What if we've been chasin' this man from the wrong direction all these years? We assumed his hideout was further west, out in the big dry. What if he came back east after we lost him? Hell, he ain't a camel. He needs water like everybody else. If he came back east, he'd have enough water to float the ark."

"You might be right, but how far could he come without bein' found? He couldn't stay hid this far east. The army surely would've located him, by now."

"Maybe he didn't come this far, but he could still come east from where we lost him. If he could make it to the Red, he'd have water galore."

"That's true enough, but I still say the stronghold's in the caprock somewhere. There's water there, too. We just don't know where it is."

Half an hour before sundown, Flop-ear made up his mind to stop. No amount of rope pitching could get him to behave, so the Rangers made camp where they were. Harley voted to shoot

The Day Hunters

the horse, but the day had about ended anyway.

#

By nightfall, the outlaws had consumed nearly half the whiskey Dukes and Cooney Bob had in the wagon. Most were so drunk they were barely conscious. But for the moment, they were content to ignore the captives. Zendejaz was sober, as always. He sat by the fire, shaving his bunions, with a knife too big for the job. At one point the knife slipped and cut his foot. Zendejaz let out a yowl. Milo had seen cuts no worse than that become badly infected. It was just a little something to hope for.

Rachel slept soundly. The bath had relaxed her, lifted her spirits somewhat. After seeing something so awful just the night before, Milo could scarcely believe she hadn't crawled back into her shell. But there she was, breathing deeply, maybe even dreaming.

Milo hadn't yet had the opportunity to tell Moody about seeing Stone Horse at the river. He'd waited all afternoon for the Rangers to come boiling into the camp to free them. But there had been no sign of them. Milo didn't think his eyes had tricked him. He was sure he'd seen the tracker. But he'd been equally sure the Rangers would've shown up by now. Where were they? How far behind? Was it only Stone Horse? How could he alone free them?

Zendejaz put his boots back on and walked away to relieve himself. With the rest of the camp in such a state, Milo saw his chance and he took it.

"I saw Stone Horse today," he whispered to Moody. "When we were in the river. I saw him watchin' us."

"Yeah," Moody said, "I saw him, too."

"You did?" Milo felt deflated. Here he'd carried a secret all day that he was certain would elevate his status, and as usual, it turned out that Moody knew all along. "Why didn't you say somethin'?"

"Same reason you didn't. Rachel didn't see him, and we

ain't gonna tell her. They might get it out of her somehow.
Nobody else saw him, or we'd be gone by now. Just stay ready,
like I told you before."

#

At daylight, Zendejaz did the last thing Stone Horse
expected. He changed his course and headed southwest. Privately,
Stone Horse had always believed the stronghold to be in no man's
land, west of the Indian territory. But the Rangers could never
travel that far north, tracking Zendejaz through the llano. They
would die of thirst before they got there. Stone Horse thought
following the Cimarron might lead the Rangers right to the place.
Now, everything changed.

He would have to leave the Rangers a sign, but the men
were in strange country. What if they struck the Cimarron further
up river? They would miss the sign, lose Zendejaz, and the
captives would surely be doomed. If he waited for them and
Zendejaz reached the caprock, they would never find him among
the many canyons there.

Stone Horse tried to think of what the Captain would do,
but it was hard to understand the white man. He saw no point
spending much time on that. He gathered stones and made an
arrow on the ground, pointing the direction the renegades had
gone. He took the pheasant feather from his hair, and stood it
securely at the arrow's point. It could be easily seen from a short
distance. He then mounted and crossed the river.

The buzzards quickly descended on the carcass of the old
gray horse. So many that some had to sit on the abandoned wagon
and wait their turn. Thirty yards distant, four coyotes had a playful
tug-of-war with the corpses of Cooney Bob, Dukes, and the Indian.
The flies buzzed, the birds sang, and somewhere high above, the
eagle screamed.

The Day Hunters

If not for a gust of wind blowing the pheasant feather across their path, the Rangers would have missed the sign completely. The sight of the tail feather floating on the breeze, sent Flop-ear into a panic. Dallied to Eli's saddle horn, he pulled back hard, nearly jerking the thoroughbred off his feet. Once Eli had him under control, Flop-ear stood wild-eyed, snorting, kicking the air. Casting about, looking for sign, Harley was the first to see the arrow.

"There," he said. "They've changed direction."

Cole didn't stop for a moment. He turned his horse and crossed the river without comment. Harley followed, but Eli dismounted to reclaim the tail feather.

"What the hell are you doin', Eli?" Harley asked.

"I'm gettin' this feather for Stone Horse. He set store by it, and he'll be glad to get it back. If he shot that pheasant in flight with an arrow, then that was a shot to be proud of." Eli put the feather in his hat band and followed the others across the Cimarron.

A cloud of buzzards scattered when the Rangers rode into the camp. There wasn't much left of the gray horse by then, mostly just head and hooves. The coyotes weren't as quick to relinquish their meal. They stood defiantly until Harley shot one, then with a yelp they ran into the trees. Cole dismounted, drawing his pistol. He searched the lodges while Harley checked the bodies. The smell was horrendous. Harley was relieved to find he knew none of the victims.

"They ain't our boys! Two white men and an injun. It ain't Stone Horse. His feet's too big. One of 'em's scalped. All of 'em gelded."

"Nothin' in the lodges," Cole said. "I guess you were right. Judgin' by the tracks, I doubt they're a full day ahead of us."

"With all them horses, they could swap two or three times a day," Harley said. "It don't look like they're in a big hurry, but if they get in one, we'll never catch up."

The Day Hunters

The tables had turned. All the extra horses had done the Rangers no good. They'd only become a detriment to them. Once again, the Rangers were out-horsed and out-gunned, their chances of saving the captives shrinking by the day.

"Dammit!" Cole snapped. "Eli, jerk the pack off that horse. Turn him loose. We'll carry our provisions as best we can. Bring all the grain for the horses. Leave whatever else you have to. From here on, we'll ride 'til we can't see. It's good trackin' through here. We've gotta catch 'em before they get too far west."

"We ain't gonna bury them bodies, Cap'n?" Eli asked.

"We ain't got time for that. There's nothin' left anyway. It's time we found out what these horses are made of."

The men hurriedly split the supplies and rode off at the gallop. Flop-ear followed a while before he realized he was free. When he did, he stopped, looked around confused, then dropped his head to graze.

With twenty-five miles behind them, the Rangers reached the North Canadian an hour before sundown. After the horses drank their fill, they were off again, hoping for another ten miles before dark. The ten miles would give them nearly seventy for the day—an outstanding feat in any cavalry. The thoroughbreds held up well. Hard travel was nothing new to them. Harley's morgan was their equal, covering the miles at an even softer gait.

They made the ten miles, but the horses had done all they could and more. After pulling the saddles and letting them roll, Harley gave each horse a good rubdown, spending an extra long time on their legs.

Eli set up the camp, while Cole climbed a tree with his spy glass. He hoped to see the renegades' camp fire, but he didn't. The night would be pitch dark. Zendejaz could keep traveling if he knew where he was going. Maybe he hadn't stopped for the night. The Rangers had followed their tracks to this very spot, but in a few days they would reach the caprock, then what? There would be no tracks to follow. Their best chance would be only horse dung, or maybe a scratch left on rock by a horseshoe. Cole was starting to believe their only hope was Stone Horse. . .and maybe some old fashioned luck.

The stew Eli put together didn't amount to much. It was mostly water with a few vegetables and some dried meat thrown in. The Rangers hadn't had a decent meal since leaving Austin nearly a month earlier. They were dirty, unshaven, and lank as could be—a subject Harley saw fit to address.

"Damn, boys, when we catch up to 'em and that woman sees us, I expect it'll scare her to death. I declare, Eli, you look like a hairy bone."

Eli chuckled, but Cole didn't. He stared into the darkness, angry and determined. Harley said it right, not *if* they catch them, but *when.* There would be no turning back now, no matter how long it took. Zendejaz would pay for his crimes with his life. When that was done, Cole would resume his search for Lean Wolf. The boys could come along or go, it was up to them. But he'd find Lean Wolf and kill him, if it took the rest of his life. He could not accept so many failures. He would rather die trying to right them.

"Cole, if looks could kill, you'd have to bury me and Eli. You might as well eat, after he's gone to all this trouble to make it look so delicious."

"I ain't hungry."

"Well, maybe you ain't, but pure meanness ain't gonna catch him. If that was the case, there wouldn't be an outlaw left in Texas once you took up pursuit."

"He's right, Cap'n," Eli said. "It ain't much, but it'll fill you up. I kept a few apples, too."

Cole grudgingly filled his plate, then walked off to be alone. Harley let him be for a while, but soon followed. He found Cole in a more passive mood than before.

"Well?" Harley said.

"Well, what?"

"Have you got it all worked out, or are you just playin' with your toes?"

"I was thinkin' about Boone and Louise. I sure missed seein' her when we were in town. Didn't think it'd hit me so."

That was a statement Harley didn't expect. He took his

time responding. "Hell, it was plain you cared for her. And she cared for you. Somethin' like that's bound to hit a man hard."

"I'm worried about the boy."

"Yeah. There's a lotta Louise in him. He's got that same chin, and crooked smile. He's a good kid."

"But he might not stay that way, bein' raised by a woman alone. Boys are hard to handle. The same thing happened to me. Now I don't know nothin' but horses and guns."

"I ain't so sure about that. You know you care about the boy and his ma. Don't be so hard on yourself. It ain't a crime to care about somethin' besides the law. The world ain't ever gonna run outta villains. There'll always be enough to go around."

"Well, I just hope Rebecca's takin' good care of him."

"She will. She's a fine gal. Smart and good lookin', but a little shy."

"I sent word to 'em in the telegram that we were all right."

Harley had to chuckle at that. "I swear, Cole. It wouldn't surprise me for you to take up preachin', if you soften up anymore."

#

Tired of the constant bickering over the woman, feeling that something must be done to bring the men under control, Zendejaz took Rachel in full view of the camp. The outlaws watched in silence, knowing that now she was the *jefe's* woman. He would never let them have her again.

Rachel hid her face behind her long, strawberry hair, crying as Zendejaz mounted her like a dog. This was the first time he had taken her, and Milo hated him most of all. He did it slow, made it last a long time. Moody hung his head and refused to look. Tears rolled down Milo's cheeks as he thought of the things he would do to Zendejaz, if he ever got the chance.

His feelings for Rachel grew everyday. Now, to watch this happen to her, was more than he could stand. He held his peace as long as possible, then, bound hand and foot, Milo jumped to his

The Day Hunters

feet, hopped across the fire, and threw himself at Zendejaz.

"Get off her, you son of a bitch!"

"Milo, don't!" Moody yelled.

Milo hit Zendejaz broadside, knocking him to the ground. His stiff rod pointed to the sky. In a moment, Ruiz and Delgado had him. Delgado jerked Milo to his feet by the hair. Ruiz punched the boy repeatedly in the ribs. Milo's knees gave out, but Delgado pulled him back to his feet. Ruiz pulled the boy's pants down, laying a knife to his privates. Moody sat and watched in horror, Fast Elk's pistol just inches from his head. Lean Wolf shouted encouragement to the men.

"Cut him, Ruiz! Cut his balls off!"

"*No!*" Rachel screamed. "*No, God, no!*"

Ruiz waited for Zendejaz to give the word, but he didn't do it. He simply mounted Rachel again until he finished. All the while Milo stood watching, his privates draped over the cold, steel blade.

Zendejaz stood up, buttoning his trousers. "She is mine now," he said. "I will kill the next man to touch her. Delgado, let the boy go."

Milo stood petrified, his pants around his knees, as Zendejaz spoke to him.

"I don't blame you. I see how you look at her. You are courageous, but foolish, though I would have done the same thing."

Zendejaz punched Milo hard in the face, his head bouncing when it hit the dirt.

"If you give me any more trouble, I will give you to these men. They will do to you like they did the scalper. But I won't let them kill you. I will never let them kill you."

Zendejaz lifted Rachel to her feet and led her to his blanket, where he tossed her down like a child would toss away a broken doll.

"You are my woman now. The others will not bother you again. I should tell you, though, that I have killed many women who have tried to escape. Don't provoke me."

219

The Day Hunters

Rachel couldn't speak. She could only stare the empty stare. Zendejaz yawned, and spoke gruffly to his men.

"Turn in. We ride at daybreak."

#

Sheriff Pence knew something was amiss. Boone showed up at the jail at seven o'clock sharp, just as he did every day, and went about his chores with his normal enthusiasm. But this morning, every little while, the boy would inquire about the time. After checking his watch for the second time, Sheriff Pence made his own inquiry.

"What's goin' on, Boone?"

"Nothin', sir. Just curious."

Sheriff Pence leaned back in his squeaky chair, and put his feet on the desk. He took a little knife out of his vest pocket and began sharpening a pencil, occasionally testing the point with his thumb. His dog, Barney, stood up and stretched, then lay back down in the corner.

"You might as well tell me, son. I'm gonna find out anyway."

"Nothin', sir. I just got somethin' I need to do at noon. What time is it now?"

"Eight-thirty. I think you've got time to tell me."

Boone hemmed and hawed, but soon realized he was cornered. He didn't want to tell the sheriff what he had in mind. He was sure he'd get in trouble again, but there seemed to be no way to avoid it.

"Dal Boyd called me a liar," he said. "I'm gonna fight him at noon behind the Rangers' bunkhouse." Boone stared critically at the floor he'd just swept, and waited for a scolding that never came.

"Why'd he call you a liar?"

"I told the boys the Captain said my name in a telegram. Dal said I was lyin', so I told him I'd fight him for it." Boone

The Day Hunters

raised his head, and looked the sheriff in the eye. "Are you gonna tell Miss Becky?"

"Oh, I don't think that's necessary." Sheriff Pence folded his knife, put it back in his pocket and swept the wood shavings from his lap. "But Dal's bigger than you, and a little older. You think you can take him?"

"Milo says if they're bigger to kick 'em in the knee first, then hit 'em till they quit. He's a good fighter. I bet he knows."

"Yep, I expect he does. But what if it don't work and you take a whippin'?"

Boone hadn't thought about Milo's technique not working. He'd only envisioned himself sitting on Dal Boyd's chest, punching him in the nose until he said uncle. Defeat hadn't entered his thinking. But as usual, when talking to grownups, the facts had now been brought to his attention.

"Well, then I guess I'll just take the whippin'. But I didn't lie. The Captain did say my name. Miss Becky told me. He ain't gonna call me a liar and get away with it."

Sheriff Pence licked the point of the pencil, and finished writing whatever he'd been working on.

"You go ahead with your chores, son. I'll tell you when it's time."

At five minutes to twelve, Boone and Sheriff Pence started for the Rangers' bunkhouse. Walking behind them were Toad Phinney, Danny Bane, and Pete Maynard, all friends of Boone. Each carried plenty of rocks in his pockets.

Dal Boyd had already arrived. He had only one friend with him. Tom Tomlinson. Tom was known around Austin as the toughest kid in town, and he didn't mind spreading his own legend. He walked around Austin daring other boys to fight him, picking on the girls and generally being a nuisance.

"If he gets in it, we'll all jump him," Toad said to Boone.

"Nobody else is gettin' in it," Sheriff Pence said. "This is

221

The Day Hunters

between Boone and Dal. The rest of you boys get up on the fence and stay there."

Tom chose to stand in defiance of the sheriff's instructions. Boone's mouth was dry as cotton. Dal looked like he'd grown some since Boone last saw him, but that made no difference. Dal had called him a liar, and he wasn't. He wasn't a liar, and he wasn't a coward. That's all there was to it. Boone swallowed hard and drew a line in the dust with his toe.

"Spit over that line," he said.

Dal did so and the fight was on. Boone threw the knee kick. It worked like a charm. He punched Dal in the face, but neither blow landed hard enough to knock him down. Dal attacked, swinging with both fists. He was slow and clumsy, only catching Boone on the shoulders. The boys on the fence booed whenever Dal connected, cheered whenever Boone did. Tom made no remark in either case.

Dal stumbled. Boone jumped on his back and tried to choke him, biting his ear all the while. Dal grabbed Boone's shirt and flipped him over his shoulder. He landed hard on his back, nearly knocking the wind out of him. Dal attempted to fall on him, but Boone rolled out of the way. Dal hit face first in the dust. Boone jumped on his back to the wild cheers of his friends. He used the same choke hold as before, but being prostrate, this time Dal couldn't shake him.

"Uncle?" Boone said.

"No!"

Boone bit down hard on the ear again. "*Ungull?*"

Sensing Boone's determination, expressing fondness for the ear, Dal relented. "Uncle," he said.

Tom Tomlinson just shook his head and walked away. The boys on the fence raised a mighty cheer. Their friend's honor had been vindicated.

"All right, that's enough," the sheriff said. "You boys go on about your business. Dal, you better have your ma look at that ear."

Danny and Pete lifted Boone to their shoulders. They

The Day Hunters

carried him down the main street of Austin, touting his victory to all who would listen. Soon a large crowd of boys gathered in front of the sheriff's office, but all the girls passing by just thought the boys were stupid.

Boone was so happy about winning the fight, he hardly knew what to do. The boys hailed his courage and sense of honor. They laughed, and whooped, and slapped his back. For a few short moments, Boone truly felt like a hero. But when he looked down the street and saw Miss Becky standing on the sidewalk watching the melee, he began to think of consequences.

He'd only done what he thought he should do in fighting Dal. But now he felt a sadness, like he'd let Miss Becky down again. How many times would she put up with it? She didn't have to let him live with her, Boone knew that. And what about the Rangers? What would they think of his behavior? Boone turned his back to the crowd and walked into the sheriff's office.

Sheriff Pence had gone back to his business. He'd no doubt seen boys fight before. He didn't seem all that impressed. As the crowd of boys outside dispersed, Boone laid down on a cot in one of the cells, and turned his face to the wall. He didn't want Sheriff Pence to see him cry.

#

Three days after Zendejaz lay claim to Rachel, Stone Horse struck the caprock country and lost the track of the renegades. He'd kept them in plain sight for nearly two hundred miles, but when they dipped into the first canyon, they vanished like smoke in the wind. Stone Horse thought they might have split up, but he could not even be sure of that. The only thing he could be sure of was that they were gone. He searched the canyon floor thoroughly, but found no sign at all.

The mare didn't like the canyon. The silence made her skittish and difficult to control. At one point she whinnied, loud and long, her sides quaking with the effort. Stone Horse held his breath in fear the outlaws would hear her cry. But if they did, their horses didn't respond. He and the mare were alone. More alone than a man could feel good about.

The country was prime for an ambush, the sloping canyon walls thick with juniper and mesquite. The trees cast eerie shapes all around. They provided plenty of cover. High ridges, perfect for a man to lie in wait and fire down on an unsuspecting rider. One could easily be trapped in such a place, by only a small number of men. Each end of the passage could be blocked and there he'd be, nowhere to run, walls too steep to climb, finished.

Stone Horse thought he'd seen enough and so did the mare. They rode out of the canyon the same way they came in, the mare anxious to leave such a spooky place behind. Once at the rim, Stone Horse searched the horizon hoping to see a plume of smoke or some sign of the outlaws' whereabouts, but again, he saw nothing that would help him. He resolved to make camp and wait for the Rangers. So many tracks would be easy to follow, if they'd found his sign to begin with. Maybe after dark, he could locate the outlaws' fire. He would have to be careful they didn't locate his.

Stone Horse unsaddled the weary mare, and turned her loose to roll in the dirt. Happy to be free of the saddle, she lay on her side, stretching and scratching, until Stone Horse had to get her up. Once on her feet, the mare shook herself hard, nearly disappearing in a cloud of red dust. Stone Horse hobbled her so she could graze at will, then set about putting up for the night.

Stone Horse felt secure in his camp. Though grass was getting sparse, there was plenty for the mare, as long as they didn't stay more than a day or two. He killed two small rabbits early in the morning, then cooked and ate them both. His fire was well hidden behind a large, downed, hackberry tree. There was little chance of the fire being seen. He and the mare lazed around the camp all morning, waiting for the Rangers, catching up on their sleep. But by midday, Stone Horse became restless. He felt he

The Day Hunters

should be trying to locate the renegades' stronghold, not just lying around scratching.

The Captain would want information when he showed up, and Stone Horse was sure he would. He'd seen the look on the Captain's face when Eli told him of the capture. It was the Captain's war face. The same face he'd seen many weeks ago on the llano. The Captain would never turn back.

Tying his scarf to a limb of the hackberry tree as a sign that he'd return, Stone Horse saddled the mare and rode south on more level terrain, trying to hold to the higher ground. He didn't want to dip into the canyons if he didn't have to, but he also had to be careful not to skyline himself riding the rim.

Often he would dismount and crawl to the rim, to survey the rocky terrain. He mostly saw birds and wildlife, of which there were plenty. A man could live well just on the mule deer he saw. If there was a reliable water source somewhere in the canyon, Zendejaz could hide out forever.

He turned and rode several miles to the west, thinking how pleasant the ride would be if he weren't in so much danger. He thought of how good it was to be alive. To ride a good horse across the vast prairies, listening to the sounds of the world.

Stone Horse loved the sounds of the world. The mourning dove and the eagle. The bugle of the elk. Wind, and rippling water. But since the whites came, there were many sounds he did not like. One was the sound of gunfire.

He could remember when he was a child, the sounds of gunfire were never heard. The whites had not come with their noisy guns yet. The guns scared the game away, and made it very easy for the whites to kill the people.

Though the Rangers often marveled at his tracking skills, they didn't take into account that he was usually tracking other Indians. The Indians he tracked did not shoot guns just to make noise. But the whites often did.

It was the distant sound of reckless gunfire told Stone Horse he had, at last, found the outlaws' stronghold.

The Day Hunters

Stone Horse rode west following the sound of the gunfire, until he reached a sheer cliff about two hundred feet from the canyon floor. Hobbling the mare, he crawled to the edge of the cliff to view the encampment. He was astonished at what he saw. Easily a mile long and a half mile wide, the stronghold had everything an outlaw could hope for. Tall grasses carpeted the canyon, more than enough to sustain the many horses he saw. Hackberry, cottonwood, even plum trees were abundant. Directly beneath him at the bottom of the cliff, flowed a sizeable creek shaded by the eastern wall and numerous cottonwood trees, suggesting the creek must flow the year round.

To the south the canyon narrowed, from what Stone Horse could see, possibly down to a footpath. The north end opened wide to a spectacular view of red caliche cliffs, green mesquite and blue sky. The western slope was long and bare, no more than a hundred feet high. Stone Horse thought the place fit for a king. It might well be compared to the garden of Eden the whites spoke of, if not for the rank debauchery taking place.

Drunken people were everywhere, running, dancing, shooting their guns. One skinny Mexican, naked but for his boots, sombrero and gun belt, fired shots in the air to mark the start of the horse races down the canyon. Couples came and went from the lodges. The camp echoed with the raucous sounds of guitars and drums, castanets and tambourines.

Stone Horse could not locate the captives. They must be in one of the lodges, but which one? The large, bright colored tent at the north end was undoubtedly the lodge of Zendejaz. Maybe the captives were there, where Zendejaz could keep an eye on them. Stone Horse did not see the *jefe*. He must be in the tent.

There were about twenty men as best he could tell, maybe half as many women. He saw no children at all. Pregnant women, he knew, were sold like mares in foal, two for the price of one.

In a few hours the whole camp would be drunk, most likely with the exception of Zendejaz himself. The white hot sun hung

The Day Hunters

low in the west. Dark shadows would soon fill the canyon. Before
they did, Stone Horse wanted a look at the pathway. He mounted
and swung wide to the south. He had no idea where the narrow
path came out, or even if it did. But he wanted to find out all he
could, before going back to meet the Rangers. Within a mile he
found the entrance, covered with foliage, almost invisible. Above
the opening on a rocky escarpment, stood a hard looking Mexican,
heavily armed.

Stone Horse needed to get closer. The Captain would want
to know every entrance and exit in the camp. He knew it was his
job to find them. The easiest way would be to kill the guard, but
that would only warn Zendejaz. Judging by the guard's position,
he could maybe enter for fifty yards or so before the man would
see him. But what then?

One thing he knew for sure about guards. They all grew
sleepy after dark. Tonight would be a rustlers' moon, hardly any
light at all. Stone Horse fell back and tied the mare. He would
wait for the rising of the moon.

#

As darkness overtook the canyon, Milo and Moody were
charged with building fires around the camp. Their rawhide bonds
had been replaced with shackles and heavy chains, so they could
work, but not try to run away. Zendejaz had the firewood cut and
hauled in from other canyons to keep his stronghold pristine.
Moody had to admit, it was a beautiful place.

"When we kill all these devils, I wouldn't mind livin' here
myself," he told Milo.

"Don't you mean *if* we kill 'em? Where the hell's the
Captain? What if they can't find us? We ain't seen Stone Horse
since the rendezvous."

"Nothin's certain, Milo. But don't forget, the Cap'n ain't
just trackin' us. He trackin' them that killed our boys. When
Stone Horse tells him Lean Wolf's with this bunch, he'll find us if
it takes forever. The Cap'n ain't one to give up. Mistuh Harley,

The Day Hunters

neither. Every day we alive just gives 'em one more day to find us."

Milo crouched by the fire, poking the coals with a cottonwood branch. Moody could see the strain on his face. He often caught the boy staring at the big tent, the tent where Rachel now lived—until Zendejaz decided to sell her. Or kill her. Moody had to wonder how much fight the woman had left in her. If she gave up, she might as well be dead. From the looks of the other women in the camp, there wouldn't be much left to live for.

The festivities were interrupted when a young Apache boy rode in, his blood bay pony showing signs of hard travel. The boy himself looked pretty well worn, possibly under the weight of the many weapons he carried. Moody counted a brace of pistols, a bowie knife, two bandoliers of ammunition, and a Henry repeater. The Apache dismounted in front of the big tent, merely dropping his reins to the ground. The pony looked too tired to wander off.

The tent flap opened and Rachel emerged, in a plain but clean gingham dress. The lights inside the tent silhouetted her shapely figure as she ushered the Apache inside. At the sight of her, Milo sank even lower.

All the renegades seemed to know the meaning of the Apache's arrival. Even the drunkest of them sobered up quickly. The buck toothed boy standing outside the tent, jumped a horse and ran through the camp, shouting, searching for Lean Wolf. He found him sleeping in a broken down wagon, at the mouth of the southern passageway.

"Wolf, the Apache has returned from the west!" he shouted.

Lean Wolf cursed the boy for waking him up, then jumped from the wagon onto the horse. He knocked the frightened boy out of the saddle and galloped to the end of the canyon, whipping the horse all the way. He slid the animal to a powerful stop, scattering the crowd in front of the tent, and was immediately ushered inside.

"What is it, Moody?" Milo asked.

"Don't know, but it looks like somethin' big. Let's see if we can get closer."

The Day Hunters

Before they could even get near the tent, the Rangers were turned back and forced to sit by one of the fires. Fast Elk stayed to guard them. Milo refused to look at the man, but Fast Elk watched Milo intently.

"Soon, Ranger, the deal will be made," Fast Elk said. "It will be me or the traders. I am only one man. There are many in the mines."

So that was it, thought Moody. The traders were coming. When? How many? And where in the world was the Captain?

"The wagons will be here in four days," the Apache said.

"*Bueno*! We are running low on many things," Zendejaz said. "How many rifles?"

"Thirty six. All Henrys. Lots of ammunition and pistols. Three hundred pounds of gunpowder."

"We have women to trade, and many horses. And two strong Texas Rangers for the mines. It would be only right for the *Tejanos Diablos* to dig their way into Hell."

The Apache merely grunted his response. The women in the tent held his close attention. Two lay on big pillows, twirling each other's hair, while Rachel moved from glass to glass pouring whiskey.

Zendejaz laughed. "There are women in the camp you can have," he said. "But these belong to me. Go. Enjoy yourself. Someone will feed you."

With one last look at the women on the pillows, the Apache grunted again and stepped outside.

"I will have to leave to find traders," Lean Wolf said. "Ellsworth has kept me too busy."

"No," Zendejaz said. "Stay here awhile. Ellsworth may yet be alive. I don't believe the boy. If he is alive, he may still be looking for you. Let things cool down. He will never find us here."

#

229

The Day Hunters

Stone Horse was well into the passageway when he heard two men talking at the guard post. One of the men was very excited, talking loud and fast. A shipment of rifles and trade goods was on its way from Fort Sumner. It would be delivered in four days. Surely there would be a big fiesta when the wagons arrived.

Stone Horse kept still and listened until the talking stopped. He assumed one man had come to relieve the other, then left. Occasionally, the guard would walk to the edge of the passage, inadvertently kicking gravel over the precipice. But that soon ceased. After a long silence, Stone Horse thought the guard was either sitting down or asleep. Or both. He took his chance, slowly making his way through the gap until he reached the opening to the canyon.

Just outside the opening, off to one side, stood a broken down old wagon. Stone Horse inspected it quickly, finding only a few blankets inside. The blankets were still warm. Probably a quiet place to bring a woman, or maybe post a guard. Either way, it was something to remember. A spot to keep an eye on.

He had gone as far as he dared. He hadn't located Milo or Moody, but captives or not, the Rangers had been searching for the stronghold a long time. It was the search for this very place that resulted in the deaths of the five Rangers. Four days from now there would be even more guns in the camp. The Captain had better move soon.

Stone Horse sneaked out of the gap and back to the mare, where he wasted no time hitting the saddle. The rustlers' moon teetered high above in a cloudless sky, as he picked his way across the dark prairie. He thought he would reach the camp by breakfast. The idea was making him hungry.

#

Milo and Moody were left alone by the fire, after the camp quieted down. A few men were still roaming around trying to find a willing woman, but most had already been confiscated. By and

The Day Hunters

large, the camp was serene.

"We've gotta get outta here," Milo whispered. "Once those traders get here, we'll be lost for good. And what about Rachel?"

"Don't know. It looks bad, but I don't know what we can do. We couldn't shoot our way out, even if we had the guns. We can't climb out, and there's guards at both ends o' the canyon. We come through a maze gettin' here. I ain't sure I could find our way out again."

Milo had taken about all he could stand, and Moody well knew it. He'd seen hardened men give up under conditions not nearly as bad. He was proud of Milo's courage and self-control. After all, this was just his first trip to the field. But every man had his limits, and it looked like Milo had about reached his.

"We can't quit," Moody continued. "If we do, Miss Rachel will, then you won't have her. It's plain you want her. I think she wants you, too. That was a brave thing you did, jumpin' Zendejaz. I expect she thinks you're a hero."

"Hero, hell. I'm scared to death."

"Well, don't let *them* know it. The traders are still four days away. The Cap'n and Mistuh Harley maybe ain't as far behind as you think. They'll be here," Moody said, though he had begun to have his own doubts.

Moody heard a few catcalls from down the canyon. He looked up to see a great hulking shape walking toward them. It was not the first time he'd seen it.

"Oh lawd," he said. "It's Big Iris again."

Milo chuckled at Moody's predicament. Big Iris had been on Moody's trail ever since they'd arrived at the stronghold. She came straight to the fire, kneeled down between the Rangers, and cackled, "Wanna see my titties?" After which, she bared her bosom to their shock and amazement.

"No, ma'am!" Moody exclaimed. "You better go on now, before you get us in trouble. Go on, now."

"Good lord!" Milo said.

Big Iris cackled even louder. "You like 'em? Wanna touch 'em?"

The Day Hunters

"No, ma'am!"

Big Iris unbuttoned a few more buttons and bent closer to Moody, who tried hard not to run. When she did, a large butcher knife fell from her dress. She laughed at Moody's surprise, winked at him knowingly, and said, "Well, goodbye then." Big Iris struggled to get to her feet and skipped back down the canyon, her bare bosom swinging side to side.

"What the hell was that?" Milo whispered.

"Be quiet." Moody opened his legs and let the knife fall between them. Later, when the fires died down, he would slip the knife into his boot.

"You think we can trust her? She's crazy."

"That might be, but did you see that wink? She knows what she's doin'. Maybe she thinks we can help her. And we will, if we can. Let's try to get some sleep."

It was a vain hope. Neither man could sleep in light of what had happened. The captives now had a weapon. . .and an ally.

#

Rachel was mortified by the acts the other women expected of her. She'd been pushing them away since arriving at the stronghold, but Zendejaz only laughed at her dilemma. Such goings-on were common in his tent. She felt her life had become Hell on earth. Her hope was dwindling fast. Here she was, held captive in a secret place she couldn't find her way out of in a lifetime. Sooner or later, Zendejaz would get tired of her. He would turn her over to the men in the camp, as he did all the women. And now the traders were coming. God only knew where she might end up.

Lying beside Zendejaz, listening to him snore, Rachel could smell the sweet bath soap he used, the tonic in his hair, mint candy on his breath. Zendejaz was a far cry from the stinking riff-raff he surrounded himself with. But that made him no less a devil in Rachel's eyes. She now saw Moody and Milo as her only hope.

232

The Day Hunters

And precious little hope it was.

Moody was a calm, steady man, but so far it had been Milo who stood up to the outlaws. Rachel knew it was just greed that kept Zendejaz from killing him. A schoolgirl could see how Milo felt about her. She had her feelings for him, too. Rachel had to admit, he was handsome and brave, but she didn't want him killed on her account. Sometimes, young men were too impetuous for their own good.

The Captain they spoke of, and his friend Harley Macon, now seemed like characters in a fanciful story. A story that one dreamed was true, but down deep knew that it wasn't. Rachel felt she'd been waiting for someone to save her all her life. She'd hoped for a husband to save her from her father, then continued to hope for someone to save her from her husband. The Indian's bullet had ended her husband's drunken abuse, but the abuse itself was now even worse. Now there were even more men to take her. To take the only thing she had to give.

Sound asleep, Zendejaz rolled over and wrapped her in his arms, his swollen manhood pressing against her hip. Afraid to move for fear she'd entice him, Rachel let the tears run down her cheeks. God, how she wanted to kill this man, and all the men who rode with him. Even the women in the camp had been driven to depravity. Rachel did not want to be like one of them. Death might be the only thing to free her from such a life. She knew Milo would save her if he could, but how. . .and why? Was he really in love with her, or did he only want what the others wanted? Men could change for the worse. Her husband had proven that. But right now, the Rangers were her last chance to be free. Maybe Milo wanted to free her just because it was the right thing to do. It was a pleasant thought, but how could she believe it? She'd never known a man to do anything just because it was right.

Rachel heard the fresh horse turds plop on the ground outside the tent, so close she could even smell them. The horse was tied right next to the flap, just a few feet from where she now lay. Lord, she wanted to run to that horse, to mount him and ride for her life. She wanted to feel that power beneath her as she raced from the canyon, the cool wind blowing through her hair. To be free again, free from the nightmare of her life. But the dream of freedom vanished when Zendejaz woke up and slid his hand between her legs.

She stiffened when he touched her, but it only made him laugh. He gently brushed his fingertips up and down her thigh, stopping just before he reached the place that made her jerk. Each time her apprehension made him laugh again.

Zendejaz pulled her legs apart, positioning himself between them. Fully aroused and completely exposed, he teased Rachel, rocking back and forth on his knees. She turned her head to look away, but he grabbed her hair and slapped her hard. Rachel listened to the other women breathing deeply in their sleep, as Zendejaz took her.

#

Eli Plummer dozed off while squatting to empty his bowels. So tired from the hardships of relentless pursuit, he merely had to stop moving to relax and give in. Eli tried to remember his last good night's sleep, but the memory escaped him. The Rangers had only stayed two nights in Austin. Most of the first one he'd spent in the whorehouse. Most of the second he'd spent worrying about the upcoming patrol. It must have been well before that.

The smell of salt pork and potatoes frying almost made him think he was home again, sitting in his mother's clean kitchen. His mother cleaned house every minute she wasn't doing something else, standing firm on the "cleanliness is next to godliness" theory. Eli was aware he was far from clean or godly. A hot bath, a full belly, and a soft feather bed, now seemed more glorious to him than anything he'd ever wanted before. Or would likely ever want again.

Eli was a man who liked his privacy, consequently choosing a spot well hidden to do his business. So well hidden, in

The Day Hunters

fact, that Stone Horse all but ran him over as he loped toward the camp. The mare jumped sideways at the sight of Eli, who was so startled at the sudden appearance of the mare that he nearly fell in his own leavings. Stone Horse barely noticed Eli. His face was set like flint. Eli quickly pulled up his pants, and ran to the fire to get the news.

"Captain!" Stone Horse shouted. "I have found it. I have found the stronghold."

It was exactly the news Cole wanted to hear, yet it stunned him. He couldn't quite get his mind to accept it. He just looked at Stone Horse, as if trying to believe it was true.

"You found it, Horse?" Harley said. He and Cole looked at each other dumbfounded, like maybe they'd just witnessed a miracle.

"I found it. Lean Wolf is there with them."

"Lean Wolf?" Cole snapped. "Are you sure?"

"I'm sure. He joined them back at the soldier camp. He is the rider who came from the north."

Cole's face turned dark with anger. "How far?"

"Half a day. A big canyon. Water, grass, lots of horses. A shipment of rifles is coming in four days from Fort Sumner."

"Milo and Moody?"

"I did not see them. There are many lodges. They must be kept inside. I think they will be traded when the rifles come."

"By God," Harley said. "How many gun hands?"

"About twenty. They were having fiesta. It was hard to count. Maybe half as many women."

"Guards?"

"At the north and south end. The south is only wide enough for a horse. The north end is big."

"Well, I'll be damned," Harley said. "I'd say it's high time we ride on over there, and deal out a little justice."

"Deal out justice?" Cole said. "Ain't you forgettin' there's only four of us?"

"No, I ain't forgettin'. And I ain't forgettin' why we came, neither. Five dead Rangers. That melted woodcutter and his little

235

The Day Hunters

girl. Now they've got our boys and who knows what else. We've got right on our side, Cole. I say we go kill 'em all."

"We will get there after dark, if we wait until midday to leave," Stone Horse said.

"It will be easier to get close in the dark."

"Well," Harley said, "let's eat then while we're waitin'."

Eli returned the pheasant feather to Stone Horse. He smiled gratefully as he wove it back into his hair. The two filled their plates and coffee cups, then sat down to eat their breakfast. Harley and Cole filled theirs and walked away.

"Looks like we're up against it," Cole said.

"Yeah. Whatever we do, we've gotta do it before the guns get there. I wonder how many hands are with the delivery."

Cole took notice of the smirk on Harley's face. "Now what the hell are you thinkin'?"

Harley licked the pork grease off his fingers. "I was thinkin', how interestin' it might be to hijack a shipment o' rifles."

The Day Hunters

Chapter 22

The Rangers circled far south of the stronghold to avoid any hint of detection. Cole wanted a view from the west side of the canyon, as that was the direction the guns were coming from. Tying their horses in an arroyo about a mile from the western rim, they slipped off their spurs and proceeded on foot.

They made the last hundred yards on their bellies at dusk, but it proved to be unnecessary. From their position on the rim, they could see both guards. Each held a post lower than the rim of the canyon. The rim sloped off to the north and south, the southern guard holding the higher ground of the two. But neither man could see over the rim.

"Zendejaz chose a dandy place," Cole said. "But he don't know nothin' about postin' guards. Why wouldn't they take the higher ground?"

"Cocky," Harley said. "He thinks nobody can find him out here. Up to now he's been right."

The camp was quiet, with no more than the normal evening activities going on. The men yarned and smoked, and cleaned their weapons, but to Cole's dismay, there was no sign of Lean Wolf. Several women cooked at the fires. A few were hanging out their wash between the lodges. A large band of horses grazed throughout the long canyon, ten of them the horses that were left in Moody's care.

"I wish I could see our boys," Cole said. "I hope they're here."

"They *are* here," Eli said. "Look yonder."

A team of stout mules stepped into the firelight pulling a heavy wagon load of wood. Milo and Moody sat atop the wood pile, along with an Indian, armed with a shotgun. A short, fat man drove the wagon.

"That is the idiot man driving," Stone Horse said. "And Fast Elk with the shotgun."

Climbing down from the wagon was difficult, the Rangers

237

being shackled and chained. Moody hung his leg chain on a piece of firewood and fell from the wagon, landing hard on his shoulder. Fast Elk threatened him with the shotgun, poking him vigorously until he regained his feet. The boys unloaded a pile of wood at the fire, then moved down the line, repeating the task.

"They're still with us," Harley said. "What about the woman, Horse?"

"Zendejaz took her. She is his woman now. I think she is in the big tent."

Most of the lodges were directly beneath them at the bottom of the western slope, though a few were on the other side, closer to the creek. The big, bright tent was hard to miss. Cole thought it was a perfect target.

"You don't suppose we'd be lucky enough there'd be some dynamite in that shipment, do you? If we could blow that gap on the south end, we might could trap 'em. Cut 'em down as they come out the north."

"Interestin' theory," Harley said. "I'm surprised at Zendejaz. This place is hard to find, but even harder to defend. Hell, one good rifleman could control that gap, if it's only wide enough for a horse. Why, if we had a few more men, we could ride through this canyon like the 8th rode through Kentucky."

"Well, if we tell 'em you're here, maybe they'll surrender."

"Might be better for 'em if they did. We may be shorthanded, but in a couple days, we'll have the guns. And whatever else is in them wagons."

"Yeah. I wish we could let the boys know we're comin'. I'd hate for 'em to try somethin' rash, now that we're so close. Let's wait a while. We'll watch 'em change the guards, then fall back to the horses. Eli, you and Stone Horse head back and get somethin' cookin'. Me n' Harley'll be along."

#

Lean Wolf couldn't shake the feeling that something was

The Day Hunters

wrong. He'd lived his whole life by his wits and his luck. Right now everything in him said run. He owed Zendejaz nothing. All their trading had been plain and straight. There were no loose ends to unravel, except that he knew the stronghold's location. But so did others. If Zendejaz killed all who knew it, he would soon be out of business.

Many suspected traitors were buried throughout the maze of canyons. Most, in Lean Wolf's estimation, were probably unjustified. But if Zendejaz even remotely suspected treason, the perpetrator would pay the ultimate price.

Few of the delivery escorts ever left the canyon. Zendejaz would see something in their eyes, hear something in their voice to make him suspicious. He would murder them or turn them over to Ruiz, in which case they would be better off dead. Lean Wolf had no problem with people being murdered or tortured, as long as it didn't happen to him.

Not for a minute did he believe Ellsworth was dead. His spirit told him otherwise. He still had the same feeling he had while being chased. The feeling that Ellsworth might show up at any moment and put a rope around his neck. The same spirit that told him to run *then*, was telling him to run *now*. But no one just rode out of the stronghold. Zendejaz would not allow it. Once you were in, you stayed in, until Zendejaz let you leave.

Lean Wolf saw the young Mexican girl step out of the lodge and straighten her skirt. He determined right then he would have her. He needed something to take his mind off his worries. Giving the girl an evil smile, he took her by the hair and walked her to the broken down wagon. She'd just left the blankets of another man. He could smell the man smell on her, but he didn't care. Camp women were for general use and he intended to use this one. He intended to use her hard.

Sunup found the Rangers ten miles from their camp in the

The Day Hunters

hidden arroyo. Even at such an early hour, they knew they were in for a long, hot ride. The arroyo held a little water, enough to fill all the canteens, but they would have to be careful how they used it. A dry prairie lay in front of them. It might be the last water they'd see for a while.

They traveled at a steady pace, through the morning and the heat of the day, stopping only when they had to, eating Eli's dried apples as they cut down the miles. Stone Horse, as always, rode far ahead. The Rangers had hardly seen him since leaving the camp. About all they saw were rattlesnakes, jackrabbits, and a lonesome eagle, flying high above the troubles of the world.

When the sun dipped below the horizon, Cole ordered a halt, setting up camp to wait for Stone Horse. He arrived about an hour later.

"You seen 'em?" Cole asked.

"I've seen them. Camped five hours from here. Two wagons. Eight men."

"Eight o' them and four of us. Just the way I like it," Harley said.

"Get some rest," Cole ordered. "We'll leave at midnight. Take 'em first thing in the mornin'."

The wagon camp was quiet as a tomb. A single guard sat cross-legged on the only high ground to be seen—a little knoll hardly worth noticing. The guard, like most men at that hour of the morning, looked more asleep than awake. The rest of the men were wrapped in their blankets, likely dreaming of the women at the stronghold. The Rangers held an eastern position, waiting for the sun to rise at their backs.

"Well, there they are," Harley said. "How you wanna do it? Sit back and pick 'em off, or ride in shootin' like the old days?"

"If we ride in, we might lose somebody," Cole said.

The Day Hunters

"We're already shorthanded. But if they take cover under those wagons, we might be here all day."

"Hell. Let's get it done. We need to get our boys outta there."

"All right. Horse, when the sun comes up, you take the guard. Keep it quiet. When you get him, we'll ride in. Be careful not to hit the wagons with your gunfire. There's likely ammunition in 'em. We might blow 'em up. We may need everything in 'em to take that stronghold. Let's get ready."

#

The guard sitting on the little knoll woke suddenly to a warm, wet feeling. For just a moment, he thought he'd wet his pants. He'd been drinking the night before, and as a result, sometimes found it hard to wake up in time. But when he looked down, he saw his shirt covered with blood. He hadn't wet his pants. His throat had been cut. The Indian pushed him over onto his back and wiped the knife on his shirt sleeve, the only part of his shirt not already bloody. The guard palmed his pistol, trying to draw and fire, but couldn't get his fingers to close on the grip. The Indian's face became distorted and blurry. The guard tried to ask the Indian to help him, but the Indian only stole his gun belt and walked away. He heard cursing and shouting, hoof beats and gun fire, then darkness swallowed the morning sky.

The outlaws reacted quickly to the sound of the charging horses, but they were no match for the Texas Rangers. The first shot of the engagement, fired by a bald outlaw with a wooden leg, accidentally killed one of their own. The man simply stepped in front of the bullet while rising from his blankets. Cole dispatched the shooter, racing in, firing two pistols. Harley killed two more as they scrambled to get under the wagon. Neither man had any fight in him. They merely tried to hide like cowards. The remaining three ran for the horses. Cole and Eli each took one down before they got there. But the third man *did* reach the horses. He even managed to gain a few yards, before Stone Horse shot him down with his rifle.

The men quickly dismounted and searched through the wagons. They were anxious to see what was inside. Six cases of Henry rifles, seven shotguns, twelve pistols of varying caliber, several hundred rounds of ammunition, and three hundred pounds of gunpowder.

Four saddles, clothing, blankets, sugar, flour, coffee, salt, lard, and a barrel of soda crackers. Axle grease, a wagon tongue, lamp oil, a box of books, and a clarinet. Plenty of whiskey, and two barrels of water on each wagon.

"By God, there's somethin' for everybody," Harley said.

"I'd say the clarinet ain't for Lean Wolf."

"Not likely. Let's hitch 'em up, and get outta here."

"Damn, Cole, can't we have a little coffee first?"

"We'll have coffee up the trail. We need to get movin'. These wagons are gonna slow us down."

"I guess we ain't gonna bury this bunch neither," Harley said.

"Dammit, we ain't got time!"

"Yeah. Well, this is gettin' to be a bad habit, *Captain* Ellsworth."

The statement was like a slap in the face, but Cole wasn't about to slow down, now. What if Lean Wolf left the stronghold before they got back? What if the trade actually took place somewhere else, to keep the location secret? The renegades were at last all in one place, and that's just where he wanted them.

"Turn them saddle horses loose. Throw their gear in the wagons. Let's go."

The outlaws' horses wandered through the camp, looking curiously at the dead bodies as the wagons rolled away.

#

The Day Hunters

Eli found it alarming that, in just a few days, the Captain had left so many bodies to the buzzards. The Captain had strict rules about burying people, and now he was breaking those rules himself. It seemed there were no rules at all in this pursuit, only an objective. . .to find Lean Wolf and kill him.

He finished cutting the hole in the last of the powder kegs, and stuffed a long rag into the hole to act as a fuse for the fifty pound bomb. The Rangers would leave one wagon in the arroyo, and unload all but the powder from the other. The raid would take place after the changing of the ten o'clock guard.

"I'll take the guard at the north end," Cole said. "Horse, you take the south. Make damn sure he's dead. How long to set up the bombs?"

"Twenty minutes, maybe," Harley said. "We'll start layin' 'em out down south, and work our way north. And that's the way we'll blow 'em. That'll give our boys time to do somethin'. But Horse, you wait 'til they're in the gap to blow yours. Maybe get some of 'em that way."

"Eli, try not to hit the lodges when you roll 'em," Cole said.

"We don't know who might be inside. But likely they'll be out in the open after the first blast. When you blow the first one, me n' Harley'll close the front door. When you blow the last one, grab your horse and come a shootin'. Any questions?"

"Yeah, I've got a question," Harley said. "Would you like a drink o' whiskey before we go?"

"Yeah, I would. Eli?"

"I'd like two, Cap'n, if we've got the time."

After the shift change, Stone Horse expertly finished the guard, easily pushing the knife between his ribs into the heart. The man died without a sound. Stone Horse dropped his body into the gap. The wagon rolled up just a few minutes later.

"Put it about thirty feet inside," Harley said. "If we drop it from above, it might bust and we'd just get a fire. It'd burn bright, but not long. We've gotta close this gap. You won't be able to light it, Horse, so when they try to escape, shoot it with your rifle. After it blows, pick off whoever's left. . .if there is anybody left."

Harley nodded to the tracker and the wagon rolled away. Stone Horse spread his blanket and knelt down to pray, for courage in battle, for courage in death. If it came tonight, let it be swift.

#

Cole waited impatiently for the shift to change, but the oncoming guard was late. If all was proceeding as planned, the guard at the south entrance should be dead by now. Harley and Eli should be setting out the bombs. But what if that guard was late too? What if the shift schedule had been changed? He'd have to take the guard soon, for fear the man would catch a glimpse of the Rangers on the rim.

Cole decided he'd waited long enough. He crept toward the guard, taking cover behind the rocks. The guard was angry, cursing his relief. No doubt he had things he'd rather be doing. His anger distracted him and Cole moved. He clamped a hand over the guard's mouth and cut his throat. Blood gushed from the gaping wound. The man was dead when Cole lowered him to the ground.

Just at that moment, the relief guard appeared. He called to his friend and Cole answered. Startled, the guard wasted the second it took Cole to draw. The sound of his gunfire vanished in the first explosion.

Harley came racing down the slope with Cole's horse in tow. Cole swung into the saddle before they came to a stop and spurred the horse into a gallop.

"Horse get his guard?" he asked Harley.

"He got him. Looks like yours brought a friend."

"Yeah. Let's go."

"Good luck," Harley said.

The Day Hunters

The first explosion stunned the camp. The second sent it into complete chaos. The people were shouting, running, shooting, hiding. They ran in and out of the lodges, not knowing which way to go.

Moody stabbed the first man he ran into. Milo strangled the next one with his chains. Relieving the dead men of their weapons, Moody scanned the camp for targets, while Milo headed straight for the big tent. *He had to get Rachel out of there!*

He ran as fast as his shackles would allow, but to him it felt painfully slow. Before he reached the tent, two galloping horses came through the north entrance, the riders crouched forward, screaming like madmen. It was Harley and the Captain, riding and shooting as if they couldn't be killed. Harley even gave him a nod as he passed.

Milo reached the tent at the boom of the next explosion. When he tore open the flap, Zendejaz shot him. The bullet hit him in the shoulder and rolled him outside.

Zendejaz stepped out and threw down on Milo. But before he could fire again, Rachel grabbed one of the many guns he'd been loading, and shot him through the back of the head. The outlaw's handsome face disappeared in a bloody spray. He fell to the ground, nearly landing on Milo. Rachel stood behind him, horrified, holding the smoking gun in both hands.

"Get some o' them guns. Let's go!" Milo shouted.

Rachel took two pistols and ran out of the tent, leaving the other women huddled and crying in panic.

The last two powder kegs didn't explode. They broke open while rolling down the slope, showering many of the lodges with fire. Emmett ran from his hiding place, screaming in terror, completely engulfed in flame. Harley took careful aim to put him out of his misery, but decided to save his bullet.

The Day Hunters

Ruiz slowly stepped out of the darkness. Moody's broad back was his target. As he leveled his pistol, Big Iris tackled him, biting him hard on the nose. Ruiz fired two rounds into her ribs, before Moody shot and killed him.

Moody ran to the woman and rolled her onto her back. She looked into his eyes, a sweet smile on her face. "My daddy died fighting for the nigras," she said. Then she was gone. Moody thanked her, and gently closed her eyes. If he lived, he'd see she got a fine burial.

#

Four riders pushed hard through the passageway, whipping for more speed with every stride. They were close to the exit when they heard the rifle, then the bomb went off. The explosion didn't do much damage to the passage, but it brought down enough rock to kill the first horse and rider. The horses screamed and whirled in the gap. One horse reared, unseating his rider. The man's bare foot hung in the stirrup. The horse dragged him through the gap, beating his head on the rocks at every turn.

Stone Horse ran to the other end, firing into the gap as he went. He shot the second rider in the back and killed him. He saw no point in wasting ammunition on the dragging man, but the first rider to get out of the gap escaped him. It was Lean Wolf.

Lean Wolf turned and fired his pistol. The bullet hit Stone Horse in the belly. He dropped his rifle, struggled to keep his balance, then fell from the ledge out of sight.

#

Nearly the whole camp was in flames when Eli rode into the fray. The herd of horses raced out of the canyon, just as he rode in. He had to fight his own horse to keep him from following the bunch.

"Harley, you and Eli take them lodges by the creek," Cole yelled. "If Lean Wolf's in 'em, try to take him alive."

The Day Hunters

The two wheeled their mounts and galloped across the canyon. Harley reloaded his pistol as he rode, guiding his horse with his knees.

"Sounds like the Cap'n's got hangin' on his mind," Eli said.

"Really? When'd you notice?"

#

Milo searched frantically for a place to hide Rachel. They ran around a burning lodge, where they saw Fast Elk trying to mount a horse. He wasn't having much luck. The horse was in a panic, fighting the bit, circling around Fast Elk. When the renegade saw Milo, he ceased the effort and raised his pistol. Pushing Rachel behind him, Milo fired again and again, palming the hammer of his pistol until the gun was empty—as empty as Fast Elk's dead, hollow eyes.

#

Lean Wolf galloped his horse through the canyon, desperate to reach the north end and freedom. In the light of the burning lodges, Cole recognized him. He drew a full pistol and charged the renegade, firing to bring down his horse. Lean Wolf's horse buckled with the impact of the bullet. He turned end over end, throwing Lean Wolf directly into Cole's path. A bullet struck the ground just inches from his head. Lean Wolf rose to a knee and fired his pistol. The bullet hit Cole in the hip and knocked him from his horse. He fired once more as Cole tried to rise, but he shot too fast. He only burned the Ranger's ribs. It was his last bullet.

Cole tried to collect himself. He was still reeling from the fall. Lean Wolf pulled his knife and attacked the Ranger, screaming the war cry at the top of his lungs. Cole steadied himself and emptied his pistol, each shot blowing away a small piece of Lean Wolf, until the renegade dropped dead at his feet.

The Day Hunters

Cole fell back and lay quiet, exhausted, listening to the gunfire dying down. He felt as if he'd just finished something he'd spent his whole life doing. At last, it was over.

"We got 'em, boys," he said to the sky. "We got 'em. Got 'em all."

#

Harley and Eli rode through the camp, finishing the wounded outlaws. When they reached the old wagon, they found Stone Horse there, shot through the belly, impaled on a broken wheel spoke.

"Oh God," Harley said. "Horse? Are you dead?"

"Not yet," Stone Horse replied, his voice just a ragged whisper. "Did we get Lean Wolf?"

"Yeah. We got him. We got him thanks to you."

"Should we try to lift him off?" Eli asked, turning his back to hide his face.

"No. Let's just let him be."

"Will you give the mare to my woman?" Stone Horse asked. "She can sell the foals. I don't. . .want her to live at the fort."

"Why, Horse, I've known you all this time and didn't even know you had a woman," Harley said. "We'll see she get's the mare. What's your woman's name?"

"I call her. . . High Wind. When she is angry, she. . .talks a long time. I. . .have a little girl, too. Her name is Pretty Water. I think. . .she will like the mare," were his last words.

"Well, let's get him off there," Harley said. "Be careful with him."

#

Cole slowly opened his eyes, the sun just peeking into the canyon. Moody's face hovered directly above him. "You be still, Cap'n. Your hip's broke. Mistuh Harley and the boys gone to get

The Day Hunters

the wagons."

"I'm sorry about this, Moody. We lose anybody?"

"Yessuh. Stone Horse. We buried him over by the creek."

Cole felt numb. How many people were dead because of his bad decision? How could he ever live with it all?

"We got 'em all but Delgado, Cap'n. I guess he escaped when the horses stampeded."

"What about the women?"

"Four o' the camp women survived. All of 'em crazy as bull bats. But Miss Rachel gonna be fine, I think. She takin' care o' the other women."

"Moody, make sure all these people get buried."

"I will, Cap'n. I'll make sure. You just get some sleep."

#

Harley and the boys arrived with the wagons, late in the afternoon. Cole was awake, though he'd been in and out all day. He was starting to take the fever. Moody had many of the bodies buried. He was having coffee when the wagons rolled up.

"How you makin' out, Cole?" Harley asked.

"I've been better. I was gettin' worried, you've been gone so long."

"Took a while to find a way in. We couldn't bring the wagons down the slope."

"Milo," Cole said, "come over here."

Milo approached, not knowing what to expect.

"Howdy, Captain. Boy, was I ever glad to see you."

"How's your shoulder?"

"Okay, I guess. It's just a burn. It didn't bleed much."

Cole propped himself on an elbow and offered Milo his hand. "Moody told me how you behaved through all this. I'm proud to have you in my troop."

"Why, thank you, sir." Milo felt a little embarrassed. The many times he'd doubted himself didn't make him feel so well

249

The Day Hunters

behaved.

"You just rest, Cole," Harley said. "We'll get these graves finished up and pull out in the mornin'."

The Day Hunters

EPILOGUE

Cole awoke between cool, clean sheets, in the infirmary at Fort Belknap. Boone and Rebecca were there to greet him. They'd arrived only that morning. Rebecca sat quietly pouring over a copy of Maguffy's primer. She wore a smart traveling suit with a matching hat, a color Cole didn't know the name of. The skirt, however, was a perfect length to show just enough of her well-turned ankle. Boone sat beside her, fidgeting, pulling at his collar.

"Boone? Rebecca? What're you doin' here?"

"We come to take you home," Boone said, proud beyond belief that he'd been chosen for the task. He stood in his chair and came to attention, a move he regretted when he saw Rebecca's reaction.

"What? Take me home?"

"Harley sent us a telegram, Captain," Rebecca explained.

"He said he needed someone to see you back to Austin, whenever you're ready to travel. How are you feeling?"

"All right, I guess."

"We want you stay with us 'til you're better. Miss Becky said you could, if you want to."

Cole was taken completely by surprise. He had no idea what to say. Or how to feel. It was all happening too fast. He knew his Rangering days were over, no matter what happened with the governor. His hip would never be the same. The doctors told him the bone was shattered. It would be a while before he could travel, even by stage.

But he had to admit, Rebecca was a sight to look at. And she'd taken the boy in. Louise's boy. That said a lot for her character. Not many single women, and even fewer respectable citizens, would have taken the child of a drunken saloon girl. Such an act took courage, a virtue he had always admired in Louise.

"I expect I'll be quite a burden for a while. I doubt you'll have time for that."

The Day Hunters

"We'll make do," Rebecca said. "You'll need someone to look out for you. At least, for a while, I mean. We want you to come home with us, Captain. Maybe we'll start to grow on you."

"Just like I done," Harley said. He leaned on the doorjamb, cleaning his fingernails with a pocketknife. "Let's face it, Cole. It's time to settle down. The boys went with some of the troopers to gather all them horses. When they get back, Milo and Rachel are bound for Cleveland. I expect he's seen enough o' the wild west. Moody and Eli are gonna have to find somethin' else to do. We ain't gonna be Rangers anymore."

Boone waited eagerly for Cole's answer, a hopeful plea in his eyes.

"Well, I suppose I will need some help. I guess a man could do worse than a pretty gal and a good boy. Maybe we could give it a try."

"*Yahoo!*" Boone shouted.

"Boone. This is a hospital."

"Sorry, ma'am."

"It's time for me to get goin'," Harley said. "Rebecca, I got you a room behind the sutler's store, while you're waitin' on Cole to come around. It ain't much, but it's clean. I paid you up for a week."

"What're you gonna do?" Cole asked.

"Well," Harley said, "I think I'll take a ride to Tennessee."

Made in the USA
Lexington, KY
29 March 2014